"A wonderfully different zombie novel. Well worth the price and time."
- Jason Scott, author of *Hotel Hell*

"It [is] difficult to write a stand-out book. Glenn Bullion has given it a damn good try and for me it is a success."
-The Aussie Zombie

"Not your ordinary Zombie Apocalypse... I give *Dead Living* an enthusiastic 5 stars."
-Debi Faulkner, author of *Summoning*

"An eerie, compelling story worth checking out."
- Todd Russell, author of *Fresh Flesh*

DEAD LIVING

GLENN BULLION

A PERMUTED PRESS BOOK

ISBN: 978-1-61868-642-8

Dead Living
© 2016 by Glenn Bullion
All Rights Reserved

Cover art by Mooney Designs

PERMUTED
PRESS

Permuted Press, LLC
permutedpress.com

Published in the United States of America

For Katie, of course.

Also for Bubba, Rizzi and Scooter.

Special Thanks: Debi Faulkner and Brian Frederiksen

CHAPTER 1

Joe Thompson lowered the prongs on his forklift and set the crate near the end of the trailer. He backed out of the thick heat and wiped a bead of sweat from his head. The loading dock itself was much cooler. It was beautiful outside, a cloudless seventy-five degree day. A great day to be anywhere except at work loading freight.

It was the Saturday before the last week of the month, always the busiest shipping week. Someone had to draw the short straw, and this weekend, it was Joe. He tried to use his pregnant wife as an excuse, but she was still a few weeks from her due date, and the excuse didn't fly. He knew they needed the money. He shot his supervisor Danny a dirty look as he climbed off the forklift. He knew he should feel bad for Danny too—he had to work every single weekend—but Joe was having trouble being sympathetic.

Anthony, the driver for the trailer Joe had just loaded, called his name. Joe was lost to the sounds of the warehouse. The hum of air compressors was always in the background, along with grinders, welders, paint sprayers. His plant made industrial driers for plastic, and it was his job to crate and ship them.

"Hey, Joe!" Anthony yelled. "You awake over there?"

"Oh yeah, yeah. All done. Just some paperwork. Over here."

Anthony was one of the regular drivers, and Joe had known him for almost two years. Joe noticed he had a bandage around his arm as they walked back to the desk.

1

"You alright?" Joe asked. "Your wife beat you up again?"

Anthony shot him a look. Anthony's wife was an amateur bodybuilder, who was nearly twice his size. Secretly, Joe felt bad for him. Joe was still head-over-heels in love with his wife Sarah, even after seven years. He couldn't wait to add to their little family in a few weeks. At least half the time he was excited; the other half he was terrified. Anthony, on the other hand, didn't have many good things to say about his wife.

"No, she didn't beat me up, wise-ass," he said. "A homeless guy bit me."

"Bit you? Are you serious?"

"I'm dead serious. The bastard was drunk or something. Bit me while I was getting in my car."

Joe laughed. "You should get your wife to bend him in half, teach him some manners. Did you call the cops or anything?"

"You want me to call the cops on a homeless guy? And stop talking about my wife, or I'll get her down here to smack you around."

Joe watched him as he signed a few forms. His hand shook slightly and he looked pale.

"You might want to go to the hospital. You don't look so good. I mean, worse than usual."

"Ha ha, you little bastard. Wait till you see how you feel in a few months with that newborn baby. Wave goodbye to sleep now."

Joe smiled. "I'll just wake Sarah up."

"Yeah, good luck with that."

They shared another laugh, then Joe became serious as Anthony left through the shipping door.

"Seriously, man. Go to the hospital."

"Yeah, yeah. I'm gonna take a nap in the truck, drop this load off, then I'll head over."

The door closed behind Anthony. Joe heard the door to his truck open and shut.

The break bell rang. Saturday was only a six hour shift. Sometimes Joe would skip break and punch out early. Not today. He wanted a coffee from the break room.

Their break room was simple enough. Vending machines, water fountain in the corner, some microwaves scattered around. They even had a little television on a stand against the wall. More people were gathered around than usual. Joe grew curious as he took a sip of coffee.

"What's up guys? Cartoons on?"

They didn't answer. It took a good ten seconds for anyone to notice he even said anything. Finally, his friend Brian turned around.

"Man, check this out. There's some scary shit going on."

Joe stepped forward and looked over everyone's shoulders to see the TV. It looked like a riot, filmed from a helicopter. Sadly, the scene didn't shake him that much. It seemed like every other day there was some kind of violence on the news.

What did catch his attention, however, were the words *New York City* at the bottom of the screen.

"A riot in New York? What are they fighting over?"

"Not just New York," Brian said. "*Everywhere.*"

Joe kept quiet and listened to the reporter: *"There is speculation that this is a biological terrorist attack. However, reports are now coming in that the mass outbreak of violence is happening in London, Tokyo, Sidney, on every continent. Authorities are advising everyone to stay in their homes."*

"This is un-fucking-real," Brian said.

Danny, the supervisor, walked into the break room. Joe felt an eerie sense of deja vu. The last time everyone had gathered in the break room to watch a life-altering event was on September 11th, 2001.

"Guys, I just caught some weird ass stories on the net," Danny said. "What the hell is going on?"

No one answered. They were hypnotized by the news.

It almost didn't seem real. Joe actually thought, just for a second, that this was some kind of joke. Someone had made a gag tape and put it in the VCR. But the mood of the break room told him this was no joke. He turned around and grabbed his cell phone from his belt. His first thought was to his wife Sarah.

"Hello?"

Her voice calmed him. Sarah had that effect on him.

"Hey baby. It's me."

"Joe, you won't believe this. There's fifteen cop cars down the street. Someone ran a car into a house! I think it's on fire. Can you believe that?"

"Listen honey. Are you watching the news?"

"No, why?"

"There's something really weird going on. I'm gonna cut out early today, soon. You stay at the house, alright?"

"Sure. Me and Margie are just watching what's going on outside."

Margie was Sarah's best friend. They were in high school together and had always been close. Joe liked her. She'd been helping them a lot during Sarah's pregnancy, especially with Joe working extra hours.

"Okay, I'll be home soon. Tell our son I'm leaving now."

"You mean our daughter."

Joe smiled. Eight months into their pregnancy and they didn't know the sex of their child. They wanted to be surprised. They still hadn't picked a name out for the baby, and Joe was getting nervous. He didn't want their first child to be in his mother's arms for the first time without a name. But Sarah had rejected every name they'd come up with.

"I'll see you when I get home."

"Okay, love you sweetie."

"Everyone," Danny said behind him. "I think we're just gonna close up shop for the day. Let's all just go home and take care of our own."

Some relief passed through the break room, before the television spoke again.

"The Centers for Disease Control is now issuing a public health warning. They believe whatever is causing people to exhibit violent behavior could possibly be spread through a bite or direct contact with open wounds. Again, you are urged to stay in your homes."

They showed different camera feeds taken from all over the world. Joe couldn't look away. It wasn't just mob violence he was watching. This was something different. The people didn't carry guns or knives. They just attacked people. A camera in Ontario showed a mob tackling a woman to the ground. It looked like they were trying to *eat* her.

Brian noticed it too. "What the…what in the hell are they doing to her?"

Joe couldn't believe it. The camera was quite a distance away in the sky, but they could tell what was happening. The woman struggled for only a moment, then a pool of blood began forming under her. Her attackers didn't even care. They just sat there in it.

Even the news anchor narrating the feed seemed shaken.

"Uh, I can't believe what we're witnessing here. We've heard rumors, but it looks like we have confirmation. This virus, whatever it is, however it's spreading, looks like it causes… cannibalism."

Joe shook his head. He felt sick to his stomach. Then he remembered Anthony, just talking to him five minutes ago at the loading dock.

He had been bitten by someone, and he looked *very* sick.

Joe didn't even get a chance to tell Danny when they all heard a loud crash outside. Everyone ran out of the break room and hopped down from one of the open docks.

The warehouse was located in an industrial complex. There wasn't much traffic, and every car that went by the plant was either going to or leaving a job.

Anthony had jumped the curb in his truck, ran through the fence separating them from the street, and drove right into the side of a Honda Civic that was passing by. The smaller car was pinned between the truck and a light pole.

"Holy shit!"

"Call 9-1-1!"

"That's Anthony's truck, isn't it?"

Everyone ran to the scene. A few men reached for their cell phones. Joe was in the lead. He stopped near the driver's side door of Anthony's truck and looked toward the Civic. The entire side was smashed in. He could see a woman by herself.

She wasn't moving. Her head slumped against the steering wheel. Her lifeless eyes looked toward the ground outside. Her face was covered in blood and a piece of glass stuck out of her neck.

Joe had seen her before. He didn't know her name. He would see her driving somewhere deeper in the complex. She always dressed nice, so he figured she had an office job. She would smile and wave to the guys at the picnic tables outside the plant as she went by.

Now she was dead.

Joe had never seen a dead body before. He was surprisingly numb. He could hear his coworkers around him.

"Oh shit! I think that lady's dead."

"I think an ambulance is coming. I got cut off halfway through. I lost the signal or something."

"Is Anthony alright?"

"He's moving! Hey, Anthony? You okay, buddy?"

Brian knew enough not to move Anthony until the paramedics arrived, but he wanted to talk to him, make sure he was okay. He opened the passenger's side door and leaned in.

Anthony moved his head from side to side, like he was confused. Brian saw his bandaged arm and what looked like a huge amount of blood under the gauze.

"Yo, Anthony?" Brian whispered.

Anthony whipped his head around to look at Brian. The sudden movement scared him, but not as much as what he saw.

Something was very wrong with Anthony.

His skin was pale white. His eyes were sunken with huge black circles around them. Brian could see very little of his eyes at all, almost like he had milky white contact lenses over them. His head just moved around like a baby's, like he couldn't control it.

Anthony let out a deep groan and reached out to grab Brian. He pushed against his still-attached seat belt and bit Brian right on the arm. Brian yelled and his legs slipped out from under him. He was hanging halfway out of the truck. Anthony didn't bite like a child. He sank his teeth into Brian's flesh and twisted like he was biting into a juicy steak. Brian ripped his arm away while Joe and Danny moved behind him, pulling him out by his legs. Brian cradled his arm as blood dropped to the street.

"He fucking bit me!"

Joe remembered what he saw on TV, about whatever it was being passed around by bites or open wounds.

He also remembered the part about cannibalism.

He searched everyone's faces. Clearly others were thinking the same thing, because they started to back up, keeping a wary eye on Brian.

Joe didn't back up. He pulled his shirt off and wrapped it tightly around Brian's arm. He winced in pain and just clutched his arm close to his chest. Joe grabbed him by the shoulders and led him to the curb.

"Alright man, just sit here. Keep as much pressure on it as you can. The ambulance is coming."

The crowd was divided as they watched Anthony from both sides of the truck. Joe stood next to Danny and watched from the open passenger's side door.

Anthony thrashed around wildly in his seat, his mouth ringed in Brian's blood, still chewing on the piece of flesh from Brian's arm. Joe almost lost his breakfast. Every time someone would say something, Anthony would look at them and let out a noise that shook Joe to the bone. Anthony didn't even try to form words. He just moaned and struggled against his seat belt. He didn't seem to realize that with just the press of a button he would be free.

Danny leaned close to Joe. "What the hell is wrong with him?"

"I don't know, but look at him. Something's really off."

"Oh really? You think so?"

Joe ignored his supervisor's sarcasm. "No, I mean, just *look* at him. It looks like he's-"

"Dead," Danny finished.

"Uh, guys," someone said from the other side of the truck. "You'd better get over here."

Everyone jogged around the trailer and joined the group on the other side. Joe stopped just a few feet away from the driver's side door. He could hear Anthony, still moaning and reaching out for them. But he almost seemed like an afterthought now.

The woman who drove the Civic, dead just a few minutes ago, slowly crawled out of the broken window of her car. She let out a moan just like Anthony. The entire group winced as she fell to the ground hard. She didn't hold her hands up, didn't try to break her fall. She just fell face first onto some shattered glass without a single cry of pain. She didn't even flinch. She just kept letting out that dreadful wail.

"Uh, ma'am," Danny said, "you've just had an accident. You might want to take it easy."

He took a step toward her. Joe reached out and grabbed him. He didn't think it was a good idea to even get near her.

She slowly climbed to her feet, an act itself that looked odd. It almost looked like her muscles didn't want to work. She stumbled a few times, falling against the car. Her eyes were just like Anthony's, milky white and lifeless. The piece of glass that was in her neck had fallen out, leaving a huge cut. But blood didn't gush out. It simply dripped down her neck onto her dress, like her heart wasn't even beating anymore.

She surveyed the group quickly, then lunged toward Danny. She was surprisingly fast now that she was on her feet. Both Danny and Joe barely ducked out of the way in time. She stumbled and fell once again to the ground. Danny and a few guys from the electrical department jumped on her back. She struggled to move and reached for anyone to grab.

"Lady, you have to calm down!" Danny shouted.

Joe looked up at Anthony, still trapped behind the seat belt. He let out another agitated moan and reached out through the broken window.

"I don't think they're gonna say anything. They're crazy now or something."

They heard a voice from the other side of the trailer.

"Uh, guys." It was Brian. "I'm not feeling so good over here."

Joe and a few others ran back to the other side. Joe didn't mean to, but he gasped when he saw Brian. He looked terrible. He still sat on the curb, cradling his arm in his lap. His face was pale white and covered with sweat. Joe could still see his eyes, unlike the woman and Anthony, but they had huge black circles around them.

"I think I'm gonna be sick," he said.

No one stepped toward him. Joe pointed at the ground behind him. "Just lay down, on the grass there. Help's coming."

Joe had doubts that help was on the way. If there were riots happening all over the world, would ambulances care about one little phone call at a warehouse?

He grabbed his cell phone and called his wife. It took three tries to get through. He wanted to tell her to get in the house and lock every door and window. A woman answered the phone, but it wasn't Sarah.

"Hello?"

"Margie? Is everything okay?"

"Yes, Joe, everything's fine."

He felt panic, then quickly shoved it aside. "Where's Sarah? What's going on?"

"Here, talk to him a sec," Margie said, handing the phone over to Sarah.

"Joe?"

It was Sarah. Joe closed his eyes with relief.

"Sarah. Honey, what's happening?"

"Well, uh, we're getting ready to have a baby. I tried to call you, but I kept getting some message about all circuits being busy."

"The baby? But you're still two weeks out!"

"Yeah, well, tell *her* that."

Joe had waited for this moment for months. He knew it would be one of those moments he'd never forget. He often wondered where he'd be when it happened. Maybe at home in the middle of the night, at the store, or outside doing the lawn. He even prepared himself for that phone call when he was at work. He had his drive to the hospital all planned out. They had a bag packed near the front door containing every possible thing Sarah might need. Spare clothes, a camera for pictures of the birth, a list of every single friend to call. They had a car seat already installed in the back of Sarah's car. They had planned for everything.

Now, as Joe held the phone to his ear, Brian leaned forward to vomit. Danny was struggling to keep a violent woman pinned to the ground. Anthony lashed out at everyone within ten feet of the truck. They were in the middle of an emergency.

"You're going to the hospital?"

"Yes. I tried to call Doctor Rivers, but couldn't get through to him. Meet us there. But Joe, please, be careful. There's some really weird shit happening on the roads."

"Fights?"

"It's really scary. We just missed having an accident. Some guy knocked someone down right by the car. We almost hit him. It looked like he was trying to *bite* him."

They lived in the suburbs. The riots that Joe had seen on the news hadn't spread that far yet. But it sounded like it wasn't far off. He looked up at Anthony once again. What could possibly be going on?

Joe tried to think positive, but it wasn't working. *Sarah and Margie are going to the hospital, where no doubt everyone else is gonna go. But they have no choice.*

"Okay, I'm leaving work now. I love you, Sarah. Put Margie back on."

A brief silence. He heard Sarah breathing uncomfortably in the background. He wanted to be with her desperately, to shield her and their child from the things happening around them.

"Joe? What's up?" Margie asked.

"Listen, Margie. Don't stop at any red lights. Take it slow, but don't stop for anything, okay?"

"No problem there. Whoa! Joe, we just passed three people beating the shit out of some guy against a van! What the hell is going on?"

He took a breath. He wanted to tell them what was happening on the news and at the plant, but it would take too long.

"The news isn't quite sure yet, but it's bad. Just get to the hospital. I'll be there soon."

"Okay. See you soon."

He put his cell phone away and jogged back to Danny, who was still struggling with the woman. He had his knees driven into her back now, but she still fought and wailed.

"I have to go. Sarah's in labor."

Danny nodded. "Get out of here. Be safe out there."

Joe ran across the parking lot and climbed in his truck. He sped away from the warehouse back toward the suburbs.

Two minutes after he left, Brian's heart stopped beating. Four minutes after that, he stood back up. He bit Danny and a few of Joe's coworkers. Not long after, everyone that worked with Joe that Saturday wandered the parking lot without a purpose, with no memory of their previous life. It was only when a few other delivery trucks arrived that they perked up.

Brian, Danny, Anthony, and the rest of Joe's coworkers feasted on the truck drivers until there was barely anything left.

❦ ❦ ❦

Joe sped through the streets toward the hospital as fast he could reasonably go. He kept his emergency flashers on and slowly cruised through the red lights. For a while, he drove without incident, and it looked like whatever was happening across the world had skipped over his town. But then he saw police cars with their lights on stopped at a corner. They were trying to pull two women off of a child while a crowd gathered to watch. He drove another block, and saw what looked like a riot inside a corner Starbucks.

He didn't know what was going on. But in the back of his mind he knew it was huge, world-changing big. But he didn't care about the world. He cared about Sarah. He had to get to her. He had to be there for the birth of his child. Then they would figure this whole thing out. All he needed was his family, and he could survive anything.

He narrowly missed hitting a woman as she fled from another man. He saw a motel just off the road on fire. He had to weave his way between a few cars that had stopped to look. The firemen, instead of putting out the fire, were trying to pull a woman off of one of their own.

He was a block away from the hospital when he decided to call Sarah. He didn't know anything. He didn't know what room she was in, if she went through the main entrance or emergency room.

The phone didn't even ring. It went right to a recording saying that all circuits were busy.

"Dammit!"

Joe tried to keep calm. He would park his truck, and go to the main entrance. He would ask whoever was working the front desk where his wife was. Then he would kiss her and everything would be okay.

His jaw dropped as he slowly pulled up to the hospital.

An ambulance had crashed into the front, near the main entrance doors. Fire danced from under the hood, throwing black smoke everywhere. No one was trying to put it out at all.

He didn't even bother looking for a parking spot. He pulled his truck onto the curb and killed the engine. As he climbed out he heard gunshots and a few screams off in the distance.

He didn't move for a second. Fear and confusion just locked his legs. It was only a picture of Sarah in his head that got him moving again.

CHAPTER 2

Denise Hutchins hadn't put herself through six years of nursing school to work the front desk of the hospital emergency room. But that's exactly what she was doing. Her friend Lisa had called out the night before, something about being sick with a fever. So Denise was in the middle of a midnight to noon shift, and it didn't take long to realize something was wrong.

Most overnight shifts weren't too bad. There were the drunks that were brought in to sleep it off, then released. There were some car accidents. There were the freaky sex emergencies that always gave Denise a chuckle, like the one time a woman popped a hip riding her boyfriend.

But this shift was far different.

The first patient was a woman in her early twenties, like Denise. She'd gotten into a scuffle with another woman at a nightclub and actually got bitten. Her wound was treated and she was sent on her way. Then three more people came into the emergency room with bite wounds. One woman had bites all over her body. She said two men pulled her into an alley. They didn't sexually assault her in any way, they just bit her. A bite wound on her leg was really nasty, like whoever it was that did it was biting into a tasty drumstick.

Then the man with the cowboy hat came in.

The emergency room was already half full when he limped through the sliding doors. Nearly half the people waiting to be seen had bite wounds. Cowboy stumbled in and leaned his weight on one of the waiting room chairs. He had a bloody towel pressed to his neck. The color was completely gone from his face. He looked around the room, dizzy.

"Please," he whispered. "Help me."

He collapsed to the floor. He dropped the towel, and blood poured from his neck. Everyone in the waiting room took in a breath and backed up. Denise quickly paged Dr. Blair. She ran out of the emergency room corner office and knelt next to Cowboy. She pushed the towel back to his neck and checked for a pulse. She had seen death enough times to recognize it immediately, but she had to go through the motions.

No pulse, no breathing. He was gone.

Still, he wasn't really dead until Dr. Blair said so. He, along with two nurses, burst through the swinging doors that separated the waiting room from the rest of the hospital. Denise stepped back and let them go to work.

She felt a quick stab of sadness, like she always did when someone died in the hospital. She'd wanted to be a nurse to help people, but she had learned that she couldn't be a good nurse if she dwelled too long on the people that died. She used to do that all the time. She would think about the people that died on her watch, what they did for a living, how their families would act

Not this time. She just wanted to go home. Two more hours, and her shift was done.

As she took a step back toward the front desk she heard the television in the corner.

"*...the dead are returning to life...*"

The attention of everyone in the waiting room was divided. Some were fascinated by the sight of Dr. Blair trying to revive Cowboy. Others were glued to the strange news on the television.

"*...not a hoax or a prank. Authorities still don't know if what is affecting the global population is a virus, biological attack, or natural phenomenon. But they do know that it is reanimating dead tissue. If you've been bitten by one of the infected, seek treatment immediately.*"

A six-year-old boy looked up at his father. "Daddy, Brandy bit me on the swings today. Am I going to die?"

"No, no, of course not," he said. "That's ridiculous."

"It *is* ridiculous," Dr. Blair said. He'd just finished trying to revive Cowboy, but that wasn't possible. Cowboy was dead. He gestured for one of the nurses to get a gurney, then pointed at the television. "Turn that off. There's no need to make people panic. I've been listening to that all morning. What they're saying is impossible."

There was a loud crash outside. Denise's heart thumped in her chest. Most everyone in the waiting room ran outside to see what was going on. Denise wanted to join them, but her professionalism—as well as her fear—kept her behind her desk. She was terrified. She could feel that something terrible was going on.

Dr. Blair and the rest of the crowd saw the ambulance buried in the front entrance of the hospital. The tires kept spinning, but it couldn't get any deeper into the lobby. Blair thought he saw flames under the hood.

People ran all over the parking lot. The accident was drawing a crowd on the sidewalk.

Denise just stared at the sliding glass doors from behind her desk. She could hear the television, but she wasn't focused on it. She looked at the few people still in the waiting room, including the father and son.

"It's going to be okay," she said, not believing her own words. "We'll get you fixed up and out of here."

The little boy couldn't look at anything except the dead body, still on the floor. His father tried to keep him facing the wall, but the boy would turn his head just slightly and take peeks.

Cowboy twitched.

The boy didn't scream. His jaw just hung open and he pointed. Denise followed the boy's finger.

She *did* scream. "Dr. Blair! Get in here!"

Cowboy was slowly pulling himself to his feet. Dr. Blair and two others stood at the emergency room entrance while people ran around in the parking lot. Everyone just stared in amazement.

Cowboy lunged for the closest person: Dr. Blair. He sunk his teeth into the flesh just under Blair's eye and they both fell to the ground. The father and son screamed and cowered in the corner near the television. Blair tried to push Cowboy away, but that only sent more shocks of pain through his face.

A gunshot rang out.

Denise looked to the exit doors. She recognized one of the men that had been patiently waiting in the emergency room. So many names and faces passed through her mind each day, she didn't remember his name. He had shot Cowboy in the leg.

"Sir, release that man now. Or I *will* fire again."

Denise guessed he was a cop. She prayed he was.

Off duty police officer Frank Kinkade watched for a few more seconds as Cowboy continued to chew on Blair's face. He expected Cowboy to cry out in pain, roll over and hold his leg. He did no such thing.

"Get him off me!" Blair shouted.

Frank felt silly for only a moment, then he pistol whipped Cowboy seven times in the head. He still didn't make a sound, but he did let go of Blair. Frank grabbed the doctor by the shoulders and hauled him to his feet. Blair kept a hand pressed to his face, blood squirting everywhere.

Cowboy looked up at both of them and let out an angry moan. Blood dripped from his teeth and tongue to the floor.

Frank didn't hesitate a second time. He raised his gun directly at Cowboy's head and pulled the trigger. Brain matter exploded from his skull and sprayed on the floor behind him. He fell to the floor, dead a second time.

The father and son were openly crying now. Denise couldn't find any words. No one spoke at all. The only sounds were the chaos in the parking lot and the television.

Blair was the first one to speak. "You...you killed him."

Frank shot him a look. "Haven't you been listening to the news? Hell, you checked him yourself. He was already dead."

"That isn't possible."

They didn't get a chance to continue the debate. Two women walked into the emergency room. One was very pregnant, and waddled slowly. The other had her hand on her friend's shoulders, just slowly walking with her.

"What is going on outside?" Sarah Thompson asked.

Both women stopped and cried out when they saw what was left of Cowboy sprawled on the floor. Dr. Blair was treating himself, rubbing his face with alcohol and pressing gauze to the wound Cowboy had left behind.

"My friend is having a baby," Margie said.

Dr. Blair took a deep breath. This was turning into a crisis, if it wasn't already.

"I'll take them back," he told Denise. "Get some help up here."

Dr. Blair grabbed a wheelchair and helped Sarah sit down. Denise knew this was against procedure, but she couldn't remember procedure at that moment. They didn't know the woman's name. She wasn't logged into the system. No insurance information. Nothing at all.

Sarah tried to turn her head to Denise as Blair pushed her down the hall. "My husband is coming!" she called.

Denise barely heard her.

Frank took a quick peek outside. The parking lot was empty, but he could hear the violence off in the distance. Screams, gunshots, people running, those awful moans.

He walked around Cowboy and up to Denise at the desk.

"Ma'am, I've been here for two hours now. I came here with my sister, Brandy Kinkade. They took her back a while ago. Can you tell me where she is?"

Denise was quiet a moment, just looking at Frank's face with her mouth open. He had to shake her shoulder to snap her out of it. She was embarrassed. She was a medical professional. She was supposed to have better control over herself.

"Yes, I'm sorry. Brandy Kinkade." She sat down at the computer. "Let me see."

She didn't get the chance to look.

A mob of people burst into the waiting room. Some came from the outside, while others came from the stairwell in the corner. They ran right to the father and son near the television.

The mob didn't show any mercy.

Frank raised his gun, but he held off from firing. He was afraid to draw attention his way.

He fought off the guilt and the sounds of a boy and his father dying. He quickly opened the door to the office that Denise was in. She was shutting the glass window that separated her desk from the waiting room. Frank locked the door behind him. They both climbed under the desk and just listened.

Denise kept a hand clamped over her mouth while tears streamed down her face. She heard the father and son screaming in agony, then they were quiet. She heard the sounds of the mob feasting. Disgusting, horrifying noises. She saw shadows on the back wall that hinted at the Hell that was happening. The office itself was locked, but the glass window didn't lock at all. They weren't safe.

They're just twenty feet away. We're next.

Over the sounds of the creatures eating, they could still hear the television.

"...have here footage in Brazil of an attack at a funeral. I know it's hard to believe, but it looks like the body actually climbed out of the coffin. The deceased died from a broken neck at a construction site, but it didn't seem to slow him here. Only physical brain trauma seems to put them down, whatever they are..."

Frank and Denise stayed under the desk for ten minutes. There was nothing they could do. The creatures grew bored of the cold flesh they shoved in their mouths. They rose up and wandered away, searching for their next hot meal. Some went outside, while others went deeper into the hospital.

Denise almost let out a cry when she saw a small shadow rise up on the back wall. There was a moan that was a higher pitch than the others. The mob had left just enough of the boy for him to rise among the dead.

The waiting room grew quiet, but that didn't make Denise feel better. An hour ago, she was doing her job. Now, the world was tearing itself apart. Reporters on television were interviewing witnesses to different attacks. One interview was cut short when a mob of people attacked the camera team. Frank lowered his head as their screams turned into a *technical difficulties* message.

Frank thought desperately about his next move. His sister was somewhere in the hospital. She was all he had left, after their parents died in a car crash four years ago. He had to find her, then get someplace safe. It was that simple. Whatever was going on in the world, they could figure that out later.

There was a voice in the waiting room.

"Oh my God! Hello? Is anyone here?"

Denise poked her head above the desk. A lean man with no shirt looked at the corpses on the floor. He had some blood on his hands, but didn't look injured.

She waved wildly and finally got his attention. She pointed to the door behind her. "There's a door on the side here! Hurry!"

Several moans from just beyond the double doors leading into the hospital got Joe moving. As he sprinted to the door Frank was moving to unlock it. Part of Frank, even the law enforcement part, told him that Joe was on his own. But he fought those feelings and let Joe in. He couldn't help the father and son against the huge mob that attacked, but he could help Joe.

Joe nearly fell into the office as Frank locked the door again. They quietly scurried under the desk as five more of the creatures burst into the waiting room.

The creatures sniffed the air. They knew more warm flesh was nearby. They didn't know it was just six feet away on the other side of an office wall. They didn't even know what an office wall was anymore. After a few minutes, they stumbled to the parking lot, where the scent of flesh was much stronger in the open air.

Joe looked at Denise and Frank. He saw Frank had a gun in his hand and a holster under his coat. Denise was probably a few years younger than him, obviously a nurse. She would know where Sarah was.

Denise moved her lips slowly enough for the men to read. She still didn't dare make a sound.

What are they?

Joe shrugged, but he knew they couldn't be human, at least not anymore. He knew humans could be absolutely terrible creatures. But cannibalism, feeling no pain, that was something else entirely.

He leaned toward Denise and spoke in a whisper. "Sarah Thompson, I need to find her."

"And Brandy Kinkade."

Denise closed her eyes and held her hands up. She tried to think rationally, but the fear knocked those rational thoughts aside.

"*Listen,*" she said. "The news says these things are walking dead bodies. And we're in a hospital, the worst place to be. Now, I want to help people, but I also don't want to die. We should leave *right now*. Sarah and Brandy, they're probably already dead."

Frank barely heard a word she said. He carefully reached up and grabbed the keyboard from her desk. "Look her up. What room is she in?"

Denise sighed and ran a quick search on Frank's sister. She skimmed through the doctor's notes as fast as she could.

Her voice fell. "She's in ICU."

"ICU?"

"She was bitten, wasn't she?"

He nodded. "Yes. Out jogging this morning in the park."

"Her condition got worse, so they transferred her to ICU. Listen, Frank, she's probably-"

"Where is the ICU?"

"Second floor."

Frank checked the magazine in his gun as quietly as he could.

"I, uh, suppose you don't have another one of those?" Joe asked, pointing to the nine millimeter weapon.

"Afraid not."

"Didn't think so." He looked at Denise. "Sarah Thompson."

Denise ran the search. "Nothing."

"What? I know she's here."

"She's not in the system. I'm really sorry, but as you can see, this place is falling apart."

"Come on. Beautiful blond pregnant woman, a pretty brunette would have been with her, her best friend."

Denise's eyes lit up. "Ah! Yes, Dr. Blair took her back. But she's not in the system yet. And that...that can't be good. I don't know what room she's in."

"Where the hell do they deliver babies here?"

"Third floor."

Joe looked at Frank. He wished they were going together, since Frank had the gun. But he knew that wouldn't happen. They both had different people they needed to get to.

"Good luck, man," Joe said.

"You too. Listen, whatever it is people are becoming, you have to nail the brain to take them down. I shot that guy out there in the leg. He didn't even flinch."

"Thanks."

He looked around the office for a weapon. There was nothing at all that caught his eye that he could wield. His eyes fell on a spare computer keyboard in the corner. With nothing else to use, he grabbed it and took a few practice swings.

Despite everything around them, Frank smirked and shook his head.

"Okay, hold on," Denise said. "Just hold on a second."

She grabbed the computer monitor and stretched the cables enough so she could put it on the floor. She logged into the network-based security camera system. She shouldn't have known the passwords, but Gary, the IT tech who always tried to impress her, showed her once how to log on.

They didn't like what they saw.

Denise slowly cycled through the camera feeds. Joe and Frank crouched and watched over her shoulder. Her eyes burned as she wiped away tears. The cameras showed them what she had already guessed.

The hospital was a lost cause.

All it took was bite wound victims being moved all over the hospital. The creatures were everywhere. She cringed as she watched people running for their lives down the halls, doctors that once cared for patients eating those same patients' intestines.

"I'm sorry, guys, but I can't go with you."

Frank nodded. "I understand. Get your loved ones and get someplace safe."

A sad thought crossed Denise's mind. Her mother was drunk somewhere in a bar in California. She hadn't spoken to her father since the day he'd walked out on her and Mom, almost ten years ago. Six years of having her nose in medical books didn't leave her with a lot of time to make friends.

She had no one.

Frank opened the door and sprinted across the empty waiting room. Joe was a step behind. They knew it was empty now, but it could be full of those creatures at any second. They had to be quick and quiet.

They went up the stairs without incident. When they got to the door leading to the second floor Frank peeked through the glass window. He pulled his head back when he saw a head pass by.

Frank saw two men and a woman kneeling next to a man on the floor. One of the creatures used to be a patient. His robe was open in the back, revealing a slice that went from his tailbone all the way to the bottom of his neck. Frank could see the muscle tissue exposed.

He put a hand on Joe's shoulder, not wanting him to look. Joe felt ridiculous. He still carried the spare keyboard, while Frank had a gun.

"This is my stop," Frank said.

Doubt started to creep into Joe's mind. *This is crazy,* he thought. *I'm not gonna make it.*

He had to try. His wife and child, and Margie, needed him.

Joe just gave Frank a nod. Frank pulled open the door and took his first steps onto the second floor. As Joe ran up the stairs he heard Frank shooting.

His hopes fell. How far did he really expect to get with a keyboard as a weapon?

He looked through the window leading to the third floor. Down the hall he could see someone walking, his back facing Joe. For a moment, he thought it was a normal person. Then he noticed the slow, unsteady gait. In a closet just behind the creature, a mother burst the door open and fell to the ground. Her young daughter, whom the parent had spent the last hour hiding in the closet with and treating her wounds, tore a chunk of flesh out of her mother's back. The other creature turned and joined in the attack.

"My God, this can't be happening."

A hand grabbed his shoulder from behind.

Joe spun around and cocked the keyboard back, ready to strike. Denise held up her hands and shielded her face.

"Hey, hey! It's me!"

He let out a breath and lowered his weapon. "Shit, lady! What are you doing here?"

"I, uh, don't really have anywhere else to go. And you need help. You gotta find your family. Hell, that's my job here. I'm supposed to help people."

Joe was surprised. He didn't expect help from anyone. He gave her a smile and looked at the fire extinguisher she carried. It was no doubt a little sturdier than the keyboard he had.

He stuttered. He didn't know what to say. "I...well...thank you. I owe you one."

"I'm Denise."

"Joe."

Denise pushed her face to the glass. She looked away when she saw the disgusting feast still happening at the end of the hall.

"Okay, the maternity ward isn't too far away. It's just two halls over to the right. But...I don't know what we're gonna find there."

He took a breath. "You ready?"

She nodded.

Joe opened the door. The two creatures at the end of the hall looked up. They climbed to their feet and started walking quickly.

"Come on," Denise urged.

They took the hall slowly but steadily. It took everything Joe had not to break into a run. He heard the two creatures trying to catch up behind him, but he told himself they were slow. If they ran, they would make noise, and who knew what they would run into?

As they approached one hall intersection Joe saw a hand grab the corner of the wall, then pulled around the corner. Denise recognized the man as Dr. Jay, a nice man who always told her how pretty she looked.

He looked at her now and wailed. His eye hung halfway out of the socket. When he opened his jaw to moan, the eye fell out completely, held only by the optic nerve.

Denise was now convinced that they were walking corpses.

Joe, who hadn't kept track of the news, was stunned. He knew they didn't feel pain, but this was too much.

He raced toward what used to be Dr. Jay and swung the keyboard as hard as he could across his face, breaking the cheap plastic. Dr. Jay stumbled backwards and fell awkwardly on his leg. Joe heard it break.

That still didn't stop the doctor. He slowly crawled toward them, drooling blood on the floor.

"The ward's one more hall over," Denise said, grabbing his arm. "Let's go."

As they passed an exam room, Denise saw a nurse she used to eat lunch with ripping the tongue out of someone's mouth. The nurse, with the scent of warm flesh in her nose, left her cooling meal and stood up.

"We have to hurry before we attract too much attention," Joe said.

"We're here. Just this next left."

When they reached the intersection they stopped. Joe looked down a long hall with rooms on both sides. A creature had a woman pinned to the wall, teeth in her throat, about halfway up the hall.

"Dr. Blair would have brought her here."

Joe looked behind him. Three creatures were still slowly approaching, their arms outstretched. He took the fire extinguisher from Denise.

"I guess we have to look in every room, right?"

She nodded.

They started searching rooms. The first room they saw that wasn't empty had a creature eating someone's foot. Joe ran forward and smashed him in the head with the extinguisher.

The noise attracted the attention of the single creature ahead of them. The three others still tailed them as well.

"They're gonna pin us in," Denise said.

Joe wasn't worried too much about the creature ahead. He could simply knock him over and run. But Denise was right, they needed to hurry.

They approached a large room to their left with a huge viewing glass, and a mini lobby across from it. The single creature was twenty yards away. Joe took a quick look.

It had been the hospital nursery.

It wasn't a nursery any longer.

Rows and rows of tiny beds were knocked over. He couldn't see what the creatures were doing, but they were on their hands and knees, reaching into the beds. Not a single baby made a sound.

Joe lost it. He leaned over and vomited. The creature approaching them was getting dangerously close. It actually seemed to get faster as it drew near.

"Joe, we gotta move. Come on."

He snapped. As he wiped his mouth, he could only think one thing. *Is my baby in there?*

He ran forward and swung the extinguisher as hard as he could. The creature fell to the ground, a huge dent where its forehead used to be. But Joe didn't stop. He hit the thing eight more times, until its brain leaked out of its crushed skull.

Denise was crying. Joe was hunched over, vomiting again. Thick, almost coagulated blood was smeared on his chest from destroying the thing. She ran up to him and grabbed him by the shoulders.

"You have to get it together!" she almost screamed at him. "We have to keep-"

She cut herself off when she saw movement to her right. She looked into the room next to them, and recognized Dr. Blair.

Joe's murder of the creature attracted the attention of five more of them, all coming out of different rooms. They were moving much faster than the others. Joe and Denise were trapped now.

"Come on!"

She dragged Joe into the nearby room and locked the door behind them.

Dr. Blair was standing near the window, just swaying back and forth, with his back toward them. Blood covered the bed and walls. There was movement on the floor. The angle they had from the hallway didn't let Denise see it, but someone else was in the room.

Joe thought maybe he had died and gone to Hell. He thought back to his chaotic day. The warehouse, then the hospital. He didn't remember dying along the way, but that was the only way to explain what he was seeing.

His beloved wife Sarah crawled out from next to the bed. The gown she had on was twisted and covered in blood, and showed most of her front. Her stomach was split open. Intestines dragged along the floor as she let out a moan that threatened to send Joe over the edge.

He couldn't move or think. All he could do was look into the hollow face of his once beautiful wife. He didn't hear the crowd of walking dead gather outside the locked maternity ward room. He didn't hear Denise next to him urging him to do something. He wanted to crawl to the corner and die, but his legs refused to carry him anywhere.

He thought of the last time he saw her. It was at the front door, where they hugged and kissed goodbye before he left for work that morning. He had no idea then that it was the last hug and kiss they would ever share.

Denise plunged the scalpel she found on the table next to them deep into the skull of Sarah Thompson before she could crawl any closer. She fell lifeless to the floor, the womb where their baby once grew exposed.

Dr. Blair shuffled forward. He had more bite wounds than when Denise saw him earlier. His neck was ripped open, exposing tissue and muscle. Joe didn't even realize Denise had taken the extinguisher from him. She beat Blair in the head till he fell, then beat him some more.

Denise looked at Joe. She knew he was out of it, just leaning against the locked door. He seemed oblivious to the pounding coming from the other side. She gently grabbed him by the shoulders and leaned him against the closed bathroom door.

She knew they weren't getting out the way they came in, not with all the creatures on the other side. She stepped over Blair's corpse and looked out the window. The emergency waiting room was its own little addition, and the roof to it was just outside. The window didn't open large enough to walk through. It only cracked a little, to get air. She swung the extinguisher through the glass, being careful not to cut herself. She ran back to get Joe. The pounding on the door was getting louder.

"Let's go," she said. "We can climb out on the roof here and jump down. It's not a short fall, but we'll figure something out."

Joe blinked twice. Tears stained his face. "I-I think I'll stay here."

"What?"

"Sarah…she's gone."

Denise grabbed his face gently. She had just stabbed a woman in the head and beat a man to death. She was amazed she was keeping it together as well as she was.

"Joe, she would not want you to die here."

Before he could respond, there was a voice in the bathroom behind him. "H-Hello? Is someone out there?"

Joe thought he recognized the voice. He turned the handle to find the bathroom locked.

"Unlock the door."

The door opened to reveal Margie. She was a mess. Her shirt was torn, blood smeared down her face. Her pretty blue eyes were bloodshot from crying.

In her arms, she held a tiny baby boy. He slept peacefully, wrapped in a blue blanket.

"What in the *hell* is happening?" Margie asked.

Denise shook her head. "People are dying, and getting back up. We have to get out of here."

Margie looked at the locked door in front of them. It actually shook from the pounding.

"Not *that* way."

"No. We can get out through the window."

As Margie moved out of the bathroom Joe pointed at the newborn baby. "Can I hold him?"

She gently placed the hour old baby into his arms. "Of course. He's yours."

Joe was lost in his own world for a moment as he looked at his son. The baby yawned for just a moment, then went back to sleep.

The sounds of fists at the door brought him back to the real world.

"Joe!" Denise called from the window. She had already put a sheet over the sill to cover the shattered glass. "Come on!"

Margie was out on the roof. She helped Denise climb through. Joe moved with new-found purpose. He very carefully handed over his son through the window to Denise, then climbed through himself. He heard the door splintering behind him. He almost expected something to grab his foot as he stepped onto the roof, but that didn't happen.

They had a better view of the surrounding area. Buildings were on fire. The hospital parking lot was empty of people, except for a few bodies littered about. Some car alarms went off, and they could see the ambulance that had crashed into the hospital earlier was completely engulfed in flames. There was the occasional scream and some small explosions off in the distance, plus the wails of the creatures.

Margie ran to the edge of the roof. It was a good twelve foot drop to the ground. She had no idea how they'd pull it off with a baby.

She turned and screamed when she saw the creatures at the window. Joe spun around.

They weren't coordinated or organized enough to get through. They tried to climb out at the same time, bumping into each other and falling down. But one did manage to make it. Joe acted fast. He ran forward and grabbed the creature before it could stand. He dragged it along the roof and slid it right off the side.

"They'll figure out how to get out eventually," he said. "What are we doing?"

An engine fired up in the parking lot. Denise looked down to see Frank Kinkade sitting behind the wheel of a minivan. He backed out of his parking spot, running over a dead body as he did so.

"Frank!" she called. "Hey, Frank!"

He stopped the van and looked around. It took him a moment to find the voice. He looked up at Denise.

"Can you give us a hand up here?"

Cop or not, Frank was tempted to drive away. He wanted to live through whatever was happening. The more he stopped to help people, the less of a chance that would happen. But he saw Denise and the man whose name he didn't know in the waiting room. They had another woman and a baby with them. He'd never forgive himself if he didn't help.

"I'm gonna back up as close as I can," he shouted. "Hurry up!"

Frank parked under the roof close to the front of the emergency room. Margie jumped on top of the van first and accepted the baby from Denise. Denise was right behind her. Joe was ready to make the leap when he saw Frank pull his gun and aim right at Joe's head. He fired a single time. Joe flinched as the round went past his ear and struck the creature between the eyes behind him that managed to climb out the window.

"Hurry the fuck up!" Frank said.

The women made it inside the van first. A creature shambled toward them from the waiting room as Joe landed on the ground, but a shot from Frank dropped it.

Joe jumped in the side and shut the door. Six creatures seemed to come out of nowhere. They pounded on the sides and back, trailing blood across the van. A creature that used to be a security guard lost its fingernails as it dragged them down the side. The rear window cracked, sending spider-lines across the glass. The baby was awake and crying in Margie's arms.

"Go, go, go!"

Frank hit the gas. He weaved his way in and out of parked cars and ran through a row of bushes next to the sidewalk. He drove past car accidents, creatures shambling through the streets, people dying in the alleys. Margie was in the front seat, Joe, Denise, and the baby in the back. Everyone cried except for Frank. He wanted to join them, but knew he had to keep his composure, even after he saw his sister eating the hand of a doctor in the intensive care.

The world is falling apart, he thought.

"Frank, thank you, thank you so much," Denise said. "Your sister?"

He didn't say anything, just shook his head.

"I'm so sorry."

Frank ignored her. "Look, everyone. I don't know what's going on, but my grandfather used to have a house way up in the woods in Cumberland. I'm going there. You guys can come with me, or I can drop you off somewhere."

"You're a police officer," Denise said. "You're just gonna run?"

He shot her a nasty look in the rear view mirror. "I don't see you back there taking temperatures."

She was quiet.

"Margie," Joe said. He still had trouble talking, but he had to know. "What happened?"

The memory was still fresh in her mind. She wasn't sure if she could talk about it without breaking down.

"I lied, told them she was my sister, so I could be there. Sarah...Sarah died. Dr. Blair, he tried his best, but everything was so screwed. There were people right outside the delivery room, killing each other. She had an aneurysm or something, right when the baby was born."

She cried a moment. Denise put a hand on her shoulder from the back seat.

"He was right in the middle of a C-section. He told me I had to leave, but I wasn't going out there, not with those things. He almost had the baby out when...when Sarah reached up and bit Dr. Blair. She was dead, but she still got up." Margie paused a moment. "I-I cut the cord myself, grabbed the baby, and hid in the bathroom. I could hear Sarah eating him just outside the door. I think he got up too. They beat on the door. They sounded so awful. Something would distract them for a while, but then they would come back and beat on the door some more."

Margie cried at the memory. The entire hour she was in the bathroom she expected them to bust the door down and kill her and the baby. She could hear people being attacked and killed just outside in the hallway.

She suddenly remembered something Sarah said. "Joe, right before the doctor put her under for the C-section, Sarah said 'Tell Joe Aaron'. Do you know what that means?"

He sobbed. Sarah and Joe came up with hundreds of names for their baby over the past eight months. One of the early ideas they liked, but shied away from later, were names that could fit a boy or girl, like Aaron or Erin. Aaron had the bonus of being the name of Joe's father, who Sarah adored as her own before he died.

Joe held out his arms for his son. Denise handed him over, and the baby stopped crying.

"It's okay, Aaron. I'll take great care of you."

Frank made it to the highway. It was almost as bad as the streets near the hospital. Cars were on fire, dead bodies on the shoulder of the road. He even had to maneuver his way around a big rig that was on its side with its trailer blocking most of the highway.

Everyone in the van was quiet. Frank didn't like it, and turned on the radio.

Two deejays debated and theorized as they took calls from several listeners.

"*I'm telling you, these things are walking dead bodies. My neighbor got bit by one, and I can see him now from my kitchen window. He's just standing in his backyard wandering around.*"

"*I've heard the same thing here. It looks like even people that are dying of natural causes are getting back up. Only damaging the brain seems to do anything. I mean, what is going on here?*"

"*You think it's a terrorist attack?*"

"*I doubt it. This is worldwide, and no one has claimed responsibility. Maybe God's just pissed off at us.*"

"*Whatever it is, for anyone listening, just stay inside. They're dangerous, but they don't seem that smart or fast. I've had a few callers say they've seen a few that can run, but not any faster than you or I. So please-*"

They were cut off by the sound of glass breaking.

"*Andrea, are you okay? Oh my God-*"

Those were the last words. Denise put a hand to her mouth as they listened to two men dying over the air waves. There were screams, then they turned into more of a liquid, gargling sound as their throats were ripped open. They could hear whoever Andrea was feasting.

"We're all gonna die," Margie said.

Joe found strength, and it wasn't a mystery where it came from. He looked at little Aaron, still sleeping in his arms.

"We're not gonna die," he said. "We *will* get through this."

"Amen to that," Frank said. "I hope you guys like the outdoors, cause that's where we're headed, at least until this blows over."

They continued on the highway in silence. Each one of them pondered their future.

CHAPTER 3

Frank was wrong.

It didn't blow over.

It didn't take long for the world to die. Two weeks after the dead began to rise, the news stopped broadcasting altogether. There were the assaults on supermarkets and department stores. The power went out slowly across the world, as fewer and fewer people were around to maintain the facilities that had spoiled society for a century.

There was no stopping the walking dead. For every person that died, there was one more walking corpse to avoid. Even deep in the country and small towns, the dead walked. For reasons that science was never able to determine, they didn't decompose like normal corpses.

The living did just as much damage as the dead. People killed each other for food and supplies. The world of the dead brought out both the best and worst in people. Unfortunately, the *worst* seemed to have the greater numbers.

Time passed, but for survivors, time was meaningless. What did the passing of a day, a month, even a year, matter to people surrounded by walking corpses?

A lot of time passed for Joe Thompson and his new family.

Joe was in the middle of a nightmare, a variation of a nightmare he'd had throughout the years. He was in the middle of a busy city street, but he didn't know what city it was. The walking dead surrounded him from every angle, every building,

35

every alley, led by his wife Sarah. She wasn't a walking corpse, like the others. She was alive and beautiful. As she got closer she began to slowly decay in front of his eyes, before shoving a hand inside his stomach.

"Dad! Dad, wake up."

Joe woke up with a start. He sat upright and looked around. It was pitch black, but the familiar feel of the couch under him told him he was in the living room, in his home for the past fourteen years. His body told him it was late. The sheet he'd found on their last supply run felt good against his skin. He couldn't see Aaron, but he knew where he was standing, right in the hallway that led to the three bedrooms. Denise and Margie shared one bedroom, while Frank and Aaron both had their own. Joe had shared with Aaron for a long time, but was more than happy to give it up when Aaron wanted a little more independence.

"You alright, Dad?" Aaron asked.

"Yeah. Just having a bad dream. Nothing new, I guess. Especially with Frank's cooking."

Aaron laughed. "You want me to stay up with you a while?"

Joe smiled in the dark. That was Aaron, a caring soul. They'd all done their part in raising him, and he was turning into a fine young man, even in the world they lived in. Sadly, Joe didn't know how old his son was. Thirteen, maybe fourteen years old.

"No, you go and get some sleep. We'll hit the lake, bright and early. Catch us some breakfast."

"Alright. Love you."

"Love you too, son."

Joe listened as his son walked down the hall and back into his bedroom. All their ears had gotten sharper over the years, especially at night with only candles and moonlight to light the way. Aaron climbed into bed and shifted around for a minute. It was quiet, until a male voice cut through the air.

"Hey Joe. You mind keeping it down out there? Some of us who aren't pussies are trying to sleep."

Joe smiled. "Bite me, Frank."

The women laughed in their bedroom.

He stood up from the couch and stretched his arms over his head. He knew he should try to get more sleep, but after the nightmare, he wasn't quite ready to put head to pillow just yet. He easily navigated around the coffee table and loveseat and walked outside to the porch.

It was a beautiful night. The full moon hung high over the lake that was just outside the house. Joe walked to the edge of the dock and sat down, letting his toes touch the surface of the water. The breeze felt great.

He leaned his head back and closed his eyes. The sounds of the lake and nature soothed him. Crickets chirped, birds flew overhead, fish hopped out of the water. It was hard to believe that just four miles away, in the nearby town, the corpses walked the streets.

The corpses never wandered back into the woods. Every now and then, a lone straggler would show up. But Frank always thought it was just a hermit who'd been deep in the woods, and not a sign of a corpse invasion. So far, he'd been right.

Joe didn't ever think he'd be the outdoors type. All things considered, he liked their lifestyle. Fresh water in the backyard, peace and quiet. Food could be a little rough. There were times he thought he'd die if he ate one more fish. But Margie did most of the cooking, and did a great job, even if she hated lighting the grill.

It took them a while to get used to the changes. Night was very black with no electricity. All the chores had to get done before sunset, or they didn't get done. Sleep schedules changed, no more sleeping in till mid-morning. Everyone was up at dawn. When supplies ran low, they had to brave the nearby town to get the things they needed. They hadn't driven the van in years, relying on bikes for transportation.

Their new life could be hard. But they were alive.

He felt a hand on his shoulder. He didn't even hear her coming. His heart skipped a beat as he turned and saw Denise.

The moonlight hid certain parts of her while giving a gray hue to others. She wore her favorite summer nightgown, and looked great.

"Sorry, didn't mean to scare you."

He laughed. "It's okay. Just enjoying the night air."

"Want some company?"

"Sure."

She sat next to him. Joe was suddenly conscious of what he was wearing, which was just a pair of shorts. Her nightgown rode up her legs a little, and Joe caught himself trying to steal a look at them.

"I couldn't sleep," he said.

Denise had the hint of a smile. "Yeah, we heard."

"Sorry if I kept you up."

"Look Joe. If you want we can take turns on the couch. I don't mind at all."

"No, I'm fine. But thank you."

They were quiet for a moment. Joe enjoyed watching the moonlight bounce off the ripples in the lake. He enjoyed spending time with Denise, more than he admitted. He owed her a lot. Not just for saving his life, but Aaron wouldn't be who he was without her.

"It's gonna get cold soon. I'll start working on some wood tomorrow."

She nodded. "We might have to head to town soon too. Some of our blankets are falling apart."

Denise scooted an inch closer and carefully leaned her head on his shoulder. The closeness made Joe's heart pound just a little harder.

She wasn't sure when she fell in love with him. She had long arguments with herself that it even *was* love.

It was only when Joe and Frank returned home two days late from a trip into town that she realized she couldn't live without him.

It was Frank's house they were living in. He had also taught everyone how to fire and care for a gun. But it was Joe who was their leader. It was just something about him, his calm manner in which he approached everything. He had a quiet leadership that Denise didn't think he was even aware of. Everyone was in a panic those first few days after the dead rose, and Joe had pulled them through, all while looking after his motherless newborn baby son, Aaron.

There was a time Denise thought she'd never laugh again. He was somehow able to make everyone laugh. *I love you*, Denise thought. She had that thought so many times. *Now if only I had the guts to say it.*

"I, uh, I think Frank and Margie are having sex."

"What?" He turned toward the house. "Right now?"

"No, not *now*, nutball. Just, you know, having sex."

Joe suspected as much. The other day, while getting the cooking fire ready, Frank had to get more wood. Nothing unusual about that, until Margie volunteered to go with him. Joe had thought maybe there was something going on there.

"Maybe you'll get your own room soon, after all."

They shared a laugh and she moved her head more onto his shoulder. She ran a hand through his hair.

"You're gonna have to let me cut your hair tomorrow," she said. That was as good an excuse to touch him as any. "It's getting long."

"Maybe I'll just cut it all off like Frank and Aaron."

Frank had decided he had enough of his thick head of hair years ago, and Aaron just had to look like his Uncle Frank. They were both completely bald.

"No, you can't do that. I like your hair."

"Why thank you."

This is it. Make a move.

"Hey, Dad!" Aaron called from the porch. "A possum got in the house. Uncle Frank and Aunt Margie are both screaming in here. He says he'll kill it with his gun if you don't get rid of it."

"Let's go save the day," Joe said.

Denise smiled. "We're heroes."

He helped her to her feet. Her smile faded when she realized he was watching her, looking at her face. She could barely make out his features due to the darkness. He didn't let go of her hands, just rubbed them gently.

He likes me too.

They walked back to the house. Joe held her hand the whole way.

🤚 🤚 🤚

The sun had only been up a little while. After catching six large-mouth bass, Joe was cleaning the outhouse, not his favorite job. Denise and Margie were in the house straightening up. Frank was chopping logs with an ax. Aaron was out in the woods practicing with a compound bow, a gift from Joe he'd found on their last trip to town. Archery was a talent Aaron was getting dangerously good at.

"Hey everybody!" a voice came from the woods. "Check this out!"

Joe and Frank looked up to see Aaron walking toward them. The first thing Joe noticed was his son covered in blood. He panicked for a moment, then saw the huge deer Aaron was carrying on his shoulders. It was nearly his size.

"Uncle Frank, can you give me a hand?"

"Jesus, Aaron," he said, dropping the ax and rushing over. "What the hell? You trying to be the Incredible Hulk?"

"I know." Aaron had a huge smile on his face. "Dinner for a week. We haven't had deer in a while. Who's the Incredible Hulk?"

The women left the house to greet Aaron. They listened with smiles as Aaron told them the story. He'd been practicing with his bow on the other side of the lake when he saw the buck getting a drink of water. He killed it clean through the trees with a single arrow from about forty yards out. Everyone was impressed.

As Aaron told the story, Joe grew unhappy. It was only when his son finished the tale that he realized why. Aaron was growing up fast.

Soon, he won't need me anymore.

"Hey Dad, you mind if I clean up and read a while? Then I'll help Uncle Frank with the wood."

Joe nodded. He grabbed Aaron's shoulder before he could walk away. "I'm proud of you."

Aaron just gave his father a confident wink. Joe tried not to laugh as his son walked around the back of the house to use the buckets of lake water they kept to wash up. If high school still existed, Aaron would be the scholar athlete, getting excellent grades, then hitting the track after school. Not the snobby popular type. Aaron wasn't like that.

"They grow up fast, don't they?" Joe said.

"It just means we're all getting older," Margie said with a smile.

"Speak for yourself. Maybe *you* all are old. I'm not," Frank said.

Joe was ready to get back to the outhouse when he saw the three of them trading looks with each other. Something was going on.

"Guys? What's up?"

Frank took a breath and shrugged at the women. "Do we want to do this here?"

Margie nodded. "Yes."

"Do what?"

Margie tried to stifle a smile as Denise took Joe by the hand. Denise tried to keep her feelings for Joe a secret, but she never did a good job.

"Joe, Aaron's gotta learn how to shoot a gun."

"He hates guns. He's scared to death of them. He can barely aim one straight."

"Hell, none of us *like* guns. Well, except for Frank the warrior here. But Joe, come on. It's *way* past time."

"We won't be around forever," Frank said. "He's mean with a bow, and I taught him how to throw his fists around. And I hope it never happens, but one day, he might be in a corner with five corpses looking at him. He has to learn how to shoot."

Aaron wasn't a stranger to the world of the dead. He'd gone along the last few trips to town. But he never had to see a corpse up close, never had to shoot one in the head.

Joe was quiet a moment. He'd always been reluctant to start on Aaron's gun training because, like Frank said, it was an admission that they couldn't protect him forever. It was easy to pretend that deep in the woods, they were protected from the Hell that had taken over the earth. But the truth was no one was *completely* safe.

Frank didn't agree with Joe when he decided to teach Aaron to read. Frank thought it was a waste of time. But Joe knew Frank was right about gun training.

"You're right," Joe said. "We all agree we need to head to town, right?"

Everyone nodded.

"Okay. We got plenty of daylight left. We'll go in together, get what we need, teach Aaron to shoot. Hell, maybe we'll even find a battery and some gas for the van."

Denise laughed. "You always say that."

"One day I'll be right."

Joe turned to leave, but Frank grabbed his shoulder. "Uh, hey. There's one more thing." He looked at Margie. She gave him a bright smile, one Joe hadn't seen in quite a while. "We have something to tell you."

✸ ✸ ✸

Aaron poured a bucket of water over his head. It felt great, although it gave him a chill as the water seeped inside his shorts.

He wiped his bald head with his sweaty shirt and carried the empty bucket down to the lake for a refill.

As he walked by the house he saw his entire family gathered near the cooking pit. They looked like they were having a serious conversation.

He knew it was one of two things. They were either doing some serious planning about their lifestyle, gathering food, the upcoming winter, that sort of thing. Or they were talking about him.

Ah man, Aaron thought. *Have I done anything wrong lately?*

He grabbed a book from his room and sat on the porch, although he wasn't really reading. He just studied his family. Aaron liked to just study and watch things. It wasn't like he had a huge option of other hobbies. He couldn't shoot a bow or read all day long.

He noticed Dad and Aunt Denise holding hands. Nothing major, just by the fingertips. Aaron shook his head. *Come on, Dad. When are you gonna tell her? It's obvious how she feels.*

He loved his father and knew him better than anyone. But Aaron was clueless as to why he held in his feelings for Denise. Whenever Dad just walked into the room, Denise would change. She would sit up straighter, puff her breasts out just a little more, smile a little brighter.

Is it possible Dad doesn't know?

Now Uncle Frank and Aunt Margie, on the other hand…there wasn't much of a secret there at all. Sneaking off in the woods together, late night swims in the lake. Aaron wasn't completely sure, but he thought he heard footsteps late one night going from his aunt's room to Frank's. He was quite sure it wasn't to play Scrabble.

He laughed to himself. He saw their mood lighten a little. Frank and Dad shared a joke, then Frank gave him a playful slug in the shoulder. His aunts hugged.

Hmmm. I wonder if Frank and Margie finally said something?

The women passed Aaron on the porch to go inside and change clothes. Frank picked up the deer and slung it over his shoulder. He looked at Joe, who was taking a seat next to Aaron.

"I'll get this deer skinned. You got the bikes covered, right?"

"Yeah, I got 'em. Just give me a few minutes."

"Alright, I'll be around back."

Aaron looked at his father. "Bikes?"

"We're all gonna head to town together today, get some supplies."

"Okay. What was the laughing and playing around about?"

He smiled and shook his head. "Well, Frank and Margie just wanted to tell us they're a couple now."

"About time."

"That's what Denise said."

They were quiet for a moment. Aaron could see his father had something else to say.

"Look, Aaron. Today, when we get to town, Frank wants to teach you how to shoot a corpse."

He winced. "With a gun?"

Joe nodded.

Aaron didn't know what it was about guns that unnerved him so much. He didn't even like holding one. It was no different than trying to get an answer out of Margie about why she was afraid of spiders. That's why he'd taken up the bow, so he would never have to fire a gun.

"Dad, I don't like guns."

"I know, I know. I don't either. But there is a lot of danger out there, and you should be prepared for it."

"I can hunt, fish, cook my own food, read a map, use the sun to get a good idea of time. Heck, give me a needle and thread and I'll fix my own clothes."

"Who taught you how to sew?"

"I read it."

Joe laughed. His son truly was amazing. Sarah would be proud.

"I'm gonna get the bikes ready," Joe said. "Don't worry, you'll do fine."

A mischievous smiled crossed Aaron's face as Joe stood up. "Okay, Dad. I won't give you a hard time on one condition."

"What's that?"

"You tell Aunt Denise that you love her."

He sat back down. "What?"

"Tell her you love her. Don't worry, she loves you too."

Joe shook his head in amusement. "And what do *you* think love is?"

Aaron thought a moment. "Love is when it hurts when the person is gone. They like, can't be apart, you know what I mean? They try to make each other happy. Oh, and they have sex a lot."

"Aaron!"

"Hey, I didn't make it up."

Joe looked through the living room window. He could see Margie and Denise in the kitchen. They didn't use it to cook anymore, but it did store all of their supplies. He lowered his voice to make sure only Aaron could hear.

"Do you really think she loves me?"

Aaron just gave him a look. "Dad, she does. Trust me."

He held out his hand. "Okay. You learn to shoot, and tonight, Denise and I will have a little talk."

They shook hands. "Deal."

CHAPTER 4

The bike ride through the woods was peaceful. It was a ride they had taken many times before, but it was rare they all went together. Aaron felt like it was a family adventure, although he knew they felt much differently.

Everyone had a large empty backpack. Aaron brought up the rear and took a quick drink of water from his bottle. He made a mental checklist of some of the things they mentioned needing. Ammunition, blankets, clothes, towels, salt and pepper, lighter fluid, shoes.

And now, condoms for Frank and Margie.

Yuck. I hope they don't keep me up all night.

Joe held his hand up as the woods began to thin out. Aaron had a sense of deja vu. This was the way they always approached town. They leaned their bikes against some trees and carefully approached the hill that overlooked Walton.

The town of Walton, once a simple place in western Maryland, was now home to nothing but walking corpses. Looters had made off with supplies during the beginning of the new world, but there were still plenty of places to find what was needed. It was just a matter of getting through the former citizens.

It always felt strange to stand on the hill overlooking town. Such a beautiful day. Not a cloud in the sky, a gentle breeze blowing. But just one hundred feet away was danger.

"Denise," Frank said. "Hand me the binoculars."

"Wait a sec," Joe said, then looked at Aaron. "Let's see what our trainee here sees."

Margie gagged a little as Aaron took the binoculars and dropped to one knee on top of the hill. "You'd think I'd be used to the smell by now," she said.

Frank gave her a quick kiss on the cheek. It felt good, no longer having to sneak around. They had only kept it a secret so they could sort out their feelings in private. At first, it was just sex, but then it grew into something more.

"It's okay. We don't come out here that often. And I don't think we'll ever get used to it." He gestured to town. "This is all just still so…unnatural."

Aaron slowly looked across the houses, the small corner businesses, the streets. He saw the world in a way his family would never be able to understand. He saw much of what the world was like in magazines and books, but had never experienced it. He just couldn't imagine millions of people all living together without going at each other's throats. As he studied the dead town, he passed over a mailbox and a fire hydrant, having no idea of what either one was.

The town looked the same as it did last time. Abandoned cars lined the streets. Vultures circled from above, then they would swoop down and eat maggots off of the undead. Nature had begun to reclaim the town; fallen trees leaned into the roofs of houses, trees and bushes were growing in the middle of the street. The only sounds were the shuffling and wailing of the corpses, and the wind as it blew through the streets.

To Aaron's family, it was a ghost town, a reminder of a life that once was. To Aaron, it was a place he never got to know, a life he never had.

He watched the undead. They stumbled and wandered around town without a purpose. Some didn't bother moving at all. One pulled himself along with his arms, as he didn't have any legs. Some of them were more decomposed than others, but they were all horrible and disgusting. It was hard to believe that they were once people, with their own thoughts and desires. Now they had only one desire, and that was to eat the flesh of the living.

Aaron took another sweep of the town. He noticed that some of the undead seemed to be stumbling in one direction. He followed with the binoculars, attempting to figure out where they were heading. Then he saw three figures in the street, running from building to building.

"Hey Dad," he said. "There's people down there."

"Let me see." Joe watched as they shot a few corpses while maneuvering around others. They were dangerously close to getting grabbed a few times.

"What's going on?" Frank asked.

"I don't believe it. I think it's Dillon and Shaffer. They got a third guy with them, don't recognize him."

"Who?" Denise asked.

"Dillon and Shaffer. Two guys Joe and I ran into last time we were out here. Good enough people, if a little reckless. Guess they have a camp around here somewhere."

Joe continued to look through the binoculars. "Well, for better or worse, they're dragging half the corpses in town along with them. We might be able to hit our normal stops a lot easier today."

"Shouldn't we help them?" Margie asked.

The men looked at each other. Joe felt a tiny twinge of guilt, but that just wasn't the way the world worked anymore. If they were in trouble against three or four corpses, that was one thing. But Dillon and Shaffer were carelessly running through town, attracting the attention of every corpse that could still see, hear, or smell.

"No," he said. "We'll hit the clothes store first. Remember, always stay together. Don't wander off. When we're back on top of the hill, we'll give Aaron a gun. Unless you want one now?"

Aaron shook his head without a smile.

They started down the hill. Joe caught Denise's arm for a moment. "Hey, uh-" he fumbled for words, "I, uh, need to talk to you tonight."

She smiled. "Sure. I'm not going anywhere."

The five quickly and quietly made their way down the hill and hugged the back wall of what used to be a laundromat. Joe took a look around the corner. There were six corpses in the way between them and the clothing shop. He tried the other side and saw a much clearer path, although a more disgusting sight. A single corpse with a raggedy police uniform slowly walked with a broken leg. A malnourished dog ate at the corpse as he walked. The dog chewed off one finger, then another. The corpse did nothing besides moan and wail, only giving the occasional annoyed glance at the dog. For whatever reason, they only craved warm human flesh, not animal.

They heard gunshots. It was hard to tell where they came from. With the eerie quiet, it could have been close to the other side of town.

They sprinted around the laundromat and across the street to the clothing store. The corpse with the dog noticed them, but Frank dropped him with a single shot to the head. Aaron flinched, like he always did. He knew they weren't people anymore; they were monsters, which his books said didn't exist.

Joe and Frank did a sweep of the store while everyone else hid against the wall behind a rack of clothes. Joe used to be able to smell if corpses were nearby. But the number of walking dead had only increased over the years, and the smell was everywhere.

The clothes store, like everything in the world, was destroyed. The large glass windows that once separated the store from the sidewalk were shattered. Clothes were scattered everywhere. Mold grew on the walls.

They didn't say a word, just watched the street. They'd been through these trips countless times. The street was empty, but that didn't mean a thousand corpses weren't just around the corner. It looked deceptively safe, but they all knew better.

"Okay," Joe said. He grabbed Aaron's and his own backpack. "Fill these two up with as much as we can. Shoes, warm winter clothes, you know the routine."

They did know the routine, and it was a sad one. Their van had run out of gas years ago, and the battery was dead. Their trips to the city consisted of filling their backpacks with whatever they needed. Backpacks only carried so much, and they were always in short supply.

Frank tossed a thick pair of jeans to Joe. He caught them and handed them to Aaron. Aaron shoved them in his backpack as tightly as he could.

"You alright?" Joe asked.

"Yeah. Those things, they just scare me a little."

Joe gave him a pat on the shoulder. Even growing up in a world of the dead, there wasn't any way to completely acclimate to the walking corpses. Everything about them was inhuman, despite the fact they used to be human: the way they moaned when no one was around, only showing excitement when they sensed warm flesh, the way they staggered, unable to control their own bodies. Aaron saw a man get killed once on a trip. It was terrifying to watch them go from creatures without a purpose to a bloodthirsty mob, in no time at all.

"Okay, we full up on two bags?" Joe asked, keeping his voice low.

Frank nodded. "Yeah. But it's not much."

Margie laughed, but it wasn't happy. "It never is."

"Okay, next stop, the Rite-Aid across-"

Joe was interrupted by gunshots. They weren't far away this time. They heard some voices just out in the street.

"Dillon! Stop shooting them in the fuckin' shoulder! Get the goddamn head!"

"I'm trying!"

Dillon, Shaffer, and their friend stopped in front of the clothing store to fire a few more rounds. Joe heard a skull explode and a body fall. Dillon turned and saw Joe and his family. He recognized Joe and Frank, whom he'd seen one other time in town before, but not the women or teenage boy.

"Guys! In here!"

The three men jumped over a few overturned clothes racks and joined the group.

"Frank, Joe," Shaffer greeted.

"What's going on?" Joe asked.

"The corpses are coming. A lot of them."

As soon as he said it, two shuffled on the sidewalk in front of the store. They turned and moaned. Aaron tried to fight the feeling that monsters were coming for them. But that's exactly what was happening.

Margie gave the three outsiders an angry look.

"And you thought it would be a good idea to drag them to us?"

"We're just trying to survive here, lady. More guns are better than a few."

Joe held up a hand to stop the argument, although he did agree it was a dumb move. No doubt they were just looking for supplies, but Shaffer and his friends certainly went about it the wrong way.

Frank dropped the two incoming corpses with quick shots to the head. But they could hear the wails now, just outside the clothing store. One showed up, then another. They were coming.

Joe's fear started to rise, but he held it in check. That was simply rule number one in the world of the dead. *Don't panic.*

"We won't be able to kill all of them," he said. "There's gotta be a back door to this place. Probably corpses there too, but hopefully not as many."

The third man with Shaffer and Dillon aimed his gun and finally spoke. "No. I've got a better idea."

He fired two times, but he wasn't aiming for the walking dead. He shot both Joe and Frank right in the stomach. Joe felt hot for a moment, a cold sweat forming. They both fell to the ground.

"Allister, what the hell?!" Dillon shouted.

Denise and Margie were shocked, then started to raise their guns. They were just a second too slow. Allister already had his nine millimeter raised at Aaron's head.

"No no, don't even flinch, or the kid here dies."

"You *asshole!*" Dillon shouted. "These are good people!"

Allister grabbed Dillon by the shirt collar without taking his focus from Aaron. The corpses were still coming. There were so many they couldn't see the street behind them.

"This is how it goes now," he said. "This is how you survive in this world. Get used to it."

Aaron watched numbly as the cold, calculating man led his two companions toward the back. Dillon and Shaffer looked apologetic, but didn't stop. He wished he knew how to shoot a gun, so he could fire as many rounds as he could into Allister's head.

Margie and Denise were tending to Joe and Frank. Margie was crying. Denise's medical training was trying to take over. But she knew that, here on the floor of an old clothing store, with no supplies, there wasn't much she could do.

The corpses were fifteen seconds away. Aaron got a up-close look at a walking dead for the very first time. Maggots falling off their flesh; rags instead of clothes; flesh decayed so much that bones were exposed. They moved with that slow, unsteady gait.

Aaron grabbed the gun from his father's hand.

"Aaron? What are you--"

He fired at the corpses. The gun felt heavy in his hand, and his aim was terrible. He fired until the clip was empty, and didn't kill a single corpse. It wouldn't have mattered if he did. The store was full of them.

"Get out of here," Frank said weakly. Blood poured from his stomach and formed a pool under them.

Ten seconds.

"No," Denise said. "We're not leaving."

Joe grabbed her hand. "Denise," he begged. "Please, take Aaron and get out of here."

"She said we're staying, Dad," Aaron said.

He felt hopelessness for the first time, something his father and family had shielded him from his entire life. The corpses marched toward them, and nothing was going to stop them until they had their warm meal.

Five seconds.

"Come on," Denise said, determined not to give up. "We'll drag you out of here."

She grabbed Joe's arm. He pulled her in close, so only she could hear.

"I love you."

She smiled, despite the fact that death was on top of them. "I love you too."

She grabbed one arm while Aaron grabbed the other. Margie grabbed Frank's wrists. Before they could start pulling, the undead attacked. They nearly stumbled over Frank, and two of them took a bite out of his thigh. He screamed in pain and managed to shoot the closest one in the head, covering himself with gore and thick blood.

Their time had run out. Margie tossed herself at the undead mob, trying to get them off of Frank. They swallowed her up and pinned her down. Three of them fell on top of Denise, biting her face as her head slammed to the ground. Aaron jumped on his father to protect him.

Aaron cried as he heard his family slowly dying around him. Their screams all mixed with his own. He felt his body being shifted around, and realized he was no longer on top of his father. He curled into a fetal position and covered his face. He heard Margie's cries of pain slowly die down until there was nothing. Frank died while cursing at the undead. Joe was next, screaming his son's name, followed by Denise, who had somehow managed to grab Joe's hand while dying.

Aaron didn't know that he was fourteen years old. His family, his life at the cabin, was all he'd ever known. It took two minutes to destroy everything.

He kept quiet, waiting his turn. He felt the corpses moving and shuffling around him. He heard the sickening sound of skin being pulled from bone. He felt something on his face, and realized he was lying in a pool of his family's blood.

But there was something he didn't feel.

Pain.

He didn't know how long he lay there before he risked opening an eye. Five, maybe ten minutes.

There were corpses everywhere. They stumbled and fell over each other trying to get to the warm flesh. Aaron looked at the lifeless face of his father, right before a corpse reached in and pulled out Joe's tongue.

Tears fell from his eyes. He slowly pulled himself into a sitting position, not caring that he was sitting in what was left of his family.

He couldn't think. He just stared straight ahead, not quite seeing the corpses shuffle around him anymore. This was the moment Frank used to tell him could happen at any time, but deep down, Aaron didn't honestly think he'd see.

He was alone.

The fact that he shouldn't be alive finally crept into his mind. He looked at the corpses around him. They continued to feast on his family, just a few feet away. Others wandered around the store, tripping over each other and fallen shelves.

Aaron climbed to his feet, almost slipping in the pool of blood. He tried to piece together what was happening in his mind, but he just couldn't figure it out. The walking corpses simply ignored him, as if he wasn't there. For a moment, Aaron thought that maybe they couldn't see him for some reason. Then he noticed some did look at him.

They just didn't want to eat him.

A new low moan caught his attention behind him. He spun around, and his shoulders slumped as he started to cry all over again.

The undead hadn't left enough of Frank, Denise, or Margie to reanimate. That wasn't the case with Joe. Aaron's father pulled his hand away from Denise. He slowly stood up, almost losing his balance a few times. His eyes were white marbles, and there was a hole in his mouth where his tongue used to be.

He looked at his former son, not a single glimmer of recognition in his eyes. Then he looked at his surroundings with only one goal. Fresh meat.

The rest of the undead no longer enjoyed the taste of cold flesh. They wandered off, not caring that Aaron was right there.

Aaron grabbed Frank's gun from his severed hand. With tears clouding his vision, he leveled the gun right at Joe's head.

As luck would have it, the first corpse Aaron would ever kill with a gun would be his own father.

"I love you, Dad."

He fired a single time. After his father died for the second time, Aaron leaned over and vomited.

He looked at the undead around him. He was not happy he was alive. "Why don't you kill me?"

He waved his hand in their faces and jumped up and down. Some looked at him, even gave him what might have been a look of confusion. But they didn't attack him.

As the walking corpses milled about, Aaron looked again at Frank's gun. He thought about putting the barrel in his mouth and pulling the trigger.

None of it was fair at all. Frank and Margie had finally opened up about their relationship. Joe and Denise were about to do the same. Aaron felt it. He wanted to be with them, wherever they were. He didn't want to be without his family in the world of the dead.

But he couldn't do it.

His father wouldn't want Aaron to kill himself. Joe had taught Aaron how to do everything, including how to take care of himself. He wanted his son to have a long life.

So that's what Aaron would do.

He left the clothing store, pushing a corpse to the ground as he did so. "Fuck you all."

Aaron looked at the streets of Walton one last time before he left, half expecting the undead to pounce on him at any second, right as he started to relax.

That would never happen.

CHAPTER 5

"Samantha? Hey, Samantha? You in there?"

Samantha woke up on her mattress in the corner of what used to be a high school English classroom. She didn't know how much sleep she'd gotten, but she knew it couldn't have been much by how tired she was. She looked at the dark curtains she had hung to cover the classroom windows. It was the only way she could block out the light so she could sleep. She saw a silhouette just outside.

"Yeah. What do you want?"

"It's Larry. Are you decent?"

"No. Give me a second."

Samantha always slept naked when it was hot. She slipped on a pair of panties, black shorts, and a tee shirt with a few holes in the back. A sports bra would have to wait.

She stumbled to the window and shoved the curtain aside and bright sunlight poured in. She glanced outside and saw that the people of Lexington High School were going about their lives. Michael Walker was moving some barrels of water collected from last night's rain. Susan Lively tended to the huge vegetable garden in the old football field. Paul Sorenson was chasing a chicken, with a few of the kids laughing at him. The chicken coops were on the other side of the high school, which meant that Paul must have been having a lousy morning. If she weren't so tired and grumpy, Samantha might have laughed too.

Of course, many of the people at Lexington would say Samantha was *always* grumpy. She wasn't the most popular person. Most people helped out because they wanted to. Richardson, the man responsible for turning Lexington High School into a shelter, led by example. He was always working to make the place better, and most everyone followed his lead. Samantha had only found Lexington a few years ago, and she only worked out of boredom, or because there was something to gain.

Samantha caught Larry looking her up and down. She knew some men looked at her; she didn't care. She'd spent most of her life alone surviving out in the world, only running with people when she needed to, until she'd stumbled upon Lexington. She had no desire for companionship or friends. She learned the hard way that friends were your friends as long as it was easy and convenient. When the walking corpses showed up, friendships ended very fast.

She could handle acquaintances just fine. Friends, not so much.

"Larry, I had fence duty last night. Richardson stuck me with Troy." Larry winced at the name. Troy's feelings for Samantha were well known. "So I spent every dark hour circling the fence with a man telling me how beautiful I am. I'm tired. Please tell me it's important."

"Just wanted to give you a heads up. Richardson's been looking for you."

Samantha shook her head. That meant he had another task for her. Usually when Richardson sought her out, it was to do something no one else wanted to. Samantha always would, for the right price.

"Thanks, Larry." He turned to walk away. Samantha stopped him. "Oh, hey."

He spun back around. She flashed a tiny smile. "You and your gal pal aren't as quiet as you think," she said. She and Troy had seen them while watching the fences, under the old bleachers near the smokehouse, which didn't see much use these days. "You might want to find a new spot."

His face turned red, but he managed a smile. "Uh, thanks."

Samantha closed the curtains and finished getting dressed. She couldn't decide on wearing her last semi-clean pair of socks, or wearing sandals. She settled on sandals, and grabbed her old brush and mirror from the desk she used to hold the few things she had.

Like most everyone at Lexington, Samantha didn't know how old she was. She was born after the world died, which Richardson said was twenty-three years ago. So she guessed she was a few years younger than that. She had brown eyes and dark straight hair that came down to her shoulders, with curly bangs. Her hair was starting to get long. She'd have to bug Mary Taylor for a trim. She had dark skin, but didn't know what her heritage was. She had no way of knowing that her parents had been from Pakistan, not that it mattered. Most people didn't care about race when walking corpses ruled the world.

She left the English classroom that had become her room, her sanctuary. Her room was simple enough: mattress in the corner; clothes folded neatly in stacks on the floor; a box of candles under the window; old world hygiene items on a tiny table near her mattress. There was plenty of room for her to stretch out and relax. Her room also had windows. Not everyone could say that.

It was amazing what Richardson had done with the old school. Most of the classrooms had become personal spaces, some more valued over others. The old gymnasium was their storeroom, full of clothing, guns, ammunition, candles, everything they could find. The cafeteria didn't serve much of a purpose besides a place for everyone to gather and spend time together during the winter. Sometimes Richardson would get out his guitar and play for everyone. The library was destroyed for the most part, holding nothing but trash, broken desks, chairs, and old books no one was interested in.

The halls were mostly empty. It was getting hot quickly, and most of the inner rooms were too stuffy during the day. She nodded a few greetings at the people she passed, then finally went outside through the gymnasium. She gave Helen a wave. Helen had storeroom duty, keeping track of everything people took. Samantha felt bad for her. She wouldn't want that chore. Of course, Richardson would never give her that task, since she couldn't read.

Samantha stretched her arms as she stepped into the sun. Lexington currently housed nearly sixty people. She watched them as they went about their daily routine and hoped the people appreciated what they had. She'd seen places in her life far worse.

Lexington High was located in a very unique spot in the suburbs, in the middle of a three mile stretch of road. Houses long abandoned surrounded them, as well as thick woods behind them. But that was it. There were no corpses. If they went to the end of the road in either direction, they would run into thousands of undead. But the undead didn't wander the distance it would take to find Lexington High. Occasionally small groups of them found their way, but that was why Richardson insisted on active fence duty every night. Teams of two walked the perimeter of the fence around the school, looking for corpses.

Before Samantha found Lexington, life hadn't been pleasant. Lexington had its problems, but it was better than surviving out in the wild.

She saw Richardson near the spring-house, not too far from the soccer field. They had discovered a long time ago that water flowed under them, most likely to the river deep in the woods. They'd dug up the ground and built a cinder block shack over the stream. It provided fresh water and basic refrigeration. The kids loved playing in it when it got hot.

Richardson had his notebook with him, like always. He took notes on chores, improvements to be made, everything he could think of. When he wasn't taking notes, he did whatever needed to be done. He was an older black man in his fifties, and had a way about him that kept everyone calm. He was everyone's source of strength, no question about it.

Samantha debated on approaching him. If whatever he wanted was so important, he could find her later. But he noticed her, and motioned for her to come.

Shit, what now? she thought. *Isn't a night with that horndog Troy bad enough?*

"Good morning," he said when she was close enough. "How did last night go?"

She shook her head. "Next time you draft me for fence duty, could you stick me with someone besides Troy?"

He laughed. Richardson had a warm, genuine laugh. "He put the moves on you all night?"

"I almost punched him five times."

"Well, he finds you attractive. I'm sure some of the others do too."

"The *others* stay to themselves."

Richardson smirked. Everyone knew that Samantha didn't go out of her way to make friends, and kept to herself. "I already talked to Susan. Just go see her, she'll slip you a few extra veggies."

Samantha nodded. That was how she worked. She would help out, if she had to. But the tedious work, the fence duty in particular, that required extra. Payment in the form of food, items, return favors, they were as good as gold was in the old world.

"Okay, so what did you want to see me about?"

Richardson looked around. The young twins, Kyle and Kari, chased each other across the soccer field, crossing Richardson's path. He waited until they were further away before speaking. He had no doubt what he was about to tell Samantha would be public by the end of the day. It was hard to keep a secret at Lexington. But he wanted to keep this news as quiet as possible.

"Lisa and Robert had their baby last night."

"Oh wow. That's good, right?"

Richardson swallowed hard. Samantha was surprised. It took a lot to get to him.

"It was stillborn. The child was born…already dead. It was already a baby corpse."

"Holy shit."

Richardson had been there, as well as Mary Taylor, Lisa's good friend. It was something he would never forget. The baby actually tried to bite Mary on the arm as she held it. Lisa had wanted to hold it, and Mary didn't have the heart to tell her it was undead.

"Yeah, well, Rob snapped. You know how he always carries that six shot with him?"

Samantha frowned. "Oh no."

He nodded. "He shot the baby, while Mary was still holding it. Then Lisa. I thought he was gonna shoot Mary and me as well, but he killed himself."

"Is Mary okay?"

"Physically, yes. But she hasn't been outside all day."

She was horrified. Everyone had been excited about Lisa and Rob's baby. The last birth they had was quite a while ago. It gave everybody something to bond over. But she was confused.

"What does this have to do with me?"

"Rob was on Garrett's supply team. They're heading out today. You're the only one with experience getting supplies. Hell, half the people here haven't even killed a walker. So I'm hoping you'll take his place."

She gave him a blank look. Garrett was an asshole, but he was good at what he did. They had two old U-Haul moving trucks still in working condition, and once a month they would go out and get supplies. Of course, that was much more dangerous than watching the fence at night.

"I'm not trying to be a bitch, Richardson, but that's gonna be a little pricey."

He sighed, knowing that was the response he'd get. He was still disappointed. Samantha wasn't a bad person. In fact, he trusted her with things he wouldn't trust with anyone else. But she was still something of an outsider at Lexington. She'd lived there since she was a teenager, but kept to herself. She actively refused to make friends. She had a price for everything, wouldn't do anything simply because it was the right thing.

Richardson hoped she wasn't an example of what the world was becoming.

"Okay," he said. "What do you want?"

She thought a moment. He was asking her to really risk her life. She knew she didn't have a great life, but she did want to live a while longer. The last time she went with Garrett for supplies were for her own reasons. She went looking for as many makeup kits as she could find. A ridiculous reason, but they had been for Mary Taylor, and she'd paid with a good supply of peppers and beans she grew herself.

"How many people know?"

"Just the two of us and Mary."

"They had that nice teacher's lounge on the back side of the school, right? I'll take that."

Richardson gave her a surprised look. That was the way of Lexington. Possession was the law. If someone left or died, it didn't take long for their things to get redistributed.

Still, Samantha's lack of compassion surprised him.

"Wow. Not even gonna wait till their bodies get cold?"

"Hey," she shrugged, "there's people here who would ask for much more."

He nodded. That was the truth. "Okay. I'll hold the lounge for you. Just meet up with Garrett. I think he's leaving in an hour or so."

Samantha walked away. She wasn't looking forward to the run. It wasn't the danger that bothered her, but Garrett and his boys. The last time she went on a supply run, they treated her like she was there only to look at.

For a nice lounge, I'd go alone.

Back at her room, Samantha stripped down and put on two long pairs of sweatpants, as well as two sweaters. It would get hot, but she didn't want a walker biting into her flesh. She tucked her Beretta into her waistband then strapped her favorite knife to her leg. It was six inches long, very sharp, and its smaller cousin was strapped to her wrist. She put on her hip bag with three extra clips. That was all she had.

She completed the ridiculous looking outfit by putting on a baseball cap and tucking her hair under it.

Garrett and his guys were milling around near the front gate of Lexington, where the trucks were kept. Garrett was talking to his favorite stooge, Ray. They filled the truck's tanks from gas-cans and checked their weapons. Ray gestured to Samantha as she approached.

"What can I do for you, sexy mama?" Garrett asked. He looked at her clothes. "You know winter isn't here yet, right?"

She rolled her eyes. Garrett was a large man, just a little younger than Richardson, so he'd seen a bit of the world before it died. His hair was graying, and he had the lines of a tough life on his face.

There were people Samantha could barely tolerate. Garrett was one of them.

"I'm filling in for Rob," she said.

"What's wrong with Rob?"

"I don't know. Ask Richardson. I'm just doing him the favor."

"You look stupid. When are you gonna let me sex you up?"

"I'm glad to see your head is in the right place."

"Well, *one* of them is. You know I got the only dick worth climbing on."

Everyone laughed.

Bastards. Every single one of them.

"Alright guys. And girl." Garrett winked at Samantha. "I think most of you have been through this at least one time. But I'll repeat the same shit for the learning impaired. The suburbs around us have pretty much been picked clean. There are just too many walkers to go through for such a little amount of crap, so we're gonna hit the city like we did last time."

Johnson, a rookie with fewer runs than Samantha, waved his hand. "Hey, Garrett. The city? You mean like old Baltimore, with a few million walkers? Isn't that, like, dog shit insane?"

"It's not fun, I know. But don't be a pussy. The way it works is we find a street that's not too long. Now we got eight people here. We have to work faster than hell. Two people will always be driving, keeping the trucks moving. The other six will work in two teams of three. You loot the houses, grab any damn thing you can find. I mean anything. Forks, knives, little scented candles, pillows, blankets, hammers and nails, whatever. Bag it up, and toss them in the trucks. Do *not* hit the second floors, just takes too much time. Now I know all this sounds dangerous, and it is. But the walkers move slow as shit. One street, maybe two, and that's all we have to do. The houses are all old townhomes, connected together. So we can make it fast. We ready to move out?"

Ten minutes later, Samantha sat near the back of the open moving truck. Garrett drove one while Ray drove the other. They were in front of Ray, who took the time to blow Samantha a kiss. She gave him a middle finger.

She was assigned to scavenge with Murphy and Anderson, two men she didn't like. They were near the front of the truck, gossiping about something. Samantha laughed to herself.

They're either talking about how stupid I look or how gorgeous I am.

The heat was starting to get to her. Her knife sheaths were uncomfortable against her skin. She wanted to get done, and get back to her new lounge. They took the side roads out of Lexington until they hit the old Interstate 295. Even in a relatively small suburb like Lexington there were plenty of corpses scattered around. Samantha watched them wander about from the back of the truck. Some of them made a move toward the back as they passed by, but the trucks were moving too fast. They were safe.

It would only be when they came to a dead stop in the middle of a city street that they would be in danger.

Samantha took a deep breath, trying to keep calm. Anderson and Murphy still whispered to each other. She shot them both a look. They just flashed goofy smiles.

"Alright, so what do you guys think? Maybe two minutes per house, then hit the next one?" she asked.

"Uh, yeah, sure. Whatever."

Interstate 295 was a long, old graveyard, full of cars and corpses. Garrett and Ray had to slow down and maneuver around old cars and trucks, and some of the packs of corpses got close. Samantha took careful aim with her Beretta as a few corpses tried to climb in the back. She killed five walkers while Anderson and Murphy watched.

"Hey Garrett!" she yelled. "You want to get moving up there?"

"It's not easy driving around all this bullshit!" he shouted as they passed an old Jeep Wrangler. "So keep your mouth shut back there and just be eye candy for my boys."

"Asshole."

Interstate 295 finally opened up into the city near the old baseball stadium. Walkers were everywhere, and Samantha didn't think they'd have time to scavenge more than one street.

It took ten minutes of driving to find what they were looking for: a short street with no broken down cars in the middle, townhomes on both sides. Garrett and Ray made two passes down the street, running down every corpse they could. They did a good job of clearing most of them out. They circled around one more time and slowed down. Samantha grabbed a few trash bags while everyone jumped out. Anderson shot a corpse that was trying to catch up to them.

"Alright guys, hurry the fuck up!" Garrett shouted. "One team on each side. They know we're here, and you can bet your ass they're coming."

Samantha led the way to the first house. They had to jump over three dead corpses on the way to the front door. The house wasn't even locked, and the front door was wide open.

They stepped into the living room. It was destroyed, like Samantha expected. Pictures and broken glass were scattered on the floor. The television that Samantha was told people would waste hours sitting in front of was face down on the carpet. The couch cushions were covered in dried blood. The previous owners had obviously sat there patiently, waiting to die and then to walk together forever.

Anderson tried to move around her. She stopped him with her arm. "Wait a second," she whispered.

She tapped on the wall and whistled. The undead weren't smart. If they heard a noise, or smelled a human, they would investigate, and they wouldn't be quiet about it.

She heard nothing.

"Okay guys." She stepped inside. She didn't notice Murphy quietly closing the door behind them. "Let's get those cushions. Not the bloody one. Murphy, you check the kitchen back there. I'm sure-"

Samantha didn't get to finish. Anderson struck her in the back of the head with his gun. The force threw her Beretta across the room. She fell to her hands and knees, her vision starting to blur. Before she even had a chance to think, a foot kicked her in the stomach. The air rushed out of her lungs as she fell to her side. Anderson forced her onto her back and raised his gun high above his head. He smashed the butt of it on her forehead, still covered by her cap. Her eyes shut as her head rolled to the side.

"Shit, man, don't kill her," Murphy said. "I don't want to screw a corpse."

"We've gotta make this fast. Garrett *will* leave us here. Help me with her shoes."

They each pulled a shoe off. Murphy went to a front window and watched the street. The other team had already finished one house and were starting on the next. A few corpses were near the stop sign at the corner.

"They're coming," he said.

"Yeah. I'm gonna be coming too in a minute."

"She's so pretty."

"I know. I've been wanting to fuck her forever. But she's a frigid little bitch. Ain't givin' it up for nobody."

Anderson grabbed her sweatpants by the waist and forcefully pulled them off. She didn't move an inch. He was shocked by the second pair of sweatpants she had on, and the knife he felt on her leg. "What the hell?"

"What? What's up?"

Anderson pulled her pants-leg up to reveal her sheathed knife strapped to her shapely calf. He slipped it off, making sure to give her leg a quick kiss while doing so. "Would you look at the blade this bitch is carrying?"

Murphy just laughed, but he was getting nervous. He could hear Garrett and Ray shouting at each other on the street. More corpses were showing up.

"You're not gonna need this," Anderson said, and dropped the knife next to them. "Not for what we're about to do."

"Just hurry up," Murphy said. "I want my turn."

"Don't worry. She ain't gonna feel a thing by the time I get done with her. Wake up." He slapped her across the face. She didn't move. "I want you awake for this."

Anderson started unbuckling his pants. He'd fantasized about this moment a long time, ever since Samantha first walked through the high school gate.

His fantasy was about to turn into a nightmare.

Samantha sat up like a cobra and jammed the blade she carefully worked out of her wrist sheath into Anderson's neck. The blade was only four inches long, but she severed his windpipe and hit an artery. Anderson's eyes went wide as he felt blood running inside and outside his throat.

Samantha struggled to breathe. Her whole body was in pain. Her lungs burned and head throbbed from Anderson's attack, but she never lost consciousness. It wasn't easy to fake it. She knew she had to just listen to them, figure out where they were, wait until the time was right, and then strike.

She'd had sex two different times in her life, both times by *her* choice. She would kill before she let anyone rape her, and that's what she planned to do.

She pulled the knife out of Anderson's neck. Blood gushed from his throat to her chest. Samantha looked over his shoulder to see Murphy standing there with a shocked look on his face.

He pulled out his gun.

She grabbed Anderson by the shoulders and pulled him on top of her. His body shook as he slowly died. She could feel the blood flow all over her face.

Murphy fired wildly.

He pulled the trigger until he was empty. Every round went into her human shield--Anderson's dead body. Samantha waited patiently, her heart racing with fear, but determined to get out of this alive. When she heard the click of the empty chamber, she did the only thing she could do before he reloaded. She leaned out from under Anderson and threw her knife as hard as she could. She wasn't an expert knife thrower, but luck was on her side. It pierced his skull, finding a home right between the eyes. He dropped to his knees and fell forward, driving the knife even further into his brain.

Anderson was over two hundred pounds, and his dead weight pinned her to the floor. She tried to wiggle out from under him.

Gotta hurry. Any minute, he'll turn into-

Too late.

His body jerked as he came back to life. The scent of warm flesh immediately touched his nose, and he grabbed at Samantha.

She struggled against him as he climbed up to her face. His horrible wailing filled the living room. The hole in his neck gave him a bubbly sound. He leaned forward to bite into her cheek.

She got her arm up just in time.

Anderson's teeth sank into two layers of sweater sleeve. He shook his head violently, like a mad dog, but didn't penetrate the skin. Samantha had to act fast.

Her favorite knife was just a few feet away, where Anderson had dropped it earlier.

She twisted and maneuvered, all the while dragging Anderson with her. He put one hand on her throat, not to choke her, but just to keep himself up. He cut off her air anyway. She was about to lose consciousness when she felt her hand touch her knife.

She undid the clasp and shook the blade free. Pushing his face as far away as she could, she slammed the knife into his skull, just above the ear. His jaw went loose, and she pulled her arm free.

She pushed his body away and climbed to her feet. Her lungs were still on fire, but she could breathe again. Her ribs were sore from Anderson's kick, but nothing was broken.

She left the house through the front door. Scavenging was over for the day, at least for her.

She stopped when she hit the first step. Both trucks were gone. The end of the street where they came in was crowded with walking corpses. A few stumbled out of the homes across from her. When they caught sight of Samantha, their pace picked up. It was a scene right out of her early nightmares.

She calmly shut the door behind her and clutched the knife tightly in her hand. She moved away from the walkers, further up the street, keeping an eye on every open front door.

Garrett and Ray are just making another pass. Any second now, they'll come around the corner and run all these bastards down.

She kept backing up. Thirty seconds passed. A minute. She didn't hear the trucks on the next street over. She only heard the cries of the undead.

No one was coming.

Samantha was alone.

"Fuck."

She turned and ran. The undead followed her, more than a hundred now. There were a few corpses at the other end of the street and as she drew closer, their numbers started to swell. They came from the neighboring streets, the scent of fresh meat in their noses. She was trapped.

Samantha had survived for years before she found Lexington. She had done so by being smart, and staying away from the undead. The old cities, and any major populated area, were dead zones. No one could survive in the city, not for very long.

I can find somewhere to hole up. Then figure out my next move.

The thought was ridiculous, but she held onto it. She wasn't willing to accept death yet. She knew if she could hide from the corpses, at least for a while, they'd lose her scent, get lost, and wander away. Still, she'd never seen so many undead in her life.

She felt for her Beretta. It was gone. She'd left it, along with her second pair of sweatpants, back at the first house. She couldn't get to it now. The undead were already blocking her path.

She took a deep breath and ran to the closest house. She was afraid she would see a corpse when she kicked open the front door. She didn't, but there was one at the top of the stairs. As it opened its mouth to wail at her, its jaw fell off. She wanted to shut and lock the door, but the corpse fell down the stairs and nearly collided into her.

Samantha ran through the house. She could hear the undead behind her. As she passed the open basement door, a pair of bony hands reached out for her. She screamed, more afraid than she thought possible. She kicked the corpse down the stairs and kept moving.

She burst through the door at the back of the kitchen and into the alley. The alley separated one row of backyards from another. Corpses were scattered around, but in lower numbers.

Her lungs and legs were burning. Her run had slowed to a jog. Still, she easily ran by one corpse, then another. She could see the mouth of the alley ahead.

As she jogged by a backyard with no gate, a corpse that had been behind an old shed lunged at her. They both fell to the hard ground. She tried to stab it in the skull, but was disoriented by a hard pull at her feet. She looked down to see another corpse making its way up her legs. It would only be a matter of seconds before it found a soft spot to sink its teeth into. She kicked with her legs while trying to push the one on her chest away. Its jaws snapped dangerously close to her face. She could see three more shambling slowly toward her. She felt the strength in her arms giving away at the same time her sweatpants were pulled down, revealing her thigh to the other corpse.

A shadow moved above her that was too fast to be a corpse. She heard a violent crack, and the tugging at her legs stopped. The shadow stopped above her, and she screamed as the head of an arrow pierced the skull of the corpse on top of her, stopping just an inch short of her nose.

She rolled the corpse off to the side and looked up to see a figure standing above her. Her first instinct was that it couldn't be a man. She was the only human in the city. The sun was behind him, so she couldn't see his face. It was only when he felt for her arm and pulled her up with a warm, strong grip that she knew he was human.

He had a large compound bow and a quiver on his back. He quickly shot the three oncoming corpses in the brain with ease. Samantha was impressed.

She shielded her eyes from the sun with her hand. He was definitely a man, maybe around the same age as her. He was completely bald with bright blue eyes, and just slightly taller than she was. He wore old blue jeans and a white tank top, revealing a lean upper body. She thought he looked ridiculous, totally without protection.

He did something that caught Samantha by surprise. He smiled. Then he said something even stranger.

"Good afternoon."

Her mouth hung open. Her instincts told her something was very different about him. "This city is full of walkers."

"Walkers? The walking corpses? Well, yeah. You just notice that now?"

There was a loud crash not far away. They both looked to see walkers pushing their way out of the house Samantha had run through, and both ends of the alley were blocked by corpses.

"Wow. Looks like you really got them riled up," he said calmly.

Samantha looked at him. The brief hope she'd felt when he pulled her to her feet had dissipated. Physically, he seemed fine, but something clearly wasn't right in his head. They were surrounded by death, and he didn't seem bothered in the least.

He's insane. Out of his mind.

She'd seen it before at Lexington. The world wasn't easy, and some people just couldn't handle it. Everyone lived in a world ruled by monsters, and it was easy for a mind to snap.

She turned to run. He caught her by the arm, and she quickly pulled free.

"Whoa. Where you going?"

"Somewhere safe, where there aren't any walkers. And don't touch me."

He laughed, again putting Samantha on edge. "Good luck with that. Listen, see that backyard there, with the grill on its side? Run through that house to the next street. Look for the house with *The End Is Near* spray-painted above the door."

"I can't read."

He gave her a look. "Can't read? Well, can you count?"

"Yeah, I can count, asshole."

He smirked. "Fourth house down from the end. You should see it as soon as you hit the street. I'll meet you there."

"What are you gonna do?"

"I'll slow them down."

Samantha turned and ran. She knew she owed the stranger her life, but she wasn't going to wait around for him.

He wants to be an idiot and get himself killed, fine by me.

CHAPTER 6

Aaron Thompson watched the beautiful dark-skinned woman sprint away. She pushed a stray walker to the ground and jumped over the grill, then vanished inside the house he'd directed her to.

He rubbed his head. He was as curious about her as she was about him. What was she doing in Baltimore? He had heard the trucks moving about while on his afternoon walk. He hadn't thought much of it, he'd heard them before, but this time he noticed the undead were all funneling in one direction. He guessed they were after a live meal, and he was right.

Very pretty lady, even if a little rude.

He was impressed with her. She wore two sweaters, and a cap to cover her hair. The woman obviously thought ahead.

He shook his head as he passed the undead mob. "No lunch for you today, guys."

He picked random corpses in the mob and just tripped them. Walkers started falling over each other, like the old game of dominoes he used to play with Aunt Denise.

As always, the undead made no move to harm him.

Aaron walked through the long-deserted house. He noticed a chair knocked over and an old lamp busted on the floor. No doubt the clumsiness of his guest.

He left through the open front door and saw something that made him pick up speed. At the door to his home were about twenty walkers. Three or four were pounding at the door while others were trying to climb in through the shattered windows. A

75

few undead had spotted Samantha entering the old home, and a few undead had turned into many.

"Hell, lady, what are you doing in there?" he whispered to himself.

He didn't run to the front door. He ran past the undead and the three other homes on the street. He rounded the corner and grabbed the fire escape ladder on the side of the last house. He always left the ladder down, although he pulled it up after him this time. He knew the undead weren't coordinated enough to scale a ladder, but with a live meal nearby, he wouldn't take any chances.

He sprinted up the winding metal staircase and jumped to the roof. The roof access hatch of his home was already open. He seldom closed it, except when it rained.

He quickly climbed the wooden foldout ladder down to the second floor. He heard the moans of the undead all around. The stairs leading downstairs were gone, taken out years ago by whoever lived in Aaron's home before him.

He saw Samantha near the front of the house. He watched her stab a walker that had climbed in through the window, then she tried to slide a couch in front of the splintering door.

Aaron lay on the floor and extended one arm down while bracing himself against the wall with the other. He didn't have time to set up the ladder he kept nearby.

"Hey lady!" She turned and looked up at him. "Grab my hand!"

She tucked her bloody knife into the back of her sweatpants, then got a running start near the door. She jumped and clutched Aaron's hand. The front door burst open as he struggled to pull her up. A corpse missed her foot only by a few inches.

Aaron and Samantha both lay on the floor on their backs for a minute, out of breath. The song of the undead grew louder as more of them filed into the house. When Aaron pulled himself up, Samantha was already on one knee. She had tossed her cap off, and her hair flowed down around her shoulders. She leaned

against the wall, pointing her blade right at Aaron. He went to
help her up, but she recoiled defensively and thrust the knife out.

"I just killed two people," she said.

"Uh, good for you?"

"They couldn't keep their dicks where they belonged."

"I will try to keep my dick in my pants."

"Good. I have no problem killing you."

"Okay. You're welcome, by the way."

"I didn't thank you for anything."

"I know. It's called sarcasm. Kinda like a joke."

"I know what the hell sarcasm is. I'm not in the mood."

"I can see that."

He moved in to help her up. She shoved him away. "I said
don't touch me."

"Okay, okay, lady, relax. Calm down. I'm Aaron. Aaron
Thompson."

"Samantha. No last name."

"Samantha. *Sam.* I like it. Pretty name."

She looked at him with narrowed eyes. Fifty walkers were
beneath them, and he was talking about pretty names. "Is it safe
here?"

He laughed. "Is *anywhere* safe?"

"Would you please stop laughing? It's annoying me."

He laughed again, although more subdued. "You're in a city
of the undead, and my laugh is getting to you?"

She closed her eyes and barely held in a scream. Aaron already
drove her crazy, and she'd known him less than five minutes.
"Would you, please, just shut up, and answer the question?"

He shrugged. "Sure. They can't get up here. The roofs are all
connected, but all the other hatches are closed, and they can't
climb ladders. I pulled the fire escape up. We're safe."

"Good."

Samantha leaned against the wall. The adrenaline was wearing
off, and her body began to ache. She was so tired. She still kept
a solid grip on her knife, though she didn't think Aaron would

try to hurt her. He could have already done that, but men were weird creatures. She knew Murphy and Anderson were scum, but hadn't thought them capable of rape. She's been wrong. If she was wrong this time, Aaron would end up with a blade in his gut.

"Where is your family from?" Aaron asked. "I've never seen anyone with your skin color before. Spain? Mexico? Egypt?"

"I don't know. Is it important?"

"Nah, just wondering. You don't look like a Sam, either."

She opened her eyes to look at him. It was hard to hide her annoyance. "I know. That's because my name is *Samantha*. You don't look like an Aaron."

"Oh really? What do I look like?"

"You look like a stupid son of a bitch who asks a lot of dumb questions. Look, I don't want to be your friend. I don't want to get to know you. Let's just stick to the basics, okay?"

She immediately regretted her words, but couldn't help it. Everything about Aaron was unusual, from his carefree attitude all the way down to his laugh. He bothered her.

Aaron didn't even flinch. "Well, okay then. Sounds like that's my clue to leave." He pointed to both ends of the hall. "We've got two bedrooms up here and a bathroom. The bathroom still works, believe it or not. Just gotta fill the tank up with water. I've got supplies in both bedrooms, but there's a mattress, too, if you want to rest."

He walked past her to a bedroom. She watched him grab a magazine from a pile in the corner and stretch out on the mattress.

Finally, he's not talking.

At first she thought that was a good thing, but then she heard all the undead below her. She looked down at the fifty or so that had squeezed their way into the living room. They reached up to her with wide eyes.

Sam went exploring, although there wasn't much to explore. Aaron's description of the upstairs was accurate. The rear bedroom had a mattress with no bed frame, eight large jugs of water, clothes folded neatly in open dresser drawers. It looked rather clean, except for the wallpaper peeling off the walls. The bathroom had an empty tub with a broken skylight directly overhead, letting the sun in, and a medicine cabinet that was almost falling off the wall.

She slowly peeked into Aaron's room. He had blankets and sheets folded in the corner, with a stack of books in another. He had pictures of himself along with some other people in frames on the old broken down dresser.

This didn't seem like a temporary place for him. He'd put a lot of time in it.

Does he actually live here?

Aaron kept his eyes on Sam as she studied his house. He could see the wheels turning in her head while she took everything in.

The heat must have gotten to her, as she took both of her bloody sweaters off. She leaned in the doorway, wearing just her sweatpants and a white sports bra.

He smirked and looked back down to the magazine he was reading. He thought back to a few months ago, to the last time he had entertained visitors. Two men and a woman were trying to make their way through the city. The woman was named Diane. She was very attractive, and thought she could seduce supplies and help out of Aaron. He'd tried not to laugh in her face.

Oh, Aaron, look at my tits. Can we have some water? Look at my ass, do you have any food?

It didn't work. Of course, he helped them, until they had gotten themselves killed on the streets. He helped them not because she was attractive, but because that was the kind of person he was.

He shook his head at the memory. Out of the corner of his eye he could see Sam with her arms crossed, showing off a curvy figure. She was quite beautiful, even with the huge knot forming on her forehead.

"You're reading?" she asked.

"Yes."

"What for?"

He smiled. *So much for seduction.*

Despite her harshness, for some reason, he liked her. "You sound like my Uncle Frank."

"Is he here?"

"No. My family is dead."

Sam nodded. That meant he was alone, and less of a threat. She could kill him if he tried anything.

"So what brings you to Baltimore?" he asked. "I'm guessing supplies."

"Yeah. A truck run went to hell pretty fast when two guys tried to screw me. I killed them."

"So you said."

"I need to get back," she stuttered when the word actually came to her, "home."

She was surprised at herself. She didn't go out of her way to contribute at Lexington, nor did she have any friends there. It took being stranded with a million walkers before realizing she thought of the school as home.

"Stay as long as you want. Leave when you're ready," Aaron said. "I have food, water, a change of clothes. I'll heat up some deer meat later for dinner. They walk right on the streets now."

"You actually *live* here?"

"Yes."

"In a dead city?"

He looked over his magazine to shoot her an agitated look. He didn't like her tone. "Yes."

She couldn't believe what she was hearing. "Why? How? Where do you find water? How do you even leave this house? How did you find me in that alley without getting eaten by a million walkers?"

He put his magazine down.

"Answering those questions would go past the basics. You'd have to get to know me, and we can't have that now, can we?"

Sam almost fired back a comment, but she kept it in. She slumped ever so slightly in the door frame. Aaron picked up on how exhausted she was.

"Take a nap in the other room," he offered. "It locks, so you don't have to worry about me."

She turned and walked to the other bedroom. "I'm not worried about you."

"Well, that's good."

"Don't be flattered," she called back. "It just means I could kick your ass."

She shut the door behind her. Aaron laughed, and went back to his magazine.

Sam had a terrible nightmare. She dreamed Murphy and Anderson were a little more successful in their rape attempt. They managed to get her clothes off, but instead of raping her, they turned into walkers and started eating at her bare flesh. Legs, arms, breasts, face, it was all food to them. She tried to get away, but they had torn out the muscles in her legs. She couldn't move. They continued to slowly kill her by feasting on her body, and more were coming.

She woke up and felt a hand on her shoulder, gently shaking her.

"Sam, wake up."

She sat up with a start and held her knife near her ear, ready to strike. It had never left her hand, even during sleep. Aaron jumped off the bed and backed up, his hands up defensively.

"Whoa, Sam! Calm down. You were almost screaming in your sleep. You didn't lock your door either. See? And my dick is still in my pants."

She took a few deep breaths. She noticed he had a towel on his shoulder. She nodded, the closest she'd ever come to showing meaningful gratitude.

"Come here," he said. "Let me show you something."

She followed him to the bathroom. He pointed to the tub with a smile on his face. As obnoxious as his smile was, Sam realized she liked it.

The tub was half-full of water, a hint of steam just barely visible.

"You put together a warm bath?"

"I heat the water up on the roof with my grill, then just pour it through the broken skylight. The drain actually works too. No idea where it goes, but hey, whatever. Anyway, it's all yours."

She looked at him. "What?"

"I figured you could use one. Hell, you've got blood on your face still."

Sam laughed. It was the first time Aaron heard her laugh. It was a nice sound.

She shook her head slowly, a smile still on her face. She could hear the undead in the living room beneath her. It seemed when she spoke, they made just a little more noise.

"Let me get this straight. You expect me to take my clothes off, and take a bath, with a hundred walkers downstairs, and you right outside the door? What's your game, Aaron? What are you trying to do? Get off on seeing me naked?"

Aaron was hurt. He could tell gratitude wasn't Sam's strength. Still, it wasn't exactly hard work, but it took time to heat up two buckets of water, pour them through the skylight, and then start over.

"Sam, I don't *expect* you to do anything. You want to take a bath? Fine. You don't? I'll sleep either way. You are a beautiful woman, but you're not *that* beautiful. My goal is not to see you naked. I've got more important things to do."

Her face was blank for a moment, then he thought he saw the hint of a smile. She reached out and grabbed the towel from his shoulder. "My name is *Samantha*."

It was his turn to smile. "Soap, razors, and I think some shampoo is under the sink. There's girl clothes in the rear bedroom in one of the dressers."

She laughed. "Girl clothes?"

"You know, bras, panties, stuff like that. This door locks, too."

She smiled and nodded, then closed and locked the door.

Aaron took a breath. *That is one exhausting woman.*

He listened at the door for a moment. He heard her peel off her clothes, then climb in the tub.

Good, now I can go to work.

He did have other reasons for getting her in the tub, but it had nothing to do with her being nude. He had some things he needed to get from the first floor, and the last thing he needed was for Sam to catch him walking with the undead.

He wouldn't know what he'd tell her.

He set the ladder up and climbed down to the living room. He tried to breathe as little as possible as he walked through the mob. Dangerous to him or not, they were disgusting. He leaned down to grab his fishing rod, and felt something hit the back of his head. He knew it was a maggot or worm, and quickly brushed it off.

"Maybe you all should be the ones taking a bath."

They moaned at him in response.

He gathered a few more things and went up to the roof.

It felt strange to have another guest after all this time. He could tell she wasn't too fond of him, but at least she was honest and didn't hide it. She was probably planning her trip back home, wherever that was. He knew he would help her however he could, probably even give her the keys to the car. Then he would be alone once again.

She was certainly intriguing. Aaron could honestly say he liked her, but he remembered the last time he had guests. He had to watch everything he said and did. He couldn't go on any moonlight walks with Sam staying with him.

The sooner she left, the sooner he could get back to his normal life.

Sam hated to admit it, but as horrible as things were going, she couldn't remember the last time she felt so relaxed. It had been a long time since she had an actual bath. They had makeshift outside showers at Lexington, but nothing like a bath. The warm water loosened every muscle. She washed her hair and took her time shaving. As she dried off she could hear footsteps on the roof.

She still didn't know what to make of the cute bald man. At first, she thought he was crazy, but he didn't seem to be out of his mind. He was actually intelligent and thoughtful.

Still, she couldn't shake the feeling that he was a lot more than just a hermit in the city.

She wrapped the towel around her and went to the bedroom. She picked out some undergarments, a black pair of shorts and a white tee shirt with words on it she couldn't read. It was nice to wear some clothes without holes in them.

She took another look at the undead in the living room while grabbing the roof ladder. They still waited for her. Sam had no idea how she would get back home, and tried to push back the hopelessness she felt.

But she knew she *wanted* to go home.

The cool breeze touched her face as she took a step on the roof. The sun was setting, giving the sky a pretty orange hue. The only thing that ruined the sight was the sound of the undead all around them. Once again, her jaw hung open when she saw what Aaron had done. He had yet another mattress, some lawn-chairs, a grill, some plastic sheets, more water bottles, a few end-tables, a stack of wood, and a large umbrella.

"Wow," she said. His back was toward her as he worked on the grill. "You got a little paradise going on up here."

He turned to face her with some deer steak on a plastic knife. He was surprised at what he saw. She was beautiful before, but even more so now. Her wet hair clung to her face. She had decided on a pair of shorts, and her legs were very nice and shapely. He smiled at the Baltimore Orioles shirt.

He caught himself staring, and mentally slapped himself for it.

"Want some dinner?" he said, handing her the steak. "It's actually pretty good. Salt and pepper will fix anything. You wouldn't believe how hard it is to find salt and pepper."

She took a bite. He handed her a glass of water. It *was* quite good.

Sam gestured around them. "Where did you get all of this?"

"Just around," he said, grabbing a steak for himself. "There's plenty of stuff here."

"Yeah, and there's plenty of walkers too. How do you do it? You don't even seem afraid. I know people back home who still cry themselves to sleep every night."

He bit into his steak. "We're moving out of the *basics* again, Sam."

"Samantha," she corrected once more.

There were sixty people at Lexington, and Sam figured she'd met twice that many people over the years on her own. Never once did she feel the need to explain herself to anyone. She kept to herself, people left her alone, and that was that.

With Aaron, she wanted to talk.

"I know how I come across," she said. "I really do. I know I'm not very friendly. It's just that I don't really trust people a whole lot."

He smiled and gestured around them. "Look where I live. I understand. I've got people issues of my own."

She nodded. Something about Aaron made her feel at ease, took the edge off a little. "You can take two people who have been friends forever, put them in a room of undead, and they'll kill each other trying to get out. Friendships end very quickly. I've found there's no point in having friends."

Aaron swallowed hard as he thought back to his family. "That's not true. My whole family died because we wouldn't run from each other."

"Then they were idiots."

He stopped eating and froze completely, holding her gaze. "Excuse me?"

"There's nothing wrong with not having friends," she said. "Nothing wrong at all with looking out for yourself. That's why I'm alive today." She was trying to convince herself more than Aaron.

"Sam, please don't call my family idiots. Also, the reason you're alive is because a complete stranger saved your life."

"Which was a stupid thing to do. You don't even know me. Hell, even if you did, I wouldn't risk my life for you."

He shrugged. He didn't exactly risk his life, but she didn't know that. "My family was killed by a man looking out for himself. But that doesn't mean that everyone out there is like him. I'm not a people person either, but I haven't given up on them yet. It's a shame you have. If I can save someone's life, I will."

She was quiet for a moment, and just watched him. There was a calm, a peace about him that was almost contagious.

She struggled to find words. "I don't understand you, Aaron. You seem like a good man, which is hard to find now, but you live out here with the walkers. Why?"

He smiled and took a drink of water. "The *basics*, Sam."

She almost hit him. She only had herself to blame. He wasn't going to tell her anything. Ironically, she wanted to know.

They ate in silence as the sun continued its journey over the horizon. Sam thought of how quickly life could change. The night before, she was getting ready to walk the Lexington fence. Now she was away from home with a strange man who somehow lived among the undead.

Aaron leaned back in a lawn chair and looked over a pile of books and games he'd moved to the roof earlier. He lit a candle and set it down carefully. Soon, that and the moon would be the only light they had.

"Do you play chess?" he asked.

"No."

"Checkers?"

She shook her head.

"Any games at all?"

She gave him a look. She was a little jealous of him, of his ability to smile at everything. "It's hard to concentrate on games, Aaron, when there are a million walkers between me and my home."

"And what is home for you?"

She sat in the lawn chair next to him and talked about Lexington. He listened to every word. She told him about the people, and how they actually managed to work together in the world of the dead. She told him about how Richardson had taken an old high school and made it into something special. She even described her room, and the little things she'd done to make it hers.

"It sounds like a nice place."

"Yeah, it is. I didn't really know how much till I got stuck here."

Sam tried to think of how she could get back. If she could find her way to Interstate 295, she could find her way home. She couldn't read signs, but she knew the way back from memory and landmarks.

The biggest problem was the undead in the way.

"So what do you do for fun?" Aaron asked.

"For fun? Well, I don't know. Most of my *fun* time is taken up by trying to stay alive."

"You don't have any hobbies?"

"Not really." She laughed. "Maybe that's why Richardson is always asking me to walk the fence."

"Let's play some checkers."

"I told you. I don't play games."

"Eh, you're right. You'd lose anyway."

It was a calculated statement his father had made to Aunt Denise many times when she refused to loosen up. It worked with Sam too. She looked at him a moment, then a small smile touched her face. "Teach me how to play."

They played long into the night. Sam managed to win her fair share. Aaron noticed her finally relaxing, at least just a little.

The moon was high overhead when Sam's body told her it was time to sleep. She stifled a yawn.

"Is it okay if I sleep in one of the rooms?"

"Of course, but you won't sleep. The undead will keep you up all night. Only freaks like me can sleep with the noise. You can have the mattress up here."

"And where will you sleep?"

"Right here in the lawn chair."

She didn't like that. "I always sleep alone. I don't like people near me."

He shrugged. "Okay. Either room is fine. I'm gonna sleep up here. It's a beautiful night. I'll walk you down."

"Why?"

"To make sure nothing happens to you. Why else?"

Sam held his gaze a moment, making Aaron uncomfortable enough to look away.

Richardson isn't even this nice.

She didn't understand it at all. How could someone who lived the way Aaron did be so personable? She wanted to like him, but was afraid to. She was afraid to really like *anyone*.

Sam knew that like everyone, he would find a way to disappoint her. Everyone always did. Trust was a hard thing to come by. She had to watch Richardson for years before she even began to think he was trustworthy.

Aaron led her back to the house, careful not to touch her along the way. It was pitch black, and he wanted to make sure she didn't fall to the living room. He knew undead behavior better than anyone. While their numbers were thinning from Sam being on the roof for so long, there were still a good number in the house. The undead would leave an area if they couldn't see their meal after a while.

"Good night," he said.

Sam collapsed on the mattress. "Hey, Aaron?"

"Yeah?" He had almost closed the door.

She almost said it. She almost threw out a *thank you*. She decided against it. "Good night to you too."

Aaron closed the door and stopped at the hall closet on the way out. He didn't need any light. He knew where every single thing in his house was. He grabbed an extra pillow and sheet for when Sam inevitably decided to come up to the roof.

Sam knew she didn't sleep long. The little bit of sleep she did get was full of nightmares of the undead. She could hear them as she sat up on the mattress, even with the door closed. She didn't want to admit it, but Aaron was right. There was no way anyone could sleep very well with the undead so close.

She carefully made her way through the hall and followed the moonlight to the open roof access. The undead still shuffled mindlessly in the living room. Even the sound of their footsteps made her hair stand up.

Aaron was fast asleep. He slept on the mattress with the sheet stopping at his waist. He slept shirtless, and Sam couldn't help but take a peek at his upper body. He was attractive.

A spare sheet and pillow waited in the lawn chair.

Asshole, she thought, angry that he was right once again.

As she settled into the chair she tried to think of how she would get back home.

Nothing much came to mind.

The only plan she had that was even possible was to just survive until Lexington went on another supply run. She could get Garrett's attention somehow. Lexington didn't exactly have a schedule, so she had no idea of when that would be. Even if Garrett did see her, in the vast city streets, would he stop for her? She knew she wouldn't stop for him.

"I'll never see home again," she whispered.

"Why not?"

Aaron's voice startled her. She looked down at him as he looked up at her.

"I can't get home," she said. "It's about a thirty minute drive down 295. There's no way I can walk it, not with all the undead. And shit, I don't even know where 295 is from here."

"Can you drive a car?"

"Of course I can. Why?"

Aaron stood up and stretched his arms. He motioned for Sam to follow. "Be very quiet. Don't stir the corpses up."

She followed him across the long roof, until they neared the end of the block. He carefully looked over the side.

"Do you see that red car there?"

With just the moonlight, Sam couldn't tell what was red and what wasn't. She just followed his finger to an old Honda Civic parked across the street. She had to look over the walkers to see it. "Yeah."

"That car still works."

She searched his face for his strange sense of humor. He looked serious.

"Are you sure?"

"I had a few houseguests that showed up in that thing. They stayed with me a few nights while searching for some gas. They actually filled the tank up a little, but then they decided not to listen to me, and went out looking for food. They never came back. The keys are in my bedroom. I haven't started it up in a while, but it did run."

Sam was excited, but guilt started to seep in. "Listen, I don't have anything to trade. Even if I did, it wouldn't be worth a car."

They walked back to Aaron's end of the roof. They no longer had to whisper.

"I don't know how to drive," he said. "Just take it. It doesn't do me any good."

Sam started to feel hope. *Maybe, just maybe, I can get back home.*

She looked at Aaron as he settled back onto his mattress. She was too energetic to lie back down.

"Okay, I just gotta find a map I can actually read. Hell, one street over is probably a sign pointing to 295."

"There's a gas station down the block. Maybe there's some maps there."

"Why don't you come with me?"

He laughed. "Your first joke. I'm so proud."

"I'm serious, Aaron. It'll be good for both of us."

"How so?"

"I won't lie. If I try to go alone, I probably won't make it. I have a better chance if you come along."

"Yeah, right. So if the corpses get close, you can shoot me in the stomach and leave me for dead."

"No, that's not it at all. I'm not gonna risk my life for you, but I won't hurt you."

Her honesty was surprisingly refreshing.

"And what do I get out of our little trip?"

She laughed too. "Away from here, for starters. A place where there's some people. You wouldn't believe all the things we have at Lexington. You won't have to be in danger hunting deer on the streets."

He smiled. She didn't know why.

"What do you think, Aaron? Shit, if you don't like Lexington, just hitch a ride back on the next supply run. Maybe you can score some supplies yourself."

Aaron thought about it for at least a minute without saying anything. He eventually decided he would go with her, for two reasons. The first was boredom. He'd been in Baltimore for at least four winters now, and could use a little change. The other reason surprised him, but he knew it was there.

He didn't want anything to happen to Sam.

"I'll go with you on one condition."

"What's that?"

"I get to call you Sam with no complaints."

Sam smiled. She had smiled more with Aaron in one day than she had the past year. "Deal."

CHAPTER 7

Preparations were slower than Sam expected, but perhaps that was her excitement. The mid-morning sun was up. She waited on the roof and watched walker movement while Aaron gathered some things from the house. He packed some books, bottles of water, a pocket knife, a lighter, his solar-powered watch compass, the car keys, and perhaps the most important thing, his framed Polaroids of his family. He also grabbed his quiver of arrows and compound bow.

He joined Sam—who looked impatient—on the roof.

She gestured to his bow. "Where's your gun?"

"Don't have one. I never liked guns."

"You don't like guns?"

He shook his head.

"It's amazing you're still alive."

"Can you drive that car?" he said. "I mean, *really* drive it?"

"I can go fast, if that's what you mean."

"Good. We go down together, and run like hell. We'll hit the gas station at the end of the street, so I can grab a map. I'll get us to 295. After that, it's all on you."

"I'll do my part. We'll be at Lexington in no time." She had a much better view of the car than the night before. "It doesn't have any windows. I'm not gonna be able to stop at the station long, so you'd better be quick. If we can't find a map, we keep moving."

He nodded. "No problem. You're the boss."

Aaron turned and put a hand on the roof access of the closest house to the car. Sam stopped him by putting a hand on his shoulder, then quickly pulled it back.

"Aaron, listen, and you're not gonna like this," she said, her pretty face hardening. "There's forty walkers down there on the street, and who knows how many till Lexington. I'm not a hero. If you trip and fall, or slow down at all, I'm not waiting around. I won't come back to get you. Understand?"

He smiled, which surprised her. "I know where I stand with you. You're honest."

She returned his smile, glad that was out of the way. "Okay, let's go."

The house they used to get to the street was empty. They slowly made their way to the front door. Aaron gently pushed Sam into the corner and peeked out the front window. There were plenty of walkers on the street, but most were still gathered at the other end, near Aaron's home. Only ten or so were near the car, with only three or four right in their path.

"We've got a pretty clear shot. We're gonna have a few seconds to get to the car. They smell you, right now, but they don't *see* you. Once we get to the street, they're gonna go crazy."

"Why do you keep saying *me*? They smell *you* too."

He gave her an annoyed look. "Yeah, yeah, whatever. I'm gonna open the door and take a few out while you hit the car. You ready to run?"

She nodded.

Aaron opened the door casually. Sam ran down the steps and across the sidewalk. Aaron fired three arrows at a speed Sam didn't think possible. She'd seen it the day before, but it amazed her all the same.

Three corpses fell to the ground. One was directly in front of Sam. She heard the arrow cut the air next to her ear. She hopped over the corpse and jumped into the Civic.

The undead perked up.

They shuffled toward the car, their song making Sam's hands shake. She put the key in the ignition and turned it. The engine started right up. She was shocked. In the back of her mind, she didn't think it would be that easy.

Aaron ran across the street. He didn't bother running around to the passenger's side. He jumped head first through the broken rear window and landed on the back seat. He lost a few arrows in the jump, but had plenty more.

"Go, Sam, go!"

She floored the gas, burning tire rubber as they soared down the street.

"Aaron! The window!"

He looked up to see a corpse hanging halfway out of the passenger's window. Sam tried to lean to the side as it moaned and reached for her. One of its eyes fell from its skull and landed on the seat.

Aaron casually reached over the seat and grabbed it by the back of what used to be its shirt.

"What the fuck are you doing?" Sam screamed.

He tossed it out the window.

Sam was definitely driving fast, running over any undead that were in the way. Others reached for them, but had no chance. Her heart was beating so fast she could feel it.

"Holy shit!" Aaron said from the back. "Actually never been in a moving car before."

"You're no use to me if you get bit. Be more careful."

"You know, you sure have a strange way of thanking somebody."

"No jokes! No sarcasm! Just focus!"

"Fine. There's the gas station, up on the left."

She saw it. There were plenty of walkers nearby, but they were spread out.

"What the hell?" Aaron said as they got closer. He removed his quiver and backpack.

"What's wrong?" She saw it a second after he did. There was a large dumpster in front of the only door to the gas station.

"You're gonna have to get out and help me."

"Shit."

Sam put the engine in neutral and they both jumped out. Aaron shoved a corpse to the ground as they ran to the dumpster. The recklessness bothered Sam. It was like he wasn't even worried about getting bit at all.

They shoved the dumpster out of the way as fast as they could. Aaron could hear the undead around them approaching. The closest few were maybe twenty feet away.

The gas station was a ruined mess. The maps that used to be up front near the counter were nowhere to be found. The floor was littered with old magazines, food wrappers, money, some busted ceiling lights.

"I don't see a map," Sam said. "And they're getting closer."

"On the floor," Aaron said. He dropped to his knees and started rifling through the trash. "There has to be one here."

Sam did the same. It took Sam a minute to finally find a map book of Baltimore and the surrounding area, but it felt like an hour. A corpse was at the door. Aaron shoved it to ground, like he did the other.

"Is this it?" Sam said.

He scanned the cover. "Yeah. Let's go."

They went outside. Aaron stopped Sam by putting an arm in front of her.

The undead had gathered.

There were five corpses between them and the car. Another five were approaching from one side. Two more, who used to be children, came from the other.

Sam was terrified. One of her many nightmares was finally coming true, being surrounded by undead with no way out.

Aaron just laughed. "It's crazy how one turns into twenty, isn't it?"

"Aaron-"

"You get to the car when I move, okay?"

"What are you-"

He charged at the five walkers in front of them before she could finish. They all went to the ground in a heap, including Aaron. Sam gasped, then her legs unfroze. She ran to the car and jumped behind the wheel. A corpse was trying to crawl in through the back window.

Sam didn't hesitate. She put the car in drive and sped away. The corpse lost its grip on the back and tumbled to the ground. She ran over two more as she left the station and hit the street.

Aaron didn't know why he was surprised as he pulled himself to one knee. Sam was a woman of her word. He watched as the Civic disappeared down the street, the sound of its engine fading in the distance.

Without food nearby, the undead once again had no purpose. The group that had gathered started to break apart, shuffling away randomly.

Aaron was upset. A lot of things hit him at once. His backpack was still in the car, which meant his only pictures of his family were gone.

Even worse, Sam was gone.

He had grown a little attached, even if he didn't want to admit it. He knew they weren't even close enough to be called friends, but it was nice to have someone to talk to. He'd been alone so long, he didn't realize he missed talking.

The five walkers he tackled had gotten back up. Even any undead that Aaron assaulted wouldn't hurt him. He looked at the closest one. Sadly, the walkers were the closest thing he had to friends, until Sam dropped in his lap.

"Can't say Sam isn't honest."

He had taken three steps away from the gas station when he heard the roar of an engine, followed by the screeching of tires. The roar grew louder until Sam sped back into the gas station lot. She cut the wheel and hit the brakes. The back end swung to the side, knocking a group of walkers to the ground.

"Get in!"

Aaron threw open the passenger's door and jumped in before the undead could gather. She sped away. She had no idea where she was going, but they had to get moving.

"I thought they'd be all over you," she said. "Are you hurt? Are you bit?"

"No, I'm fine." He smiled. "So much for not being a hero. Thank you."

Her anger spilled over. "What the hell is your problem? You got some kind of suicide thing going on? Don't do anything stupid like that again!"

"Sam, I-"

"Just shut up! I don't want to talk to you right now." She tossed the map in his lap. "Just tell me where the hell I'm driving."

He opened the map. "Well, that means I have to talk."

"Aaron, I swear, if you crack another one of your dumb jokes right now-"

"Turn right at Russell Street."

"I told you before, I can't read."

"The second intersection coming up, turn right. You *do* know your left and right?"

Sam ran over three walkers as she plowed through the intersection. "Another stupid comment, and I'll push you out myself."

Aaron tried to be quiet. He really did, but he didn't view the world like everyone else. To them, the world was a very serious and dangerous place. To Aaron, there was no danger, at least not from the undead. He still held onto his carefree side, the part of him that grew up with his wonderful family. Despite the rough life, his family had fun and loved each other, and Aaron had absorbed all of that. It was never too late to smile, even in the world of the dead.

He couldn't help himself. "You're really pretty when you're mad."

Despite the situation, or perhaps because of it, Sam almost laughed. She was still angry at everything. She was angry at the world for refusing to let people die a single time. She was angry at Aaron for carelessly tossing his body into a pile of walkers. Most of all, she was angry at herself for coming back to save Aaron's life.

Even as she left Aaron at the gas station, surrounded by walkers, she knew she would turn around and come back. She just needed to shake the corpse off the trunk. She had no intention of honoring her promise to leave him to die if he fell behind, and she hated both Aaron and herself for it. She didn't know what had changed in her, but she didn't like it.

I can't read the map, she thought. *I can't get very far without him. That's the only reason I saved him.*

She knew she was lying to herself.

It took a few minutes to get to 295. Sam was thankful Aaron kept quiet. She wasn't sure how much of him she could take. He studied the map, only occasionally looking at the road. She had to slow down at times to avoid dead cars, but managed to do so without corpses getting close. The Civic was much more maneuverable than a truck.

"I don't get it," he said. "Lexington is just a suburb. How is it safe?"

"It's *not* safe completely. But look at Honeyton Road, where the school is."

He found it on the map, and thought he saw what she was talking about. It was only a few turns off of 295. It was a long road, with no intersecting streets, with thick woods on both sides and the river not too far behind them.

"Deserted road?" he asked.

"Walkers show up every now and then, but not in force. We've always got our eyes open."

"Watch out for that corpse," he said, pointing. "We can't hit every one of them. The car's not in the best shape."

"Do you know how to drive? No? Then shut up, and let me do the driving."

As soon as she said it, something popped in the engine. Steam starting flowing out from under the hood.

"What? Oh no, come on now, just a little longer," Sam said.

"What's wrong?"

"How the hell should I know?"

"You said you know how to drive."

"That doesn't mean I'm a mechanic, asshole! This is your car, ya know."

The car slowed to a halt. Through the smoke Aaron could see walkers on the road ahead, plenty of them. There were a few behind them, and some on the opposite side of 295, trying to climb the concrete barrier.

"I can't believe this," Sam said.

Aaron shook his head. He let out a sigh, like this was all just a minor inconvenience.

He climbed out and slowly grabbed his things through the busted glass. He walked back to the trunk.

Sam was dumbfounded. She just followed him, her mouth open the whole time. She stayed close to his side and watched the undead approach.

Aaron looked at the sun overhead. He had a good idea of where north was, but he checked the compass on his wrist anyway, just to be safe. Sam noticed his watch for the first time.

"Aaron, come on. We have to run."

He ignored her. He placed the map on the roof of the Civic. He tried to figure out where they were by the old exit sign up ahead, which was barely hanging on the metal frame.

"Let's go, dammit!"

He took note of the wind at their backs. The undead wouldn't smell Sam.

"Perfect," he whispered.

She grabbed his wrist and tried to pull him toward the shoulder. The woods were just a few feet away. He didn't budge, and instead pulled her close.

"You're gonna have to trust me."

She shook her head. "No, I don't, Aaron. You're crazy! We have to run. I've survived longer on the streets than you, and you don't do that by sitting still."

The closest walker was fifteen feet away. Aaron didn't show the slightest bit of concern. It drove Sam mad.

"You don't run without knowing where you're running to. You want to run the wrong way?" He pointed to the other side of 295, across the concrete barrier. "Go that way, into the woods. Keep the sun just to your left. You'll run into a river."

"What are you doing?"

He rolled his eyes. "Will you just go? I'll be fine, just a minute behind you."

Sam ran. She jumped over the concrete barrier into the woods. Aaron was nervous for a moment. If she turned to look at him, she'd see that the walkers paid him no mind at all. All eyes were on her. Luckily for him, she didn't look.

He gathered his bow and quiver.

Aaron didn't understand his relationship with the undead. He wasn't sure if they thought of him as one of their own or not. It wasn't like they couldn't see him, he knew they could. He had his own theories, but he knew he would never know for sure.

He *did* know that walkers grouped together for a while would follow a leader, and he wasn't sure if they thought of him as a leader or not. So he stayed around 295 for a minute, just watching them. One of them used to be a cop, and he immediately thought of Uncle Frank. Another had been in the navy, its once white uniform now torn, filthy, and bloody. The interstate was a melting pot of undead, from all races and walks of life. Aaron felt sad when he thought about the last days of the world. These people were probably all trying to escape, and start over with life. Now, they were trapped on the interstate forever.

When a corpse tried to climb the barrier, Aaron pulled it back. A few that were already on the other side shuffled toward the woods. Aaron shot them each in the brain with an arrow.

When he was satisfied the undead wouldn't catch up, he jogged into the woods. Their moans faded and nature began to take over. He thought back to his life with his family. Crickets chirped, birds sang, squirrels ran through the trees.

In the middle of those sounds, he heard a few cries of pain.

He saw Sam leaning on a tree with her head down, holding her right foot just slightly in the air. He could hear the river in front of them.

"Sam? You okay?"

She turned to face him. Her face was twisted with pain, but she refused to cry. "I think I sprained my foot."

He bent down and took her shoe and sock off as gingerly as he could. Her ankle was already twice its normal size.

"Can you move it?"

She winced in pain, but moved it from side to side.

"Okay, probably not broken. Let's go."

"No."

"We have to keep moving. We can walk the rest of the way to Lexington, but we can't let them catch up. You can lean on me."

"Just go without me."

He ignored her. He slipped her arm around his neck and wrapped his arm around her waist. She pushed him back by the chest to look in his eyes. They were still uncomfortably close.

"I wouldn't do this for you," she said. "I would let you die."

He smiled. "You're a liar. Let's get moving."

They spotted the river, which was a beautiful sight, then turned and hobbled along next to it. Sam's ankle throbbed in pain. She felt useless as Aaron helped her walk, and hated the feeling. She had to stop for a minute every so often. They walked for hours, until the sun started going down. Aaron stopped for a rest himself. His lungs were on fire and every muscle ached.

"Do you have any idea where we're going?" Sam asked. She sat near the edge of the wide-flowing river and stuck her foot in the water.

Aaron said nothing. He sat on the ground and leaned back against a tree. He breathed deeply, then took a drink of water from a bottle they'd been sharing. He tossed it over to Sam.

He pulled the map out and sat next to her. "This river doesn't run parallel to 295. It runs away from it slightly. There's a bridge on the road your home is on?"

"Yeah, right before you really hit the walkers."

"Well, this runs to the bridge. So we're gonna pass your place by a bit. We can try to guess where it is through the woods, or just hit the bridge and use the road."

"How far away?"

He shrugged. "I don't know. It's getting dark. I want to camp here tonight. We'll definitely be there tomorrow."

She leaned away from him. "That's the dumbest idea I've ever heard."

"It's not safe to try this in the dark. I don't want to go spraining any more ankles, and we're both tired and hungry."

"It's not *safe* to sleep by a river with who-knows-how many corpses out there."

He ignored her, not in the mood to fight. He climbed to his feet. "I'll go fish up dinner. Do you think you can get a fire going? Just the wood around us will do."

"You're gonna get us both killed," she said. "I don't know why I thought you coming along would be a good idea."

Sam instantly regretted what she said. She knew she was angry, tired, and her ankle still hurt. She was taking everything out on Aaron.

Aaron was frustrated. He was doing everything he possibly could to keep her alive, and she still had nothing good to say. He looked down at her, almost with a look of disappointment.

"You know, you keep saying how you don't want any friends. I think you got that backwards. *They* don't want *you*. I honestly doubt you have a hard time pushing people away. I bet no one wants to get close to you."

He tossed her the lighter from his pack. Then he removed his shoes and walked into the cold river, which came up to his waist. He waited patiently for a fish to grab.

Sam opened her mouth. Seeing that look he gave her was worse than any sprained ankle.

Aaron, I'm sorry.

She couldn't say it out loud.

Hours passed. Sam hobbled around and gathered enough wood to start a fire. It took Aaron's lighter ten tries to start a flame, but it beat having to start the fire by hand. Sam hadn't done that in years.

Aaron hadn't said a word all night. He caught a good-sized catfish with his bare hands, and went about the task of gutting and cleaning it. He thought back to the many nights he and his father would catch fish. Aaron wished his father was with him, instead of a woman who didn't appreciate his company.

He didn't have anything at all to help cook the fish. If he were home, he'd just grill it on his roof. Here in the woods, a small tree branch sharpened to a point would have to do. He impaled the catfish onto the stick and hung it over the fire.

The night was overcast. There was no moon to keep them company. The only light was from the fire. It threw wild, dancing shadows on the trees. He wasn't sure if it was dragging Sam through the woods for hours, or the hypnotic fire, but he was very tired.

He dug out some fish meat and handed it to Sam. She took it without a word.

She finally worked up the courage to speak after taking a drink from Aaron's last bottle of water.

"What's the plan?" she asked.

Aaron stuffed fish meat into his mouth. "The plan is to get you to Lexington at first light. Then I go back home."

"You should rest first at the school."

"Yeah."

Her voice hardened. "Aaron, I'm only saying this once, so you'd better listen."

He rolled his eyes and looked at her. *What now?*

Her features softened, and she looked confused. "I, uh, well-"

"Spit it out, Sam."

She was embarrassed and afraid. She took a breath and tried to calm down. She spoke clearly and carefully. "If it weren't for you, I'd be dead, a couple times now. Thank you. Thank you for saving my life."

He was quiet, not quite sure if his ears were playing tricks on him. "You're welcome. You came back to get me at the gas station. So we're even."

"No, we're not. You've given me food and water, and let me stay at your home, when you didn't have to. And I haven't been nice to you. I'm sorry."

Sam hoped he appreciated how hard this was for her. She was opening up, and that was something she *never* did. He would ruin it with one of his stupid jokes.

He smiled. "It's been my pleasure."

He has such a cute smile.

Aaron finished his meal and pulled his framed pictures out of his backpack. He propped them up so his family could be nearby when he slept. He put the backpack on the ground to use as a pillow.

"We'll share this," he said. "We'll sleep in a line. I won't touch you or anything, I promise."

She nodded. "I believe you."

"Sleep with your feet pointing to the lake, as close as you can get."

"Why?"

"Cause if corpses come, I want you to be close to the water. They won't go in the water. I'll be in between them and you."

She said nothing, just kept an eye on him as she positioned herself near the river. Aaron lay across from her, trying not to touch her. The crackling fire was a nice lullaby, a little different than what he usually fell asleep to at night.

"So that's your family there, in the pictures?"

"Yes."

"Tell me about them."

"I thought you didn't want to get to know me?"

She turned to look at him, but only saw an ear. "Well, I do now."

Aaron smiled, and told Sam about his family, about his two aunts, uncle, and father. Sam was jealous, as she could tell he truly had enjoyed growing up. She'd spent her early years just surviving, moving from one place to the next.

He told her how they all met on the day the undead rose, and how he was born on that very same day, about how they each had shaped who he was. He rambled on until the fire nearly died, and he heard very quiet snores from Sam.

He leaned on an elbow and looked at her. He couldn't help but smile. She looked so peaceful, and beautiful.

Sam was a strong and tough woman. Aaron knew she had a tough life, and that made her who she was. Cold and distant, only looking out for herself. They couldn't be more opposite. But when the choice came to run, or come back for Aaron, she chose to put herself in danger.

He brushed a strand of hair out of her face, then put his head next to hers and fell asleep.

The stench of death pulled Aaron and Sam awake at the same time. They were both unaware that Sam had moved her head closer to Aaron, and slipped a hand under his shoulder. He helped her to her feet.

It was still night, but dawn was approaching. The fire had burned out.

Six corpses walked through the trees. Aaron quickly gathered his pictures and bow and quiver, and helped Sam take a step toward the water. Her ankle still hurt, but at least she could put more weight on it.

"They just never give up," Sam complained.

She sucked in a breath as she sank into the cold water. She had left her shoe near the fire. Her bare foot hurt as she stepped on rocks and pebbles. She almost slipped twice. Aaron kept an arm around her waist.

They crossed the river. Aaron stole a glance at the corpses, and was angry with himself when he recognized one of them.

The corpse that used to be a cop, that Aaron first saw on 295, was there. The other corpses with him just moaned and stared at Sam, hungry for flesh, but the cop looked at the river, trying to figure out how to cross it.

"Son of a bitch," he said. "A damn thinker."

Sam held onto his shoulder. "A thinker? What's that?"

He stepped away from her and nocked an arrow. He drilled the thinker between the eyes. "Let's get going."

They kept following the river, putting distance between them and the corpses on the other side. Sam walked on her own, but slowly; Aaron kept pace with her. The sun was up. He didn't think they were far from Lexington.

"Aaron, what was that? What's a thinker?"

He sighed, still angry for not seeing it earlier. He knew he'd seen the undead up close more than anyone alive, and he shouldn't make mistakes like that.

"Some of them can think," he explained. "I'm not saying they can sit and play a game of chess, but some of them can open doors, use tools, figure out simple shit. The other corpses will always follow a thinker, like some kind of herd. Very dangerous."

"I've never seen anything like that. And I've seen a lot of walkers."

"That's 'cause people always run from them, and not look."

"And you don't?"

He was quiet.

They walked for another two hours, until Sam finally saw something she recognized.

The woods cleared out to their left, and she saw the back of a house. It was a different angle than she usually saw it, but she recognized it as a house on her street.

"Aaron, we're here."

She broke away and checked out the backyard. Just beyond the house was Honeyton Road.

She was almost home.

"Just another ten minute walk down the road, and we're there," she told him, a bright smile on her face.

Aaron looked at the backyards around them. Everything was in shambles, everything deserted. Like Sam told him, he didn't see any corpses. He could still faintly smell them, so they couldn't be too far away. They had to get moving before they picked up her scent.

Honeyton Road didn't run next to the river. He wondered if the people of Lexington even knew they had a fresh water source not too far away.

"And you doubted me," he said with a laugh.

She gave him a serious look. "I won't again."

It was more like a twenty minute walk down the road. Aaron was tired and Sam's ankle was killing her.

But they made it.

CHAPTER 8

Lexington High wasn't hard to spot. The similar houses stopped, and gave way to a large building on the right side of the road. Aaron saw the tall fence surrounding it, and two moving trucks near the front gate. He actually heard voices, and even laughter. There was some banging, like someone was working with a hammer and nails.

Sam's pace picked up, despite her ankle.

Aaron slowed down.

"It's good to be back," she said. "We'll get some nice cold water from the spring-house, then-"

She turned to look at Aaron. He was no longer next to her, but ten feet behind her.

"Aaron? You okay?"

He didn't move, and Sam was actually worried. She took a few steps closer to him. "What's wrong?"

He looked past her. He had no idea what was beyond those gates, inside those walls. "Sixty people, you say?"

"Give or take, yeah."

He was quiet, then looked Sam in the eye. "It was a mistake to come here. But I really enjoyed meeting you, and helping you get here. You have a good life, and take care of yourself."

Sam's jaw dropped as Aaron turned around and started walking away. He didn't even look back.

The old Sam wouldn't have cared. She was home and safe. She would have walked through the gates without a second thought, leaving Aaron to whatever life he wanted to live.

But the old Sam was slowly disappearing, and Aaron was part of the reason why.

"Whoa! Hold on!" She hobbled up to him and spun him around by the shoulder. "What's going on?"

"I can't go in there," he said. He wiped some sweat off of his bald head.

"Why not?"

He shrugged. "I'm afraid."

She couldn't believe her ears. "Is this another of your weird jokes?"

"It's just a lot of people. I've never seen that many people in my life."

"You were in a house, surrounded by a million walkers. You could have died at any second. And you're afraid to be here with living people?"

"I know the undead, Sam. I know everything about them. I know nothing about this place."

"You can't just walk back to Baltimore. You'll be dead before the end of the day."

He smiled mysteriously. "You don't know me very well."

"Well, how can I if you just leave?"

He gave her a confused look. It almost sounded like she wanted him to stay.

"Aaron, listen. You need food and water. Stay here for a day. You don't like it, fine, then go. You'll barely see anyone, and I'll watch your back."

Aaron's stomach growled. He *was* hungry. Maybe a short rest wouldn't be such a bad idea. "Okay."

"Good." She gave him a smile and put a hand on his shoulder. "You'll be okay. I promise."

It was the first time she had ever offered a promise to anyone.

There was always an armed guard at the front gate, and this day was no different. Larry saw the two people approaching, and recognized their gait as human. That didn't stop him from pointing his gun.

It was only when he recognized the beautiful woman that he relaxed.

"I don't believe it. Samantha? Is that you?"

"It's me, Larry."

"Holy shit. Garrett told us you died." He unlocked the gate.

Aaron studied everything he could, trying to keep his nerves in check. He saw people walking in and out of the school, and disappearing around the side. He actually heard children laughing somewhere. Two men were leaning against one of the trucks, just talking.

Larry gave Samantha a hug she didn't return and looked back to Garrett and Ray.

"Hey guys!" he called. "Look who managed to not die!"

Garrett saw her and sneered. He motioned for Ray to follow, and he obeyed. Sam's posture stiffened slightly as the large man and his sidekick approached. Aaron picked up on it. He was behind Sam until then, but he moved up to stand next to her.

"I can't believe it," he said. "I thought you were worm food back in Baltimore."

"Yeah, well, it's not like you stuck around to see."

"Hey, fuck you. The streets were getting rough. We called for you guys, you didn't show up. As far as I'm concerned, you were dead." He looked at Aaron, who hadn't said a word. "What are you looking at? When did you start picking up strays, Samantha?"

"You leaving me doesn't bother me. I would have left you in a second. What *does* bother me is you being a piece of shit. Anderson and Murphy tried to rape me, so I killed them. You pick rapists for all your runs?"

Garrett laughed, Ray joining in right behind him. That only made Sam more angry. Aaron still said nothing, and watched both Garrett and Ray closely.

"Can you blame them, Samantha? You're a gorgeous woman, and I remember that winter outfit you had on. I would have screwed you too. Hell, you should be flattered."

He reached out and tried to stroke her hair. She slapped his hand away. "You don't touch me!"

Garrett reached out and grabbed her hair. "Oh, you like it rough?"

Larry felt the need to talk, but not act. He was afraid of Garrett, like everyone else. "Whoa, Garrett."

Sam's first instinct was to reach for her knife strapped to her leg, but she didn't need to.

They barely saw Aaron move.

He moved fast and with purpose, like his father had taught him. A quick kick to the groin, just hard enough to make Garrett let go of Sam's hair. He circled around and kicked Garrett in the back of the knee, bringing the larger man down to his size. Then he snaked an arm around Garrett's throat and locked the jerk's wrist in a hold his uncle showed him. He wrestled him to the ground easily. It was like his father told him. A man can't do much without air.

Everyone was stunned by the display. Ray finally came back to his senses enough to reach for his holstered gun. Sam grabbed Larry's gun from his hand and aimed it at Ray's head.

"Ray, don't move."

Ray did as he was told.

Sam knew at that moment, that not only did she trust Aaron completely, but she would also fight for him.

He obviously felt the same way.

Garrett struggled underneath Aaron. "Who the fuck do you-"

Aaron choked Garrett while applying more pressure to his wrist. Garrett let out a gasp and felt his face turning red.

"Shhhhh," Aaron whispered in his ear. He made sure only Garrett could hear him. "Just listen. If you go near Sam, if you even give her too hard of a look, I will kill you. You hear?"

"When I get up-"

Aaron squeezed harder. Just a little more pressure, and Garrett's wrist would snap. Garrett struggled to breathe as drool fell from his mouth.

"It was a yes or no question. Leave Sam alone, or I will kill you. Now, did you hear me?"

"Yes," he coughed.

A new voice rang out, near the old parking lot.

"Hey! That's not how we solve problems here!"

It was Richardson. He marched toward them. People walking by in the distance stopped to see what was happening at the front gate. Aaron didn't realize they'd attracted an audience.

Aaron let Garrett up without saying anything else. The large man rubbed his neck and wrist, not taking an eye off Aaron. He gestured for Ray, and the two walked away together.

Sam breathed a sigh of relief and gave Larry back his gun. She looked at Aaron.

"I can take care of my own fights," she said. Then she smiled and gave him a playful punch on the arm. "But shit, that was nice."

Aaron didn't smile. He kept an eye on Garrett until he rounded the corner toward the back of the school. "That's what friends do. They watch out for each other."

That surprised her. "You, uh, want to be friends?" The thought excited her more than it should have.

"We already *are* friends, Sam. I don't know when it happened, but we're friends."

She smiled, and realized she was actually happy.

Richardson stopped as he drew closer, then shook his head. "I should have known Baltimore couldn't kill you."

"I would have been dead if it wasn't for Aaron here. Aaron Thompson, this is Richardson."

Richardson looked at the both of them. Sam only wore one shoe, her other foot looking slightly swollen. She leaned on Aaron slightly, an act itself that surprised Richardson. Sam simply didn't *lean* on anyone.

Aaron looked unassuming enough. He was lean, well-built, with a clean shaven head. The bow and arrow on the ground next to him was a little strange, but Richardson had seen weirder things.

What caught his eye about the young man was his expression. Richardson had seen many faces over the years. Most of the young generation weren't pleasant. He understood why. Samantha was a perfect example. It was hard to be truly happy in the world of the dead. Yet Samantha's guest carried himself in a way that told Richardson that not much bothered him.

"Staying long, young man?"

"I'm not sure yet."

"Look, I don't like Garrett either, but we can't just go running around beating up people we don't like."

"He grabbed Sam. I just told him not to do that again."

Richardson raised an eyebrow. "Sam?"

"Only *he* gets to call me that."

He laughed. "Okay. Listen, Samantha, I'm sorry, but I couldn't hold onto that teacher's lounge. Garrett told us all you were dead. So it's already been taken."

Sam didn't care. She was just happy to be home. She looked forward to collapsing on her own mattress. "That's okay. As long as I still got my old room."

He frowned.

"Oh no," Sam said. "Tell me you didn't give my room away."

"No, no one claimed the room. It's just that-"

Sam knew how things worked. "They took my *stuff*."

"I'm sorry. You know how it is. Someone leaves or dies, we're lucky if I can even get their things to the storeroom before people take them."

She started hobbling away. She turned around while still trying to keep moving. "I've gotta go check my room. Aaron, just stay with Richardson. Don't leave, okay? We'll meet up later."

Aaron laughed to himself. *So much for watching my back.*

Richardson looked the newcomer up and down while Sam disappeared inside the school. He had never seen Sam take to anyone, *ever*, and he had known her since her late teens. What was it about this young man that made him so special?

"So, you want a tour of the place?"

Aaron shrugged. "Sure."

Richardson spent the rest of the day walking with Aaron around Lexington. Aaron hoped it didn't show, but he wasn't just impressed with Richardson and what they'd accomplished, he was amazed.

The entire high school and the athletic fields, as well as the parking lot, was surrounded by a strong fence. Richardson explained that, sadly, it was put up before the world ended. That was the sorry state of public schools during the time. Richardson had lived there since the beginning. Since that time, they dug up an underground stream and built a spring-house over it. They put together coops for the chickens they kept for meat and eggs, along with a ten foot high smokehouse to preserve meat and fish. They'd gathered portable bathrooms and lined them up when the plumbing stopped working. There was a forge in the parking lot for some simple metal work, along with a large sundial. Aaron watched as a woman walked through a massive vegetable garden, examining the crops.

The people worked hard, and Aaron even received a few simple hellos as he passed by with Richardson. Some of the ladies gave him looks he wasn't used to.

Lexington seemed nothing short of a miracle.

The halls of Lexington were very efficient. As Richardson showed him the storeroom, he could see people lived in the old classrooms. They had the makings of a simple community, which Aaron had only read about in books.

Richardson took him to the garden, where a nice old woman named Susan Lively gave them each a fresh tomato right off the vine. It tasted great.

"Let me show you our last stop," Richardson said. "Not our most popular place, but you'd better know it's there."

They walked to the back of the old athletic fields, far away from everything else. Aaron saw a hole in the ground, and was surprised to hear the familiar wails of the undead.

The hole was twelve feet deep, completely open, with enough room for about fifteen walkers. They perked up and reached for Richardson when they saw him.

"We call this the Pit," he said.

"You keep undead here?"

"Yeah. No one comes back here. We used to study them, try to figure out what makes them tick, when they'd decompose. We quit a long time ago, but the Pit's still here. One day we'll take the young kids out here and teach them about walkers."

Young kids, Aaron thought. *Never thought I'd see a place where young kids could grow up.*

Aaron spotted a walker in the Pit that caught his attention. It was a female with long white hair. She must have died exercising, as she wore torn sweatpants and a filthy tee shirt. The corpse was in good shape. It still had all its limbs and both eyes.

"You'd better cover this thing," he said, pointing at Sweatpants. "Or at least put that one down. It's a thinker."

"A thinker?"

He explained to Richardson the same way he had Sam, about how some undead could think. Richardson didn't believe it, but there was no harm in humoring Aaron.

"We've got some old fencing stored away. I'll get someone to seal this up."

As they walked back toward the school, Aaron decided he had to share his doubts. "So, what's the catch?"

"Catch?"

Aaron waved around him. "This place is amazing. What's the deal? Are you the dictator? You rule this place, have sacrifices at night?"

"Amazing? Well, we'll take the compliment. But, Aaron, some people find their way here, and leave right away. The chicken coops are falling apart. We usually have two vegetable gardens, so we can let the soil in one get its nutrients back. The second garden, it's no good, bad soil. The smokehouse? We built it with as much cinder-block as we could, but one of the guys watching it fell asleep, and a fire started, so we can't use that right now either. This whole place needs work. A lot of the people here are miserable. We had a husband two nights ago kill his wife and stillborn child. You want to know what the catch is? The catch is we live in a world where the dead walk around and eat us, making life just a little difficult."

Aaron could see the strength in Richardson. He seemed like a good man.

Richardson looked up at the setting sun. "You'd better pick out a room before it gets too dark. That is, if you're planning to stay. You can take any empty room. A lot of the good ones are already taken, but there's plenty left. Might not hurt to ask a neighbor if a room is empty or not. There's candles in the storeroom, just let whoever is on duty know you need some, although you can probably bug anyone, a lot of people carry candles."

"Thank you, Richardson. It was a pleasure meeting you." Aaron turned to walk away.

"Uh, son, one second before you go. Might not be any of my business, but can I ask what happened with you and Samantha in Baltimore?"

He shrugged. "Nothing. She stayed with me a night, and we fought our way back here. Why?"

"Well, it's just that she's, uh, smiling. I honestly don't think I've ever seen that."

"Maybe she's happy to be alive."

"Maybe."

Aaron nodded. "Again, thanks for everything."

Richardson had a good feeling about Aaron. He hoped the young man decided to stay.

Sam cursed loudly as she slid the mattress she'd taken from the storeroom into the corner of her room. It took her the rest of the day, but her room was nearly back together. She almost put a fist through the wall when she walked in earlier. The only thing the looters left were the curtains on the windows. Maybe it was a blessing in disguise, as she managed to upgrade a few items, and get a few new ones.

She found four end-tables of the same size that she put together to make one long table. She had a nice selection of clothes, although her favorite sandals were gone. Her new mattress was bigger, and still wrapped in old plastic. It had never been used. She found a nice brush that didn't look to be in terrible shape, and a medium sized mirror she leaned against the wall on her makeshift long table. She even found an old lounge-chair and tiny couch that had a few stains, but was very soft and comfortable.

It needed more work, but it wasn't a bad start.

The sun was down. Her day of work was coming to an end.

She took a breath. It was time to rest. She closed her curtains and shut the door. She started stripping off the clothes off she'd worn since Baltimore. She felt disgusting.

She was down to just her panties when she heard a voice at the door. Actually, not at the door, but just *inside* her room.

"Hey Sam, you in here?"

She spun around, not expecting to see Aaron's face. His eyes grew wide when he saw Sam's body, pretty much *all* of it.

"Wow."

"Aaron! Get out!"

He quickly pulled his head out and leaned against the door. He waited patiently while Sam put on some light clothes, and cussed at him from her room.

"Okay, you can come in."

He did so and closed the door behind him. "I'm sorry, Sam, really. I'm not used to knocking, and I thought I heard you in here."

Any anger she felt disappeared when she looked at him. She burst out laughing. Aaron looked down at himself, trying to figure out what was going on.

He had his shirt slung over his shoulder. He still wore his backpack and quiver of arrows, and carried his bow in his right hand.

"Please tell me you didn't walk around all day like that."

He dropped his gear to the floor. "I didn't have anywhere to put my stuff."

"So what do you think? Are you gonna stay?"

He frowned. "I still don't know."

She felt her heart sink. "What do you mean?"

"Sam, I've already made one enemy. And the women keep giving me weird looks."

"That's 'cause you're running around without a shirt on."

"Not just me. It's hot out there."

"Well no one else looks as good as-" She stopped herself short. Luckily for her, Aaron had no clue what she was thinking.

"What's that again?"

"Nothing."

Aaron smiled when he remembered why he came. Seeing Sam's gorgeous body, even in near darkness, threw him off a little. "Oh, hey, look what I found in the storeroom."

He pulled a game of checkers out of his backpack.

She laid halfway on the mattress on her side, crossing her ankles. He wondered if she knew how beautiful she was.

She patted the mattress. "Grab a candle and set it up."

They played for an hour or so. As the night wore on, Aaron heard the people outside pack up whatever chores they were working on and head inside. There were footsteps and voices outside in the hall. He would see the flicker of candles pass by every so often.

"So you haven't found a room yet?" she asked as she jumped two of his pieces.

"No."

"Look, don't get the wrong idea. We're *not* bunk-mates. But if you want to sleep here tonight, you can. Just this night."

"Thanks, Sam, but I know that makes you uncomfortable. I *did* find a nice place to sleep. It's not a room, but it'll do fine."

They played one more game before Aaron decided he'd worn out his welcome. She walked him to the door.

"Listen," she said before he left. "If you leave tomorrow, come find me first. Okay?"

"Sure."

She closed the door after him and rested her head against it. She didn't want Aaron to leave, and the thought bothered her.

🖐 🖐 🖐

Aaron set all his gear on the ground near the Pit. It wasn't exactly Baltimore, but he had a half moon, the familiar song of the undead, and a few magazines he found in a pile in the school.

He lit a candle, shoved it in the dirt, and rested his head on his backpack. He gave the undead in the Pit a quick glance. They didn't react, but he saw Sweatpants staring at him.

"Hi guys," he said. He spoke to them like he did when touring the streets of Baltimore at night.

If he stayed, he wouldn't be able to do that again.

"I don't know, I'm not sure if this place is *me*," he said to the undead. "The people seem nice enough, and of course there's Sam, but I just don't know."

He thought back to some of the people he had met throughout the day. Richardson, of course, was decent enough. Larry had many jobs, did a little of everything, seemed to be everywhere. Susan took care of the vegetable garden. Paul Sorenson raised the chickens. He met a woman named Carrie, who kept watching him as she walked away. A very pretty woman.

Not as pretty as Sam.

He forced the thought away, and wouldn't let it return.

"I guess we'll see, won't we?"

He read until the sounds of the undead lulled him to sleep.

CHAPTER 9

It was early in the morning when Sam stepped into one of the outdoor showers. She could finally put her full weight on her ankle. The shower was a tub suspended on a six foot high wooden frame. A hose ran from the drain which acted as a shower head. A curtain wrapped around the frame to give some privacy, but Sam never showered nude. She wore an old two-piece bathing suit. They had several of the showers lined up in a row. Everyone stood in pans so they could boil and reuse the water.

Carrie, a woman that Sam didn't like, who was a few years older than her , stepped into the shower next to her.

"Morning, Samantha."

"Hi."

Sam watched as Carrie flashed the guys smiles when they walked by. That's how she survived in the new world, and Sam didn't like it. Carrie survived using her looks and charm, which she had plenty of, flirting with men to get what she wanted.

"So where did you find the new guy? Aaron, he said his name was? I talked to him yesterday."

"In Baltimore."

"Really? The city? I didn't even know you were gone."

Sam said nothing.

"Anyway," Carrie went on. "Are you two sleeping together?"

"Only twice. At his home in the city. I slept in a lawn chair. Then in the woods."

"No, dear. I mean are you two having sex? You do know what *sex* is, right?"

Sam let loose another blast of water to rinse away the last of the soap. She felt embarrassed and wasn't sure why. "That's not really your business, is it?"

Carrie read her body language. "That means you're not. Shame on you, he's so cute. He's real nice too, which is a little weird. You don't meet nice people out in the wild anymore. What's the matter? Don't know what you're doing? Well, I bet *he* does. You think I have a shot with him?"

No, you don't.

The protective thought came out of nowhere.

She was quiet. She toweled off and left the shower.

"If you see him," Carrie called. "Tell him I asked about him."

Fuck you.

Sam dressed in some light clothes and searched for Richardson. As always, the people of Lexington flashed a few smiles, but the overall mood was somber. She didn't know it, but the mood was still heavy from losing Lisa, Robert, and their baby. She found Richardson with Larry and an older man named Travis examining the smokehouse in the middle of the old soccer field. She caught the tail end of their conversation as she approached.

"I'm telling you," Travis said, "the thing is ruined."

"Travis, come on. I know you and Larry can fix this."

"Are you kidding? I need wood, more nails, a saw that's not rusted to the teeth. This whole place is falling apart."

The men quieted down as Sam approached.

"Morning," Richardson said in greeting. "What's going on, Samantha?"

She got right to the point. "Give me something to do. What do you need help with?"

"Uh, sorry, but I don't have any paying jobs right now."

"I'm not asking for payment. Just what do you have that needs to be done? What can I do to help?"

The three men looked at each other.

"Larry's getting ready to cover up the Pit, at your friend Aaron's request. Give him a hand?"

Larry and Sam got a piece of fence and some spikes from the junk room, which used to be the old library, and headed to the Pit. All Larry wanted to do was talk about Aaron. He was the new topic of Lexington. The women all thought he was cute; the men were all amazed at how he'd handled Garrett so easily.

As they walked across the field they saw someone lying on the grass, just near the mouth of the Pit. Whoever it was didn't move.

"Oh shit, someone kill somebody?" Larry asked.

Sam recognized him as they drew closer. Her heart caught in her chest. "That's Aaron."

She broke into a jog, still slowed by her ankle. Larry was right behind her. She saw terrible scenarios in her head, like Garrett beating him and leaving him near the Pit to die.

Aaron looked up, disoriented. He was just inches away from the Pit. So close that if he rolled in the wrong direction, he'd fall in.

Sam hooked him under the arms and dragged him away. Larry dropped to a knee and looked around for anyone they might have to fight. The walkers were stirred up. They always made Larry nervous. They made *everyone* nervous.

Sam fell on her butt but didn't let go of Aaron. She pulled him close and wrapped an arm around his bare chest. He put a hand over hers, trying to catch his breath.

"What happened? Are you okay?" she asked.

Aaron tried to clear the cobwebs in his head. He'd been sound asleep until they came along.

"Who brought you out here?" Larry asked.

"Uh, *I* did?"

"Aaron, what's going on?"

"I was asleep," he said. He climbed to his feet and helped Sam up. "Is this how you wake everyone up?"

Larry finally noticed Aaron's things. "You slept out here with the walkers?"

"Yeah. I didn't find a room yet. The noise helps put me to sleep."

"Aaron, I told you we could sleep together."

Larry turned a chuckle into a cough. "Samantha, I don't think *sleeping together* means what you think it-"

An icy look from her kept him from continuing. He started securing the fence over the Pit.

"You could have fallen in," she chastised Aaron.

He playfully grabbed her shoulder, knowing she didn't like it. "Aww, would you miss me?"

She was quiet. She just looked into Aaron's eyes. "I have to go," she said, and started walking away.

He looked at Larry, who was just as confused as he was.

"Hey, Sam!" Aaron called. "If I can't find a place before the day's over, I'll sleep with you."

She turned around. "So you're staying?"

"Yes."

"Good."

She kept walking. Aaron couldn't take his eyes off her. *Definitely the most unique woman I've ever met.*

He walked to the other side of the Pit and knelt next to Larry.

"Welcome to Lexington," Larry said.

"Thanks. What's her problem?"

Larry patted him on the back. "Man, the fellas and I meet every night in the cafeteria to unwind, just shoot the shit, and watch Carrie dance, if we're lucky. There's two mysteries we always talk about. How all this bullshit started, and women."

Aaron nodded. He remembered his father and Uncle Frank having similar conversations.

"I will say this," Larry continued. "Sam keeps to herself, has so for years. But she seems pretty attached to you."

"I like her." Aaron gestured to the fence he was nailing down. "I didn't see any of that in the storeroom."

"We keep a lot of crap in the junk room, too. That's what we call it. It used to be the library. People don't have much use for reading anymore. Hell, half the people here don't even know how."

Aaron raised his eyebrows. "You have a library here?"

It didn't take Aaron long to find the old library. He saw immediately why they called it the junk room. There was so much garbage blocking the doors he had to push his way inside.

The place was ruined.

Bookshelves were broken and knocked over on the ground. Books were scattered everywhere. There were old desks and furniture with bloodstains deemed unfit to be in the storeroom. Everything had a thick layer of dust. There was broken glass, dead rats, parts of old cars. Aaron could barely take a step without nearly tripping over something.

He had already made the decision to stay at Lexington for one reason.

Sam.

He wanted to be with his friend. It was that simple.

But now, he had found his room.

"Let's get started."

Sam hadn't seen Aaron for the past three days. She knew he was still at Lexington, as everyone still talked about him. Aaron's presence made Sam more popular than she wanted to be. Everyone came to her to ask about the new guy.

She kept her distance from Aaron on purpose. She felt guilty about it, but she didn't like the way he made her feel. When she thought he was hurt near the Pit, she knew she liked him more than she wanted to. Having a friend to care for was something she wasn't really ready for.

After a morning shower and two scrambled eggs, she went to Richardson. He was talking to Susan by the vegetable garden, and she could see from their faces it was serious. Susan was having trouble with their second garden being ready by summer's end. Richardson flashed a bright smile when she walked up. Susan gave a friendly nod.

"What needs to be done?" Sam asked. "What do you got for me?"

"Take your pick. Helen needs help in the storeroom. I'm sure Paul needs help with the chickens. Larry's trying to fix the shower stall on the very end of the row. We could use some more bottled water in the spring-house. Hell, Kathy might need a break from watching the kids. Always something to do."

Sam nodded. "Okay. I'll help whoever needs it."

"Oh, hey, Samantha. If you see Aaron, tell him he did a wonderful job with the library."

She was confused. "Library? You mean the junk room?"

"It's not a junk room anymore."

Sam had to see for herself. She cut across the cafeteria and passed the ten people eating breakfast to get to the library.

She couldn't believe it was the same place.

Aaron had turned half the place into an actual working library. Tables, chairs, and bookshelves were scattered about. There were gaps from missing books and bookshelves that couldn't be repaired, and some torn spots on the carpet, but it still looked great.

The far end of the library, along the wall leading outside, Aaron had made into a living space.

He had every window open, letting in the morning breeze. There was a couch under the windows with a chair adjacent to it. A beat-up coffee table sat in the middle, with a collection of books already on it. A box of candles sat on the floor.

"Hey Sam," Aaron called, his voice echoing slightly. He had come from the librarian's office, where he was setting up his bedroom. He gestured around him. "What do you think?"

Sam had no words. She didn't think it was possible. People had used the library as a trash room for years. Richardson had thought it was sad, a place of public knowledge reduced to trash. But he had grabbed all the books he needed years ago, so he stopped caring.

"This looks *great*, Aaron."

He walked up to her so they were close. "Now we won't have to sleep together. I'm setting up a bed in the old office. It'll be great in the winter months. Oh, there's a grill right outside the emergency room door, but that's just for me and you."

She missed the fact that he thought of them as a unit. She looked around at all the work he'd done, all the things he'd gathered. She couldn't wrap her mind around it.

"How did you do this?" she asked. "I mean, shit, I know that couch wasn't in the storeroom. I would have taken it."

"Just non-stop work," he said. "The couch and stuff, I took out of an old house near the end of the block."

"You pushed a couch down the street by yourself? Aaron, there's still walkers out there."

"I was careful. Travis saw me when I got near the gate, and gave me a hand carrying it back here. That was just last night."

She shook her head. "You could have asked me for help."

"I would have. I couldn't find you during the day, and I wasn't gonna wake you up."

He saw her frown slightly. He didn't have great social instincts, but he knew they were in the middle of something, maybe a fight.

"Look, I'm sorry about sleeping at the Pit," he said. "But I didn't want to bother you, and to be honest, I'm used to sleeping near the undead. I didn't think it was a big deal."

"Aaron, it's just-" she paused, searching for words. She was ready to share something with him she'd never spoken about. "I'm not used to the whole friends thing. The last person that called himself my *friend* was before I found this place. We set up camp one night in an old restaurant, where they used to buy food. The walkers came, and he ran away without even turning around. I barely got out with my life."

"I won't do that."

"I was also mad you didn't sleep in my room," she continued. Her blunt honesty was a reason she knew many people didn't like her. "I offered my room, you should have taken it."

"Same goes for you. You ever want to sleep here, that couch is mighty comfortable. Heavy as shit though."

She laughed. They both walked to the couch and had a seat. Susan Lively, taking a break from the garden, walked in to borrow a book. Aaron gave her a polite wave as she left.

"I do need your help on something. Tell me about Carrie."

"What?"

"I'm on fence duty tonight. Carrie wants to do it with me. I've only talked to her a few times."

"They've got you on fence duty already? They either think you're very reliable or they hate your guts."

"I kinda volunteered. Leroy was supposed to do it, but hasn't been able to spend much time with his wife lately, so I said I'd take his place. Then Carrie ran up to me this morning and said she'd do it with me."

Sam was surprised. Not only was Aaron fitting in already, but he was meeting people and learning names. She didn't know who Leroy was, or even that anyone in Lexington was actually married.

"Everyone likes Carrie, especially the guys. She's mentioned your name a few times."

Aaron fought with what he wanted to ask her. "Listen, Sam, people tell me you hate fence duty."

"People tell you right." She smiled. "Why are you talking about me behind my back?"

"Would you work it with me tonight? I told Richardson I'd do it alone, but he says it's always gotta be pairs."

"You don't want to work with Carrie?"

"Not really. You're the only one I trust."

Sam felt a little uncomfortable with all of this sharing. "Same goes for you, and I don't say that lightly. I'm in."

That wasn't what he expected to hear. Everyone Aaron had spoken to told him Sam was basically for hire. She'd do things she didn't want to, but for a price.

"Thank you," he said, then remembered the bag next to the couch. He grabbed it and handed it to her. "Here. This is for you."

"What's this?"

"Some things I found last night while I was out. Thought you might like them."

She looked through the bag. There was a brush still in a sealed package, nail clippers, a bottle of shampoo, and a combat knife.

"Wow," she said. She wasn't used to receiving things from anyone, unless it was a trade. "Thank you."

"The shampoo doesn't do me any good," he said, rubbing a hand across his bald head.

Sam tried to figure out how she had gotten so lucky with finding Aaron. Maybe she was due for a little luck.

A voice cut into her thoughts.

"Hey, Aaron!" Scott called from the doors. He spent most of his time at the forge, a great place in the winter time. "You mind if I borrow a book?"

"Go ahead, just bring it back. Grab anything you like."

Sam laughed. "You've made a lot of friends already."

Aaron dismissed the idea with a wave of his hand. "Nah. Just you. I've got some people I gotta talk to, then I'll get some rest before tonight. Meet me back here at dusk?"

Sam nodded.

"Thanks, Sam. Really. I know fence duty isn't fun."

"Anytime."

She meant it.

Aaron spent the rest of the day meeting and talking to people. Richardson was right in that most of the people were unhappy. Even those who smiled the most, Susan Lively, Larry, and Carrie, seemed genuinely happy, but they always followed up those smiles with a list of complaints or needs.

Aaron wrote them all down.

He carried around a notepad and pencil from the storeroom, similar to what Richardson always did. He made a list of some of the simple things Lexington needed.

He received compliments on being the only young adult that could read and write, which he found sad.

He sought out Carrie when the sun started to set. She wasn't thrilled that Aaron had asked Sam to partner up with him for fence duty instead of her. He went back to the library and took his bow and quiver from the bedroom. Some clothes he'd taken from the storeroom were scattered across his mattress. He made a mental note to clean up tomorrow.

He read on the couch until Sam stepped into the library. She looked nice with a white sleeveless shirt and curve-hugging shorts. Her favorite combat knife was strapped to her toned leg. She had another Beretta holstered around her waist. She gave Aaron a friendly nod, then laughed at his choice of weaponry.

"Aaron, we've got guns in the storeroom. There's no need to walk around with a damn bow and arrow."

The two left the library together.

"I hate guns."

She gave him a look. For the first time, she noticed he was about six inches taller than she was. "I know you said that in Baltimore, but are you really serious? You've never fired a gun?"

"Just to kill my father."

She put a comforting hand on his shoulder, only for a moment.

The cafeteria was a maze of tables, chairs, people, and candles. It was made to hold two hundred high school teenagers. With

only sixty people, everyone had plenty of room to spread out
and have their own space. Richardson entertained a group with
his guitar, while Carrie entertained everyone else—or rather, the
males—in a far corner. She danced on top of an old table while
the men laughed and had a good time.

"Aaron!" someone called. "Pull up a chair!"

"Can't tonight!" he shouted back. "Me and Sam got fence
duty."

"Alright. I hope you don't have to whip out your bow."

Aaron laughed, and Sam smiled. He kept bumping into chairs
and tables on the way through the cafeteria. He could barely see
in front of him. Sam had to grab his hand and lead the way.

It was brighter outside, but not by much. He let her hand
drop, his own still tingling from the touch. He liked it.

"So we just walk around, keep an eye on things?"

"Yeah. All night long." She dragged out the last sentence.

"Thanks for doing this with me."

"Sure."

They circled the fence for an hour. They both kept quiet, each
lost in their own thoughts. The sounds of the night kept them
company, the birds, crickets, rustling in the trees just beyond
the fence. They passed a few other guard pairs, and gave them
polite waves. Aaron noticed Sam walked a little closer than she
did before.

"Does Carrie always do that?" he asked. "Dance on the
tables?"

"Wish she was with you now?"

"Nope."

"She's not my favorite person, but the guys love her. She
puts smiles on their faces. Everyone thinks she's bubbly and
beautiful."

"Oh, she's very pretty." He gave her a quick look up and down
in the moonlight. "You're prettier though."

She stopped along their path and leaned against the fence.
"What?"

"I'm not trying to make any romantic moves or anything. I'm just saying. You're prettier than Carrie."

Sam knew men looked at her, but didn't really care what they thought. For some reason, with Aaron, she was flattered. "Thank you."

Gratitude was getting easier for Sam.

They took a rest after a while, and shared some water. They made a loop around the school, this time in the opposite direction to break up boredom.

"Why am I prettier than Carrie?"

"Because you don't try," he said. "Carrie puts a lot of thought and effort into how she looks, which seems a little silly to me. You put thought into how you're gonna live and survive, and how to get that knife on your leg."

"So not trying to look pretty, makes me *prettier*? That doesn't make any sense."

"I know, but it's true."

Sam was quiet. *Is Aaron actually flirting with me?*

She dismissed the thought right away.

Aaron had to fight to keep alert. Sam was right, fence duty wasn't easy. He suggested they take short naps while the other watched. Troy had wanted to do the same thing with Sam when they had fence duty, but she didn't trust him at all.

She trusted Aaron. She knew he would watch over her.

When it was Aaron's turn to nap, they moved to the other side of the school, near the edge of the garden by the fence. He lay down in the grass and put his hands under his head.

"Remember, wake me up if something happens."

She laughed. "The only thing that will happen is boredom. Don't worry."

Aaron settled in and closed his eyes. She sat down next to him and mindlessly checked her Beretta.

"Hey, Sam?"

"What?"

"Would you tell me a bedtime story?"

"No."

He smiled. "My father and Aunt Denise would tell me stories before bed."

Sam tried to fight off memories of her childhood, but they flooded in. She had no memory of her parents at all. Her earliest memories were of digging food out of the trash. She killed her first walker when she was seven years old. While Aaron was listening to bedtime stories, Sam was surviving on the streets. She avoided walkers and worse, like humans with no conscience.

Familiar emotions took over. Hate and anger.

"I'm not your father or aunt."

"Are you okay?"

"Yeah. Go to sleep."

"What's wrong with you?"

"Nothing. Look, I just don't really want to hear about your family, alright?"

"If you want, I'll read you a bedtime story."

She managed a small laugh. "Oh, will you?"

"Sure. I've been going through the library. There's still plenty of great books there. I'll read to you every night if you want."

"Reading is a waste of time, Aaron."

He sat up and they locked eyes. "No, it's not. When people take over again, they'll need to know how to read and write. We can't let everything we've learned disappear."

"Take over again? Are you kidding? Aaron, walkers outnumber us. When we die, we become them. We'll never take back over."

"You're wrong. It won't happen in our lifetime, but it will happen. And strong people like you need to know how to read and write."

She was pleased Aaron thought she was strong, but she knew he was being ridiculous.

"You think reading and writing is more important than learning how to shoot a gun?" she asked as she ran a finger down his bow.

He leaned on an elbow. "Did your gun save you in Baltimore?"

"No, you did, but you didn't exactly throw a book at them."

"Okay, tell me what's important to you, for living in this world."

She sat with her legs crossed and looked at him. "Well, you have to have weapons training, and know how to find supplies. You have to look out for yourself first."

"You say that, but you came back for me in Baltimore."

She took a breath and pushed a strand of hair out of her face, to buy herself a second. "I only did that for myself. I couldn't get here without you. I used you to get here."

Aaron said nothing. He considered that a moment, if it could be true. He searched her face. He couldn't make out her expression, the moon was behind her.

"I think you're lying. I think you're actually a good, caring person. And you're afraid to admit it."

"I only care about one person besides me, and that's you."

The words slipped out before she could take them back. She felt her face growing hot, and was thankful Aaron couldn't see her clearly.

"You know I'll watch out for you too," he said.

They were having a moment, but were too inexperienced to realize it. There was some silence before Aaron picked up movement outside the fence out of the corner of his eye.

They both saw it at the same time. It was dark, but they could barely make out the shape of a lone figure on the street, walking toward the school.

Sam grabbed her Beretta, but Aaron put a hand on her shoulder. She noticed the same thing he did. The figure walked slowly, but the gait was steady.

"It's a person," Aaron said.

Sam had no intention of climbing the fence to check on whomever it was wandering the street. If it wasn't a walker, she didn't care.

It was only when Aaron scaled the seven-foot fence did she change her mind.

"Are you coming?" Aaron asked as he landed on his feet.

She sighed and scaled the fence after him. He helped steady her by the shoulders as she landed.

They both jogged down the street toward the figure. They could start to make out some details. He saw long hair and a female shape.

He grabbed her when he got close enough. The girl couldn't have been more than sixteen. He recognized her; he'd seen her earlier in the day helping to boil water. He didn't know her name.

"Are you okay?" he asked.

It took her a moment to speak. "They're all dead."

He turned to look at Sam, who was standing behind him with one hand on her Beretta and the other on his shoulder.

"What's your name?" he asked the girl.

"Nikki."

"Nikki, tell me what happened."

"Some of us went out, like you've been doing. We wanted to see what we could find in the old houses, and, they're all dead."

"*Who* is all dead?"

"Bobby, Michelle, Ashley...all dead."

"You just can't go out like me. I'm not like...are you hurt? Did you get bit?"

"No. Bobby tried to bite me, but-" she trailed off.

They heard a noise in front of them. Several walkers tumbled their way out of a house, not too far down the street. They tripped over each other, but finally managed to right themselves.

The undead were coming their way.

"That's them!" Nikki cried, and tried to run.

Aaron grabbed her firmly and held her in place. He dropped to one knee and pulled her down with him. Sam had the itch to move herself, but stayed behind both of them.

"Nikki, before tonight, have you even seen a corpse?"

"No."

"Where are your parents?"

"Dead."

Aaron sighed. He knew the school was a great place, but he could see a few of its faults. The kids would grow up learning how to grow vegetables and survive with what they had, but not be able to read or write, or kill a walker.

"Okay." He gestured with his hand toward the mass of corpses headed their way. They moved slow and steady. They were still a distance away, but Sam was nervous. "I want you to count how many you see."

"I can't!" she cried, and tried to pull away from Aaron again. He held her next to him.

"Aaron, we don't have time for this," Sam said. "What are you doing?"

"Rule number one, Nikki, is don't panic. Just think. Watch them, look at how they move. You need to be able to spot one if you're out in the world in a second."

Nikki focused on the slow mob and tried to focus her eyes in the dark. The moon provided just enough light to make out their shapes.

"There's eight of them." She hugged herself to fight the chill she was feeling. "What is that noise they're making?"

"Good. Forget the noise. It's scary, I know, but ignore it. Now one or two, you can outmaneuver and work around. Eight, you're either gonna have to run or kill them."

Nikki was afraid, but Aaron and his calm voice helped steady her nerves.

Sam leaned down next to Aaron. "We need to move. We can kill them all from behind the fence."

"Teach Nikki how to shoot."

"What? Are you kidding?"

"No. She needs to learn."

"Aaron, *you* don't even know how to shoot a gun. This isn't the time or place for this."

He stood up and nocked an arrow. He released, and his aim was dead on, even in the dark. A corpse near the front of the mob fell as the arrow pierced its skull.

"Don't need a gun."

Aaron flashed Sam a smile. Nothing about a mob of undead shuffling toward them frightened him in the least.

Sam had the feeling that Aaron was hiding something.

"Shit, what the hell am I doing?" Sam muttered as she knelt next to Nikki.

Aaron watched as Sam gave Nikki the quickest crash-course on firing a weapon in history. She told Nikki to use both hands and aim for the head. There was also recoil she had to watch out for.

Nikki killed every walker. She hesitated at the walkers she recognized, whom not even ten minutes ago had been her living friends. The last one she shot was only a few feet away. Sam had her hand on her combat knife the entire time, but there was no need for it.

She grabbed her gun from the shaking teen's hands.

"You did great, Nikki," Aaron said. "You should never be outside the school at night, or any time for that matter. At least not until you get some training."

Nikki was crying. Aaron put an arm around her shoulders and gave a gentle squeeze. Perhaps Sam was right, it was the wrong time and place, but Nikki needed to know how the world worked beyond the fence.

He felt guilty as he helped her to her feet. The kids were watching him, trying to imitate him, and it cost a few of them their lives.

Aaron and Sam walked Nikki back to the school. They found Richardson and explained what happened. He took Nikki to the cafeteria to calm her down while Aaron and Sam grabbed a few torches to burn the corpses. They stopped by the forge to light them.

"What the hell was that about?" Sam asked. They walked across the parking lot back to the front gate.

"Someone needs to teach her. Everyone's too scared to gather the kids and take them to the Pit, teach them about walkers."

"So what did you get out of that?"

"Nothing. Hopefully Nikki got something."

Sam was quiet a moment. "I, uh, wouldn't even have climbed the fence if you weren't there."

"Really? Why not?"

A sudden wave of anger overcame her as old memories flooded back. She faced him as they stopped near the dead corpses.

"Because no one would have done it for me," she said. "When I was her age, I looked out for myself. If the corpses weren't closing in, the fucking sick rapists and slavers were. Every day, a fight to find food and water. I don't need anyone to take care of me."

He shook his head as he put his torch to the first corpse until it caught on fire. "I got bad news for you."

"What?"

"*I'm* looking out for you now. So get used to it."

She was quiet as she watched him move from corpse to corpse. She replayed the scene with Nikki in her mind. Aaron hadn't hesitated to help her. He never hesitated to help *anyone*. In a world full of walking corpses and bad people, even apathetic people like Sam, Aaron tried to be the best person he could be.

She didn't like how she was starting to feel.

CHAPTER 10

Aaron knocked on Sam's door. He waved to Scott as he passed by in the hallway. Scott gave him a pat on the back for how he handled Nikki's situation last night. People were a little nervous that eight walkers were just outside the fence, and some of their young had lost their lives, but were still glad Aaron and Sam were on the fence to handle it.

Everyone already liked Aaron, and couldn't stop talking about him.

"Sam?" he said to the door. "You in there?"

He slowly opened the door. He could see Sam wrapped under a sheet on her mattress, one leg sticking out. Judging from how much leg he saw, he guessed she wasn't wearing anything. For the first time, he saw a scar on her right thigh. He had no doubt she had her share of scars.

The morning sun threw light across her room through the curtains, but she was sound asleep. Aaron couldn't blame her, as he was tired himself. He nudged her shoulder.

"Sam. Wake up for a second."

She pushed his hand away, then shot upright when she realized she wasn't alone. She looked at Aaron with wide eyes and pulled her sheet to her chin. "Aaron, what the hell are you doing?"

"I knocked this time," he said. He sat in the chair opposite her mattress. "I really did. You didn't answer."

"That's 'cause I was *asleep*. We were up all night. Shit, how are you even awake?"

He tried to keep his eyes steady. "Do you always sleep with nothing on?"

Her face grew hot. She pulled her leg under the sheet. "I'm getting sick of you seeing me naked. Turn around."

He complied as she got dressed.

"How's the girl? Nikki, is that her name?"

Aaron thought it was strange that Sam barely knew anyone.

"She's fine. She's with Susan, at the garden. Just trying to keep her head on straight."

"Hell, aren't we all?"

"Yeah. Listen, Sam, I need your help with something."

"What's that?"

"I need you to teach me how to drive a truck."

Sam laughed. She grabbed him by the shoulder and turned him around. Aaron gave her a nod. Even with only a few hours' sleep and bedhead, she was beautiful. She ran a brush through her hair.

"What are you talking about?"

He held up a piece of paper. "I've been asking people about things we need. I'll go get everything, but I don't know how to drive."

"That's not gonna happen, Aaron."

"Why not?"

"Everyone likes you. I know that. But you've only been here a few days. Richardson isn't gonna let you drive. Besides, he only gives the keys out to Garrett and his little puppet Ray."

"I saw what happened the last time they took the trucks out. You got left with me."

"I know. I don't like the rules. I'm just saying, forget about it."

"I'll go talk to Richardson."

Sam smiled. "This I gotta see."

They found Richardson near the back gate of the school chopping down a tree while Larry split wood. They had an audience. Some of the kids were playing and watching them.

"Hey, Richardson," Aaron called. "Can we talk for a second?"

Richardson buried his ax into the tree and warned the kids not
to touch it. He approached Aaron and Sam while wiping sweat
from his forehead.

"Best time to cut wood," he said. "It's not too hot yet. How's
Nikki doing?"

Aaron shrugged. It was strange how everyone thought he
knew everything. "She's with Susan. She'll be alright. Listen, I
want to take one of the trucks out."

Richardson chuckled. Aaron was irritated at everyone laughing
in his face.

"No can do, Aaron."

"Look. Just tell Sam to teach me to drive. I'll go out alone, no
big deal. No one gets hurt."

"And what if you get yourself killed? You think about that?
Then we're out a truck, and a person everyone looks up to."

"I'm not gonna get myself killed." He paused a moment.
"People look up to me?"

"No one ever goes out alone, Aaron. That's why we have
teams, led by Garrett and Ray."

"Assholes."

Richardson tried to hold in his laughter. "Anyway, ask them if
they'll let you join them, if you want to get out that bad."

"Aaron doesn't go without me," Sam said.

Aaron turned to look at her. He knew they were friends. Still,
her loyalty was surprising. It wasn't long ago that Sam told him
to his face she would leave him to die if she had to.

"Sam, thank you, really, but I'll be better off taking the truck
out alone. Just teach me how to drive right here."

"You go out, I'm going out with you."

"No."

"You don't tell me no. I do what I want. Who do you think
you are?"

"Hey!" Richardson said. "How old are you two again?"

Aaron and Sam looked at each other. He went first.

"You said the corpses first rose up twenty-three years ago? I'm twenty-three then. I was born on the first day."

"And I'm twenty. Maybe twenty-one?"

Richardson shook his head. The joke sailed right over their heads. "Look, I know you think Lexington might not be as bad as Baltimore, and you might be right. Still, there's no way you, by yourself, even if you could drive, can get anything from around here."

"You'd be surprised."

Richardson rolled his eyes. He couldn't believe he was going to waste gas for this. Part of the reason he was compromising was Sam. Aaron was bringing a side out of her he'd never seen before. She was focusing that strength of hers on a friendship, instead of what deals she could make.

He looked at her. "Samantha, you know where the keys are. Take Aaron to wherever he wants to go. Show him it's pointless, then come back here. If you spot some easy gas, grab it."

Richardson went back to chopping wood without another word. Sam gave Aaron a smile, pleased at her little victory.

"Like I said. You go out, I'm going with you. You ready?"

Aaron said nothing. He was frustrated. He just wanted to help, and Richardson and Sam were actually preventing him from doing so. He understood Richardson's thinking, but he didn't understand Sam's.

"Why are you coming with me?" he asked.

They entered the school. She led him through the hallways to the old office where Richardson kept the truck keys.

"Cause we're friends."

"I know. Larry and Richardson are friends too. I bet they wouldn't risk their lives for each other though."

She shrugged. She didn't feel like analyzing her feelings for Aaron now. "I'm safe with you. You're safe with me. I don't want you going into walker territory without me."

Aaron watched her as she fished the keys out of an old desk drawer. He knew he was a lucky man.

"Fair enough."

The drive through Lexington wasn't too long, only about twenty minutes. Like driving on the interstate, there were times Sam had to slow down to maneuver around old cars, fallen light poles, masses of dead bodies, and packs of walkers milling about.

Aaron helped her navigate with a map he'd found in the library. He wanted to head to an old Home Depot. He helped his family raid one when he was just a child. He knew all these years later there might not be anything to get, but even just a little wood would help out. Susan needed two-by-eights and soil for flower beds in the vegetable garden. Travis needed plywood and tools to fix the smokehouse. Larry needed two-inch hose to fix two of the broken shower stalls. Everybody needed something. Lexington was a good place. It kept people alive, but people were shaken up. The death of Nikki's friends was enough to get people talking and afraid. Hope was starting to dwindle, and Aaron wanted to make sure that didn't happen.

His own spirits fell when Sam pulled into the back of the Home Depot parking lot.

There were walkers everywhere. Maybe a few hundred or so stumbled around, and surely there were more inside the old store. Cars and trucks were turned over on their sides. Old carts littered the lot. One walker pushed one in a circle constantly, nearly tripping over its own feet.

Aaron would have laughed if he weren't in such a bad mood.

"See?" Sam said, gesturing in front of them. "Nothing here but corpses."

Aaron said nothing. He'd hoped that the corpses would be manageable, that he and Sam could just park the truck by the front door and quickly load up. Two sets of hands were better than one, and with her help, he'd have no problem crossing items off the list he'd written.

But the corpses weren't manageable. Even if every single person at Lexington High came along, with weapons, they would all die within an hour.

He wouldn't risk Sam's life.

To drive the point home, walkers made their way to the truck. They started beating on the sides. It was just light tapping at first, but as more walkers came, the louder it got. A few started beating on Sam's window. She started driving slowly to throw the corpses off.

"I'm sorry, Aaron," she said. She put a hand on his arm. "But you probably needed to see this. It's why we risk our lives getting supplies in the city. You getting things for just yourself in Baltimore is one thing, but for sixty people? Not quite the same. We can't stay here, they'll be in this truck in minutes. We gotta head back."

Aaron didn't argue.

He wasn't happy, but he wasn't done yet.

Oh well. Plan B it is.

He had seen where Richardson kept the keys to the truck. He also watched every move Sam made while driving.

He glanced at the Home Depot in the side mirror as they drove away, knowing he'd be back again soon.

Sam was pulled from her sleep by someone knocking at her door. She slowly looked around her pitch black room. It didn't feel like dawn. It was still the dead of night.

The knock came again, more forcefully this time.

Aaron, I'm gonna kill you.

"Hold on!" she shouted. She didn't care if she woke up her neighbor in the classroom next to her. "Give me a second to get dressed."

She dressed in clothes that were so old and torn she wouldn't have a choice but to throw them away soon. She was surprised

Aaron hadn't just barged in like he always did. She opened her curtains for the moonlight and opened the door.

It wasn't Aaron.

"Richardson?"

She'd seen Richardson angry before, but it was rare. He knew he always had to be positive, keep the happy face. Everyone looked to him as the leader, and as a leader, he couldn't afford to be seen angry or unhappy.

This was not one of those times.

"Where is he?" he asked.

Sam wiped the sleep from her eyes. "Is it still night?"

Richardson stepped inside and gently closed the door behind him.

"*Where* is he?" he repeated.

"Who?"

"You know damn well who. Aaron."

Like Sam always did whenever someone pointed anger at her, she got angry back. "I don't know. It wasn't my turn to babysit him."

"Stop feeding me that shit, Samantha. You two are best buddies now. You're always spending time together."

"He doesn't *sleep* here, Richardson. He lives in the library."

"I know."

Sam felt a knot in her chest. "And he's not there?"

Richardson took a deep breath, trying to get his anger under control. "When did you see him last?"

"We had dinner together in the cafeteria. He said he had some things to do, and he'd see me later."

"Did he say anything about going out on his own, or just flat out leaving?"

"No."

"Well, one of the trucks is gone. I talked to Gabe who was watching the gate. Aaron left, and told Gabe *I* said he could go. And dumbass Gabe believed him."

Sam couldn't believe what she was hearing. "What?"

"He *left*, Samantha. He stole our truck, and he's gone."

She was stunned. She felt miserable as she sat on her mattress. *He's gone.*

"He wouldn't just leave," she said. "He'll be back."

Richardson almost laughed. "Oh, he will?"

"Yeah."

"And why is that?"

"Cause we're friends."

Richardson looked down at Sam. He'd never told anyone before, but when Sam first came to Lexington, he almost thought of her as a daughter. It was only when Sam made it clear she wanted nothing to do with anyone that he kept his distance.

He sat next to her.

"Samantha, I'm so glad you finally made a friend. And I don't know him too well, but I think Aaron is a good man. I don't think he'd steal a truck and run, but you know he isn't coming back."

She turned to look at him. The moonlight revealed just enough of her face to show her pain. "Why do you think that?"

"Because he's dead by now, whatever it was he was trying to do. He didn't even take his bow with him. And everyone says he doesn't shoot a gun? He's already dead then."

His words made sense, but Sam couldn't bring herself to believe them.

"No. He's not dead. He lived in Baltimore, with the walkers. He's tough."

It broke his heart to see her upset. He didn't think anything could ever upset her.

"I'll leave you alone," he said. "Sorry to wake you. I was hoping Aaron had said something to you."

"No, nothing."

Emotions Sam had little experience with attacked her. She was angry, afraid, hurt.

Why would Aaron leave? What is he doing? Why didn't he ask me to come with him? Why didn't he say goodbye? I'm supposed to be his friend.

Richardson quietly left without another word. Sam felt a tear rolling down her cheek. She didn't know why she was crying, and that made her even more angry. She balled her fist and punched the wall just under the window. The pain shot through her hand as she shook it. The tears flowed freely, although she lied to herself and said they were tears of pain.

👋 🙌 👋

Aaron parked the truck near the front of the Home Depot. He only had the moon to give him light, but he thought he did a good parking job, considering it was his first time. He killed the engine and left the truck, knocking over a walker in the process.

He pushed his way through the horde of undead to the broken sliding glass door. It was pitch black inside. The stench of the undead was far more potent inside the old store. That would be the hardest part of gathering supplies, just pushing undead out of the way, and not vomiting from the stench.

He would have to wait until morning. He couldn't see one foot in front of him inside.

He knew this wouldn't be a short trip, so he came prepared. He grabbed a bag of vegetables Susan had given him, and used the open door to climb on top of the truck. He took a bite out of a tomato and pulled out a book he'd brought along. He'd read in the moonlight many times in Baltimore. It brought back memories.

While he read about the history of the former United States of America, his thoughts kept drifting to Sam.

He forced the thoughts away each time, but only for a few minutes until her lovely face popped into his mind again. He felt silly, as they ate a wonderful dinner of squash and chicken a few hours ago. They talked and laughed, and Aaron successfully dodged some nasty glances from Carrie from the other side of the cafeteria. Sam offered to knock her out, to which Aaron politely declined.

After Aaron's family was murdered, he made sure he stayed alone. He didn't hate people. He believed people could be great or terrible, but didn't want to spend too much time with anyone to find out which they were. With the undead, he was safe.

Then Sam fell in his lap.

It was a strange trap. The more time he spent with her, the more he wanted to spend. He felt terrible leaving her behind at Lexington, but she would never understand the relationship he had with the undead. Would she?

He knew she was special. He finally had a best friend. He liked Richardson, and thought Lexington High was a great place. It was an example of the good people could do, but he knew if Sam weren't there, he wouldn't be either.

His thoughts constantly shifted between trying to read under the moonlight, and Sam. He took a short nap until the sun finally peeked over the horizon.

Time to get to work.

He pulled his list from his pocket and gave it a quick glance as he pushed his way into the store. Hammers, nails, wood, saws, axes, push-lawnmowers, it was quite a long list. He'd be busy for a while.

The Home Depot had been looted before over the years, before the undead mass grew too large, but there was still plenty to find. Aaron had no trouble finding everything on his list. The hard part was getting it all into the truck. He knew he knocked down a corpse that used to work there at least twenty times. There were just so many of them.

He carried two large bags of gardening soil on his shoulders and walked slowly back through the store. He knew the nutrients in the soil were long gone, but loose dirt was loose dirt. As he walked down one of the aisles less crowded with undead, he saw something that caught his eye.

It was a gas-powered generator.

It was a mid-sized model, large enough to be on wheels. He'd never used one before, but remembered his father and Uncle

Frank talking about them many times, and how they wished they
had one.

An idea came to mind, something he read about in an old
magazine.

He smiled, then patted the shoulder of a former employee.
The walker gave him a moan.

Sam sat on the front steps of the school, only a short distance
from the front gate. She sat there all day, only moving to eat a
quick lunch. Everyone that walked by saw her mood and wisely
decided to leave her alone.

The hours passed. Sam knew the longer Aaron was gone, the
less chance he had of being alive.

She fought emotions so long throughout the day that she
grew numb. She sat there watching Gabe nap in a chair by the
gate. He would turn every now and then and give her a nod, but
knew better than to approach her.

As the sun started to set, the people of Lexington wrapped
up their chores. The children vanished inside. Not many people
stayed out after dark, as there just wasn't anything to do, and
deep down, people were still afraid of the dark.

Garrett and Ray walked by. Sam expected them to keep
moving, but her mood took a turn for the worse when they
slowed down. Garrett gave her an ugly smile.

"So your bald boyfriend stole one of my trucks?"

"He's not my boyfriend, Garrett. And he's coming back."

"He's already dead."

Ray laughed. Garrett kept taunting her.

He gestured to himself. "You've had all this in front of you
since you got here, and you go and make the wrong choice."

She rolled her eyes. "Would you just get out of here? Leave
me alone?"

"You won't be able to resist me forever, beautiful. You'll be mine one day."

They walked away, laughing the entire time.

Later in the evening, Paul Sorenson took over for Gabe watching the gate. Sam guessed it was a nice break for Paul, instead of hanging out with chickens all day, slaughtering them for meat and taking their eggs.

Paul didn't keep track of the gossip that floated around Lexington. Instead of sitting by the gate, he sat next to Sam.

"What are you doing out here, girl?" he asked. "Figured you'd be inside with your new friend. It's a hell of a job he did with that library."

"He left."

Paul scratched his blond head. "Is that why everyone is running around here so sad today?"

"I guess so. It's, uh, definitely got *me* down."

"Hell, girl, you're always down. Everyone here is scared to death of you."

"Thanks, Paul."

"Don't mention it. Yeah, that Aaron fellow, he's a good guy. A little strange, but I like him. He actually helped me clean up the chicken shit yesterday morning. No one ever wants to help me with that."

"Why do you say he's strange?"

Paul looked back at the pretty young woman, trying to find the words. "Hard to say. He's just so…happy, I guess. I hear he lived in Baltimore?"

"Yeah."

"Right in the middle of all the walkers?"

She nodded.

"Well, that's fuckin' strange. Shit, isn't he afraid of them? Just don't make much sense to me."

Before Sam could say anything she heard an engine off in the distance. She'd heard the sound many times over the years, and recognized their truck.

"Unbelievable," she whispered.

Paul didn't see the truck until it turned into the school and stopped at the main gate. "Speak of the devil."

Aaron waited while Paul ran forward and opened the gate for him. He drove the truck slowly next to the other one, shifting it back and forth as he crept forward. He still wasn't comfortable driving.

Sam didn't move an inch from the steps.

"Hey there, Aaron," Paul called as Aaron climbed out of the truck. "You have everyone here worried sick."

"Hi, Paul." They shook hands. He ran a hand over his head, which was slowly growing some hair. "I just needed to get some stuff, that's all."

"Gabe's pissed at you, you might want to steer clear from him. Richardson gave him a tongue-lashing for letting you leave with the truck."

"I'm sorry. But I had to leave, and I knew Richardson would throw a fit. A little white lie never killed anyone."

Paul slapped him on the shoulder. "You got balls, young man, I'll give you that."

"I got supplies for you. Wood, nails, should be enough to rebuild that second chicken coop."

He raised the truck door so Paul could see for himself. The older man's jaw dropped. "Aaron, this is...wow."

Aaron gave Paul a slap on the back and went back for the truck keys. He almost ran right into Sam. She stood there rigid with her arms crossed.

She wanted to reach out and hug him. She also wanted to slap him across the face. She compromised, and did nothing.

"Where did you run off to?" she asked, danger in her voice.

He was confused. He had planned as much as he could. He took the truck, knew he'd have to stay out overnight, knew he'd have to face Richardson when he got back. He didn't think Sam would be mad at him.

"Getting supplies," he said. "Things we all need."

"You could have been killed. Why didn't you take me with you? We go out, you see how dangerous it is, so you decide to go out by yourself?"

"I don't want you to get hurt."

"And I don't want *you* to get hurt. That's why we go together. Do you see how this works? How are we supposed to look out for each other if you do stupid shit like this? I'm new at this friends thing, but I don't think this is how it works."

She walked away. She didn't even look in the truck to see the many things Aaron brought back. He took a step forward to stop her, but decided against it. He'd seen Sam's temper, and figured it was best to let her cool down.

Hell, I'm lucky she didn't stab me with her knife.

Paul shook his head and leaned an arm on Aaron's shoulder.

"Girlfriend mad at you?"

"We're not a couple, but she is a woman," Aaron said. He gestured to Sam as she disappeared around the side of the school. "I don't get it. I know she's had a tough life. I can't even imagine the things she's had to go through, and the people she's had to deal with. But she's pissed for not letting her come with me to get supplies? She's mad at me for watching out for her?"

"She's protective of you, that's all."

"That's a weird way of showing it isn't it? Getting mad and walking away?"

Paul nodded. "It's refreshing, I think. The world has changed, damn walking corpses everywhere. I know you don't remember any of the old world, but women were a mystery then too."

There was a voice behind them.

"Aaron."

They turned to see Richardson peering into the back of the truck. Aaron tried to read his face, pick up on what was going through his mind. His expression was blank.

Richardson had trouble believing what he saw. Garrett and Ray, in supply runs covering their last six months, couldn't get as much as Aaron did in a single day.

The truck was almost completely full. Wood, tools, drums of water, blankets, clothes, soil. There was a little of everything.

"How the hell did you get all of this?"

Aaron didn't just stop at Home Depot. He'd hit a few other places too, including a Target and a Walmart.

He was anxious to get started on his project.

"A lot of luck," he lied.

They locked eyes. Aaron could see a spark of anger.

"Would you mind walking with me a minute?"

Shit. Here it comes.

Aaron turned to Paul as they walked away. He knew the supplies wouldn't stay on the truck long.

"Paul, I have some things near the front covered with a blanket. That's all my stuff, something I'm working on. Watch it for me, okay? Don't even let anyone see it."

Paul nodded. "Will do."

As soon as Richardson and Aaron were away from the front gate, Richardson blew up.

Sam navigated the halls of Lexington with a candle. She didn't see anyone at all until she made it to the cafeteria. Two people she didn't know were sitting by themselves, enjoying a quiet conversation. She passed through the cafeteria and headed for the library.

It had been a few hours since she fought with Aaron at the front gate. She was calmer now, and felt some guilt. She couldn't help being angry at him, but she knew she didn't handle that very well. She needed to talk with him, clear the air.

She was surprised at what she saw in the library. It was late, so she didn't expect to see anyone. She thought Aaron would be asleep in his bedroom that was once an office, and would take pleasure in waking him, like he always did her. Instead, he was sitting in his living area on the couch. There was a single candle on the end-table and a book in his hand. There were children gathered on the floor around him, half of them asleep. Sam recognized Nikki in the crowd.

He was reading to them.

Sam walked close enough to hear and quietly leaned against a bookshelf. She watched him for a few minutes as the children hung on his every word.

Aaron noticed her, just barely in the shadows. He flashed a smile and closed his book.

"Okay guys, let's take a little break," he said. "Hell, maybe we should call it a night. Your parents would kill me if they knew you were here this late."

There were a few protests, especially from the ones that didn't have parents. But in a few minutes the kids were ready to go. Not all of them brought candles. He motioned for Nikki. "Do you mind helping the kids get to their rooms?"

Aaron planned to give Nikki a lot of chores, maybe even bring her in on his project. He wanted to help get her mind away from her recent tragedy.

"I can do that," she said. She leaned in close to his ear. "Samantha's been mad at you all day. Watch yourself."

"So I hear."

Nikki rounded up the kids and lit a candle. The ten or so children left as a group.

Sam and Aaron were alone.

"Looks like the kids really liked that," she said. She sat on the couch.

"Yes. Something called *Harry Potter*." He took a seat in the chair. "It's actually really good."

There was silence. Sam thought she knew what she wanted to say, but now her mind was blank. Aaron spoke instead.

"Listen, me and you, we're okay, right?"

"Yeah. I said my piece. I didn't like you going without me."

"It's just that, you're my best friend. So I'll come to you before anyone else here, but I'm gonna keep you out of danger."

Sam leaned forward and held his gaze. "Look, we're a team. It's sweet you want to keep me safe, but this isn't a safe world. That's not what I need. Next time, you take me with you. Okay?"

"Richardson already gave me the lecture."

She laughed. "What did he say?"

"Eh, something about trust, and teamwork, how I was irresponsible. Then he offered me Garrett's job of supply runs."

"You're joking."

"Nope. It was pretty funny. I told him no."

"I don't blame him. I've never seen anyone get around the corpses like you."

I should just tell her.

He pushed the thought away quickly. He never told anyone his secret. He was afraid of how they'd react. Would people push him away for being different? Would they try to study him to figure out why the undead ignored him? He didn't think anyone at Lexington would try to hurt him, but he had learned over the years that human behavior was unpredictable.

"While I was out, I got you some stuff."

She said nothing. She watched him get up and disappear into the darkness, in the area of his bedroom. There was some rustling around, then Aaron reappeared dragging a box behind him.

Aaron pushed the box in front of her. "Go ahead. Check it out."

She pulled out a medicine cabinet. It looked brand new. Aaron had no trouble finding one that had never been used, still wrapped up, at Home Depot.

"We can nail that up on your wall somewhere," he said. "I see you have that small mirror in your room. Well, this is better."

Sam looked at him. She was speechless.

"There's more in there," he said. "Keep digging."

She pulled out some curtains and a chess set.

"I saw your curtains were getting nasty. And the chess set's for us. I'll teach you to play sometime. Then we can play checkers *or* chess."

She didn't know what to say. No one had ever been so nice to her before. She knew part of that was because she kept people at a distance. She tried to keep Aaron at a distance when they first met, but that was useless now.

She really liked him. That terrified her.

"Uh, Sam?" Aaron said. She just stared at the chess set. "You alright? I mean, we don't have to play chess if you don't want."

"I'm going to bed," she announced. "Thank you for everything. Really."

She packed up her presents and left without another word. She didn't even bother lighting a candle. Aaron watched her go. He was too confused to say anything.

"Just remember, women are a mystery," he reminded himself.

CHAPTER 11

Four days passed. Sam saw Aaron in passing, but they hadn't spent any time together. She missed him. Aaron was learning more about Lexington, while Sam was asking people what she could do to help. In the past few days, she had helped Susan plant more seeds and pick vegetables off the vine, and helped Larry clean out the spring-house.

It was a good feeling, she discovered, earning her keep.

It was the middle of the day. Sam was working with Mary Taylor in the storeroom. They were cleaning up, moving things around, still trying to organize the supplies that Aaron had brought in.

Sam didn't talk much. She took direction from Mary, and gave any kind of help she needed. They were dragging a mattress across the old gym floor when Mary spoke.

"So, you pretty much know Aaron Thompson better than anyone, right?"

Sam rolled her eyes. Everyone was still smitten with Aaron, even more so since his return with the supplies. The only person she knew of that hated him was Garrett.

"I guess so."

"What's the meeting about then?"

They stacked the mattress against the wall and went back for another.

"Meeting?"

"Yeah. He's called a meeting for tonight in the library, at sunset. He wants everyone there, even kids. I thought Richardson called all the meetings. Hell, when's the last time we even had a meeting?"

Sam had to think. "Not too long after I first got here. I didn't go."

"You don't know what it's about?"

"Nope, not at all."

Sam was curious. What could Aaron possibly want to say to everyone?

"You'll show up to this one, won't you?" Mary said with a smile.

"What's that supposed to mean?"

"It means you got a thing for Aaron."

"What the hell is a *thing*?"

"You know, a crush."

"What's a *crush*?"

Mary shook her head. Expressions some of the older people used were lost on her too, but she at least knew what a crush was.

"You like Aaron more than just a friend."

"You mean like bunk-mates?" She laughed. "No."

Sam was quiet. In the past, she would have been content to let the subject drop. But she needed to convince Mary, as much as she needed to convince herself.

"Even if I did," she said. "I'm not exactly the girlfriend type."

"Oh, that's right. That would mean you'd have to let your guard down. Let someone get close to you."

Sam said nothing.

"Samantha, I'll tell you right now. If you want Aaron, you better go get him. This is too much of a messed up world to just wait around. We could all die tomorrow."

"I don't *want* Aaron. We're friends. We're not bunk-mates."

Mary just smiled.

Aaron had been busy since the early morning hours. His project was complete and ready to go. The only thing he and Nikki had left to do was arrange the chairs in the center of the library. That was harder than he thought. There weren't many chairs floating around Lexington. It took him over a day to get sixty, and he wanted a few extras in case Richardson was wrong about the population count.

Nikki looked at the mystery Aaron had covered, just in front of the chairs. He had shown no one. There was a thick blanket covering his surprise. She knew it was on wheels, as she'd seen Aaron pushing it around earlier.

"Are you happy with these chairs?" she asked.

Aaron looked them over. Seventy chairs, all laid out in seven rows of ten. "Yes, that's great. Pull a few to the side up front here. I'll get Sam to sit with me."

"You two make up?"

"I think so. Haven't seen her for a while, but I don't think we're fighting."

She looked at Aaron as he took another peek under the blanket. She knew he was trying to keep her mind off what happened to her friends. He was a nice man. She could see what Sam saw in him.

"Thanks for looking after me," she told him.

"Hey, no problem. Thanks for helping me here."

She smiled, knowing Aaron probably didn't even need any help.

There was a knock at the library door. Aaron hadn't blocked it off like he wanted to, but had written a sign earlier.

"Did you put that Keep Out sign I made up out there?"

"Yeah, but I told you, Aaron, not everyone can read."

Nikki spaced the chairs out while he went to the door. Richardson stood there with his arms crossed. Aaron opened the door for him.

Richardson got right to the point. "I hear you're calling a meeting tonight."

"Don't worry. I'm not looking to step on your toes. I just have a few things I want to run by everyone."

Richardson noticed the chairs and the surprise under the blanket. "Can I ask what this meeting's about?"

"You can *ask*."

"But I won't get an answer?"

"Exactly."

Nikki laughed.

Richardson took a breath. "Twenty years ago, when the world was still trying to figure out what the hell the walking corpses were, we had a *meeting*. Turned out a lot of the people living here didn't want to stay. Those people had a spokesman, too. They wanted to take almost all our supplies and leave the rest of us with nothing. We're not talking that type of meeting, are we?"

Aaron put a friendly arm around Richardson's shoulders, making sure to keep him clear of the surprise. "Trust me, nothing crazy. Just some important issues."

Richardson was wary. He liked the young man, but was still a little miffed at the stunt he'd pulled with the truck, even if it was for a good cause. But Sam trusted him, and she didn't give out trust easily. He'd also done a lot of good in such a short amount of time.

"I guess I'll be here at sunset."

"Good, good. We'll be here. Oh, hey, Sam's coming tonight, right? I haven't seen her, but she's coming?"

"We don't really hang out together, Aaron. If I see her, I'll tell her you personally asked for her to come, even though you wouldn't go to her yourself."

"Okay, thanks."

He ushered Richardson out the door. He was back to the chairs when he looked at Nikki.

"Wait. Did Richardson just make fun of me?"

"I think so."

"The bastard."

She laughed. With Aaron around, it was sometimes easy to forget there was a world of walkers just a street away.

Aaron had checked the generator outside the library emergency exit door for the sixth time when he heard the first few people arrive. It was Larry and Susan. Nikki invited them to have a seat. Larry looked at the long electrical extension cord running across the floor as Aaron came in from outside.

"Hey, Aaron," Larry said. "What you got under the blanket? What's with the cord there? You finally pay our power bill?"

"Oh, you'll see."

Without Aaron asking her to, Nikki greeted people as they came in. Aaron tried to gauge the mood of everyone. Some were annoyed at being called to a meeting, while most were just curious. The children ran around the chairs as everyone settled in.

Richardson arrived and took a seat near the back. He was definitely curious, and stared at the cord with surprise. He gave Aaron a slight smile. Aaron wondered if he had a clue of what the surprise was.

Sam walked in. Aaron went to greet her, but Nikki was already moving.

"Hey, Samantha!" Mary called. "Come sit over here with us."

Aaron raised an eyebrow. It looked like Sam was finally making some friends. Nikki grabbed Sam by the hand and gave Mary an apologetic look.

"I'm sorry, Miss Mary. She's already got a seat."

Mary had the hint of a smile. "Of course she does."

Nikki led Sam to her seat near the front next to Aaron, then went back to the library door.

Sam gave Aaron a smile. As the room filled up, his cheeks turned a shade of red.

"You okay? What's going on?"

"I've never seen so many people at once in my life."

"*You* are the one who called us all here."

"I know."

The light was slowly fading outside. Larry went to light a candle.

"Hey, Larry, no need for light."

"How the hell are we gonna see you running your mouth up there?"

Aaron said nothing.

A few minutes later Richardson looked around. Most of Lexington had arrived. He noticed Garrett and Ray weren't there, but he didn't expect them to be. A few others he knew were starting fence duty.

"I think this is as full as we're gonna get," he told Aaron. "So what's up?"

Everyone quieted down, and all eyes were on Aaron. He couldn't even move a muscle for ten seconds.

"Uh, hi, everyone," he managed to say.

Sam laughed quietly just in front of him. Nikki took her seat in the front row.

"Okay. Everyone, uh, have a good time."

He had planned everything, except the words. He could hear confused grumbles as he trotted back to the emergency exit and started up the generator on the first pull. He closed the door behind him to soften the noise.

He pulled down the screen that had shown countless videos and presentations in the old world. It was dirty in spots, and had a few tiny holes, but would still get the job done.

He pulled the blanket off the cart on wheels, his surprise. On the top shelf was a DVD player he'd found at Walmart. On top of that was a projector. On the bottom shelf was the largest set of speakers he could find. He had to push six corpses out of the way just to get to the speakers in Walmart. Apparently Walmart was a popular place in the old world.

He had to read the DVD player instruction manual three times over the past week before he understood it enough to hook up the wires. At first, there was picture, but no sound. Then he had the picture upside-down. He thought he'd never get it right.

But it was finally showtime.

He listened to everyone as he turned the projector and DVD player on. Only the older residents had any idea of what he was doing. He looked up to see Richardson and Travis smiling.

Some of the children jumped when the opening theme of *Star Wars* started playing.

"You gotta be shittin' me," Travis said.

It was actually too loud. Aaron turned the volume down, then sat next to Sam.

"What the hell is this?" she whispered.

"It's a movie. *Star Wars*. Relax. It'll be fun."

She smiled, and pointed at the screen. "What do those words say?"

"Damn, I forgot about that." He jumped up quickly. "Sorry about that, everyone. I'll read what we got up there."

Aaron didn't really pay attention to the first half hour of the movie. He was too busy watching everyone else. He wanted to give everyone some fun. He had read about old theaters and listened to his family talk about their favorite movies plenty of times. He'd never seen one himself, and knew he wasn't alone in Lexington.

He was glad to see everyone enjoying themselves.

The only thing that ended up having to go were the uncomfortable chairs. Most everyone pushed them to the side and sat or laid down on the floor.

The children especially looked like they were in a trance.

Sam was quiet nearly the entire movie. She sat next to Aaron, almost putting her head on his shoulder a few times. Near the end she leaned over to whisper in his ear. "Why did you need me up here with you?"

"I'm more relaxed when you're with me."

She gave him a long look as Luke Skywalker blew up the Death Star.

After the movie ended, Aaron gave Nikki some candles to light. He quickly turned off the generator and ran back inside. Everyone was laughing and talking about the movie. The children were asking to watch it again.

"And that's our meeting," Aaron called. "Thanks for coming."

Not everyone left right away. People stopped by to shake Aaron's hand. Some even gave him a hug. Carrie stole an extra-long hug. He made sure Nikki got her share of attention too.

Richardson approached him, just shaking his head. Aaron spoke before the older man could unleash his temper.

"I found everything when I was out. I had to take some gas, but don't worry. I can always find more."

Richardson said nothing. He just looked around at his people. He'd known a lot of them most of their lives. He tried to do the best for everyone, to keep everyone safe and happy. Aaron's simple act of showing a movie had meant more than the young man could possibly know.

He shook Aaron's hand, then Nikki's, and left.

After an unexpected meet and greet with most of Lexington, only Sam, Nikki, and Aaron were left in the library. He lit a candle and placed it on the end-table next to the couch.

"That was a lot of fun," Nikki said.

Aaron nodded. "Yes. I think that went pretty well."

Sam sat next to Aaron on the couch. "So this is what you've been working on the past few days?"

"Yep. I found the generator while I was getting supplies, and it just clicked. Hell, we can use it for other things too. Just gotta keep the gas flowing."

"I'm gonna get something to eat," Nikki announced. "Do you need me for anything else?"

"Nope, Nikki. Thanks. I couldn't have done all this without you."

Nikki blushed and left.

They were quiet for a moment. Sam wanted to spend time with her friend, but didn't quite know what to say.

"I haven't seen you around the past few days," she stuttered.

"Yeah, I missed you too."

"That's not what I said. I just meant..." She didn't finish.

Aaron laughed. Sam always had such a tight grip on her emotions. She wouldn't even admit to missing anyone. "Do you like that medicine cabinet? Larry told me he helped you put it up."

"It looks great. Thank you again."

There was some uncomfortable silence until Aaron stood up and threw his hands together. "Okay, so what do you want to do tonight? Go for a walk? Get some air? You got anything planned?"

"No, no plans." Sam was surprised. She thought Aaron would want time alone after the busy night he had. "You want to spend time with *me*?"

"Of course. So what are we doing?"

She kicked her shoes off and grabbed a book from his collection on the coffee table.

"Read to me."

"*Harry Potter*? You want to listen to me read?"

"Yes."

"Sure."

Aaron watched as Sam tossed her legs up on the couch. She looked gorgeous. He could see she was finally getting comfortable around him.

He sat on the floor and leaned back against the couch. He could feel her arm on the back of his shoulders. It felt strange, as his audience was usually in front of him.

Sam didn't say a word for three chapters. She just closed her eyes and listened to her friend's voice.

"I'm glad I met you."

It came out of nowhere. He turned to make sure she was talking to him. Their eyes met and she gave him a slight smile before shifting on the couch.

"Me too, Sam."

She fell asleep not too long after. Aaron laughed to himself while closing the book. It wasn't long until he was leaning back, their heads touching. He fell asleep right along with her.

CHAPTER 12

The sounds of quiet whispers brought Aaron out of his sleep. His neck hurt from sleeping on the floor. It took him a moment to realize someone was pressed against him.

Sam slept soundly in Aaron's arms, an arm and leg draped over him. Some of the children were playing not too far away. Aaron had told them they could use the library whenever they wanted during the day, which meant that everyone in Lexington was already awake.

He locked eyes with Nikki, who was on babysitting duty. She looked through a children's book while trying not to laugh.

"I think she likes you," she whispered, pointing at Sam.

He never thought he'd ever wake up with a beautiful woman in his arms. If the children weren't watching, he might have let her sleep.

He gently shook her shoulder. "Uh, Sam?"

She stirred slightly, and gave him a gentle squeeze. She was aware of the position they were in, half her body thrown over his. She liked it.

She heard the children giggling, and jumped up. They started laughing like only kids can, loud and long. Nikki couldn't hold it in anymore.

Sam looked at their young audience. Most of the kids were afraid to look her in the eye before. Now they laughed right in her face.

Aaron smiled too as he climbed to his feet. He grabbed his book from the floor and tossed it on the table.

"I must have rolled off the couch in the middle of the night," Sam explained, loud enough for everyone to hear. "Sorry about that."

Aaron nodded. "Hey, I slept fine."

He could see the embarrassment on her face. She looked over at Nikki and the children. "Well, I'll see you later."

Sam left through the emergency exit into the morning sun.

"How long have you all been here?" he asked Nikki.

She smiled. "Long enough to know there's no way Samantha just falls off the couch. She looked *very* comfortable."

"Aaron, could you show us the talking picture again?" one of the children asked.

They cheered with excitement. Nikki watched Aaron for his reaction.

"If I can find some more gasoline, I'll definitely show you again. But we need the gas for other things right now."

They groaned a bit. Aaron smiled. He was glad they liked the movie so much.

He gave Nikki a nod. "I'll be out lending a hand if you need me."

She waved and looked at the children. "Okay. We'll be in here playing hide and seek."

The kids cheered again as Aaron left.

He worked for the next few hours, helping anyone that needed it. Everyone wanted to talk about the movie he'd shown, and how much it meant to them. A few of the older crowd shared their first experiences with movies. Travis said he kissed his wife-to-be for the first time watching a reshowing of *Gone With The Wind*.

As Aaron worked throughout the day, he noticed Richardson sitting near the garden, where the teenagers used to play football in the old world. He sat on the bleachers, writing in his notebook. He didn't move the entire morning.

It was the middle of the afternoon when Aaron approached him. Richardson didn't see him coming and jumped.

"Shit, Aaron! Don't sneak up on people."

"Sorry about that. Everything okay?"

Richardson gestured to the spot next to him. Aaron took a seat, glancing at some of the notes and sketches Richardson had in his book. He was always thinking of ways to make things better.

"Is everything okay?" Richardson repeated. "It's kinda hard to say. I mean, a person dies, they get back up. That's not really okay."

Aaron didn't respond. He just watched Susan move through the garden and pick vegetables.

"That was a good thing you did last night," Richardson said. "We're starting to get to where there's more young people than old. I bet half the people here had never even seen *Star Wars*."

"Glad everyone liked it."

Richardson continued to just look around. He closed his notebook and dropped it to the bleacher seat in front of them.

"I was here when it all started. *Right* here, in this spot. My ten-year-old niece had a soccer game. I picked her up and brought her here so my brother and his wife could set up a huge birthday party for her. One of the girls on the team was infected. We thought it was just another soccer fight. You wouldn't believe how competitive the girls used to get." Richardson smiled for only a second, then frowned once again. "My niece was bitten, and I had to kill her myself. I never saw my brother and his wife again. I still don't know what happened to them."

Aaron waved around them. He wanted to get Richardson's mind off the past. "Looks like you've done a great thing here. I've seen plenty of places out there, but nothing like this. Most people will kill each other over scraps of food."

"This place will die eventually. The walkers will get in, our luck will run out. We all know we're on borrowed time."

This didn't sound like the upbeat leader Aaron had gotten to know.

"Then do something before that happens."

Aaron pulled his own memo pad from his back pocket and opened it.

"Grow, expand," he said. "Block off both ends of the street. Make sure every single house is clear of walkers. Make this whole area yours."

Richardson smirked at Aaron's notes. He was still impressed the young man knew how to write. "Got any more bright ideas in there?"

"We need more gas and generators, or a windmill."

"Now how do you even know what a windmill is?"

"My father taught me. We always talked about making one. We need to get power back here. Just some little things to make life easier. Wouldn't you rather use a chainsaw than an ax to cut down trees?"

"Last time I checked, Aaron, getting a chainsaw from the hardware store isn't the easiest thing to do with a million dead corpses in the way."

"That's the easy part."

"Oh yeah? How?"

Aaron said nothing, and Richardson knew he was hiding something.

He didn't get a chance to press the matter further.

They both heard shouts in the distance. Carrie was running and shouting at the top of her lungs.

"Travis is hurt! We need some help!"

Aaron and Richardson exchanged looks before jumping off the bleachers and sprinting to Carrie. Susan had already made it to her and held her by the shoulders.

"Carrie, what's going on?"

She could barely catch her breath. "Travis. He was trying to fix the smokehouse by himself. He fell off the ladder. The side wall came apart and fell on him."

They ran toward the smokehouse. Most everyone was funneling in that direction. Aaron could see a crowd gathering. Travis was motionless under a pile of cinderblocks, the ladder on top of him.

No one dared approach him.

Even Richardson stopped at the front of the crowd, at least ten feet away from the injured man.

"What's going on?" Aaron asked.

"He'll probably turn into one of them," Susan said.

Aaron rushed forward and started moving cinderblocks.

"Aaron! Be careful!" Richardson called. "If he bites you-"

Aaron ignored him. He moved as quickly and carefully as possible. He threw the ladder to the side and started clearing the area around Travis, making sure not to touch him. As he worked, a new set of hands joined in to help. He looked up to see Sam.

They didn't say anything, just looked at one another for a second.

Slowly, other people started to help. Richardson joined in, then Larry, then Susan. Soon, at least ten people were clearing away the rubble. After they were done Aaron knelt next to Travis.

He didn't move, but Aaron could see he was alive. His chest moved slowly. He had a head wound that bled, but the worst injury was his right leg. It was bent backwards at the knee, and they could see the bone.

Carrie took a few steps back and vomited.

"Travis? You okay, buddy?" Aaron whispered.

He started to stir. "I think I fell."

He tried to move. Aaron put a hand on his chest.

"No, no. Don't move. Just be still."

A voice came from behind Aaron. "What should we do?"

He thought back to some of the training Aunt Denise had given him so long ago. He knew they had to keep Travis conscious, perhaps set the bone. Beyond that, he didn't know what to do, and Travis' leg didn't look to be in any condition to be set.

Richardson searched the faces of the crowd. Most of Lexington had gathered. Nikki was near the back with the children, trying to keep them from the grisly sight.

"James! Where are you?"

An elderly man pushed his way through the crowd. He had very pale skin and thinning white hair.

"I'm here, Richardson. I'm here."

He froze when he saw Travis. Aaron could tell from the man's face he didn't like what he saw.

"Severe dislocation. Probably compound fracture."

Richardson nodded. "Okay, what do we do?"

James said nothing, just motioned for Richardson to follow. A younger man that Aaron didn't know left the crowd and joined them. Larry did too, a meeting of the minds.

The crowd started whispering amongst themselves. Sam stood close to Aaron and put a hand on his shoulder.

"James used to be a doctor back in the old world. The young guy there is Eric. James is training him."

Aaron didn't like what was happening. James almost didn't even look at Travis. He didn't check his pulse or for signs of a concussion.

"Let's go see what they're talking about."

Sam tried to protest, but Aaron was already moving, and she wouldn't let him do anything alone. The three men lowered their voices as Aaron and Sam approached.

"What's going on?"

The three men traded glances.

"We're trying to figure out what to do with Travis," James said.

"How about helping him?"

"How do you figure we do that?"

"You're a doctor, right?"

"Look, this isn't exactly a hospital. We can try to set the bone, elevate his leg. But if it gets infected, and he dies, then we're all in danger."

Aaron searched everyone's faces. "I can't believe what I'm hearing here. So you don't want to go over there and help him? Is that it?"

"Aaron, keep your voice down," Richardson said. "We're just trying to think of everyone. We'll do what we can, but we should probably isolate him. I know it's sad, but he could very well die."

"Okay, if this was the old world, what would you need?"

James thought a moment. "Morphine, antibiotics, bandages, stitches. After the puncture wound heals, we'd have to put the leg in a cast."

"I'll go out and get what we need."

Larry shook his head. "Aaron, the local hospital is crawling with walkers. And James, do you think even if there were drugs there, they'd still be any good?"

James scratched his chin. "Morphine does have an expiration date. But if it's stored properly, kept out of direct sunlight, there's a chance."

Aaron looked at James. "Okay, what am I looking for?"

"You can't go alone."

"I do better alone."

Sam gave him an angry look.

"You don't know hospitals," James said. "You won't even know where to look."

Aaron opened his mouth to argue, but James was right. He wouldn't be in any danger, but it would take him forever to find medicine or supplies.

"I'll go," Eric said.

"No," James said. "You stay here. You watch after Travis. Get some help getting him moved. Make sure he stays conscious, concussion or not. I'll go with Aaron."

Aaron turned to the Lexington crowd. Carrie had soaked a rag in cold water and set it on Travis' head, which was more than anyone else had done. He spotted Garrett and Ray by themselves, whispering to each other.

"Hey, Garrett," Aaron called. "You up for a supply run?"

Garrett looked at Travis. "For that dumb old fuck over there? Fuck him, and fuck you."

He spit on the ground and walked away, Ray a step behind.

Aaron shook his head. *What an asshole.*

"I need volunteers," he said. "James and I are going to the hospital to get supplies for Travis."

Larry tapped Aaron on the shoulder from behind. "I'm in."

Nikki pushed her way through the crowd. "If you're going, Aaron, I'll go."

"No, Nikki, you're needed here."

"I'm coming," Sam said.

He looked at his best friend. "I guess telling you *no* is a bad idea?"

"*Very* bad idea."

To Aaron's surprise, half of Lexington stepped forward, all volunteering. He was amazed. He knew the world of the dead brought out the worst in people, but it could also bring out the best. Lexington proved that.

Aaron's eyes fell on Scott, who ran the forge. He had the look of a man who could take care of himself.

"Okay, Scott, you're in."

Larry took a deep breath. "I'll drive."

Aaron walked over to Travis, who actually had a smile on his face, despite the pain. Carrie held his hand, which might have had something to do with his good mood.

"You just do what Eric says, okay? We're gonna go get what you need."

Travis nodded. "Thanks. Don't get yourself killed for me."

"We'll do our part. You just stay awake and be strong. Eric's gonna have to set your leg, and it'll hurt like hell."

"Yeah, I know. Fell off a swing and broke my arm when I was a kid. No stranger to pain here."

Aaron smiled, then looked at his crew. James, Larry, Scott, himself, and of course, Sam. He gave them a nod, then they headed to the storeroom for guns.

Richardson watched them leave. He knew they all wanted to help Travis, but he also knew if Aaron wasn't leading the way, there wouldn't have been as many volunteers, especially Sam.

The young man was slowly becoming their leader.

Fifteen minutes later Larry drove the truck while everyone else was in the back. The back door was open, and walkers grasped at the truck, but they couldn't get a good grip. They moaned in frustration as the fresh food drove by, and they were unable to do anything about it.

James leaned against the side. Scott was near the front, where the open sliding door separated the back from the front cab. Aaron and Sam sat next to each other, a fact the older doctor noticed.

"It's been a while since I've been outside the school," James said.

Aaron smiled, which only made James more nervous. Everyone was afraid. They had different success in hiding it, but they were still afraid. Sam did the best job of keeping it under control, but her constant unsheathing and re-sheathing of the knife strapped to her leg was a giveaway.

"It's not so bad out here," Aaron said. "Just don't get bit."

James wanted to talk. It was how he dealt with being nervous. "I heard you lived in Baltimore for a while. How did you manage that?"

"Very carefully. Sam saved my life."

James looked at the attractive bronze-skinned woman. She was dressed exactly the same as the last time she went out. She had two layers of clothes, two knives, a hat covering her head, a Beretta tucked in her belt. Everyone in Lexington had noticed the change in Samantha since Aaron had arrived. She smiled a little more. James even caught her playing with the kids once or twice. She had softened a little, but he had no doubt about her ability to kill a corpse.

The truck bucked as Larry ran over a few wandering corpses. Sam watched their bodies on the street as they drove. Larry had to slow down for a turn, but the walkers still didn't pose a threat.

That would all change when they had to stop.

"So what's the plan, James?" Scott asked.

"I have no idea of what shape the hospital is in. There's plenty of supply rooms, we just gotta hit them and get what we need." He patted the two backpacks he brought with him. "Got plenty of room."

Scott gestured to Aaron. "What's with the bow?"

"Huh?"

"Everyone here has a gun or two. Why did you bring a bow and arrow?"

Aaron ran a finger down the string of the bow. "Never liked guns much."

James smirked. "I didn't either, until the heart attack victim I was working on shot up and tried to bite my face off."

"Guys," Larry said from the front. "We're almost there."

Sam leaned close to Aaron. "Stay close to me. I'll watch your back."

He grabbed her hand and gave it a squeeze. There was a time she would have pulled it away. Now she relished his touch, and squeezed back.

"Me and you, fighting our way through corpses. Things don't change much, do they?"

Larry drove slowly enough around the hospital to get a good look, but fast enough that walkers couldn't reach them. The parking lot had surprisingly few walkers. Most of the windows on the first floor were broken. Some were boarded up, an eerie glance into a past fight for survival.

"Okay, James, you know where you're going in here?" Larry asked.

"Well, it's been a long time, but I know where the supply rooms are. I just hope the inside is as clear as the outside."

Larry shook his head. "I wouldn't bet on that. I'm sure a hospital is a good place to find a lot of dead people."

"The front door looks clear. Park as close as you can."

Larry stopped the truck near the door and everyone jumped off the back. There were two corpses slowly approaching from in between a few abandoned cars, but they were a safe distance away.

Scott lifted his gun to fire, but Aaron motioned for him to stop. "Save your bullets. Noise draws them."

They filed inside the hospital. James tried to keep his composure. Another lifetime's memories flooded back to him. The last time he was at the hospital was on the first day the dead rose, when he was a young know-it-all doctor. The bloodstains on the walls, the mess of papers on the floor, he was part of that a long time ago.

It was dark, but there was enough light coming from outside that visibility wasn't a problem. A lone walker was behind the front desk. She clutched a phone in her hand while spinning slowly in a circle. When she saw the humans she moaned and bared what was left of her teeth.

"Keep moving," Aaron said. "We can move around. They're only a danger if they're in a group."

Larry gestured to his right, down a long hall. "You mean like *that* group?"

Aaron turned. Eight or so corpses moved slowly toward them. They were a mix of old doctors and patients, still in the hospital after over twenty years.

"Damn," James said. "There was a supply room down that hall."

Aaron knew he could just walk forward and knock every single corpse down. They wouldn't hurt him. But then his secret would be out.

"Are there any others we can get to fast?"

James thought a moment. "The second floor. Follow me."

He led them down another hall toward the stairs. There were a few walkers in the way that Sam put down with single shots to the head.

James reached the stairwell door first, and was too anxious to open it.

"No, wait!" Aaron said.

He was too late. James swung the door open, and two corpses fell out of the stairwell. They tackled James and pinned him to the ground. Their teeth barely missed his throat.

Aaron and Sam acted fast. She drove her knife deep into the side of one of their heads. He grabbed the other by the back of its shirt, and just threw it off. Sam stabbed the other through the temple. Her knife still had gore from the first kill.

"You okay?" Aaron said, helping James to his feet. "You can't just rush around. You get bit?"

James shook his head. He felt like he was going to vomit. "I'm sorry. I'm fine...just not used to being out here."

Sam carefully leaned into the stairwell. It was completely dark, but she heard nothing. Still, she had to be sure. She let out a small whistle, knowing any walkers in the stairwell would moan.

"It's clear."

"That's a strange way of handling walkers you have there," Larry whispered to Aaron as they entered the stairwell.

"I've been yelling at him to be careful since we met. He won't listen to me," Sam said.

Aaron moved past Sam to take the lead. They were blind moving up the stairs. Despite using the hand railing they almost tripped a few times. Sam bumped into him as he stopped near the second floor door.

He peeked through the small pane of glass carefully, and saw movement straight ahead near the end of the hall. It was more movement than he thought they'd see. He knew walkers liked to be near each other. But to be in that large a group, without any food around, could only mean one thing.

"Shit. A thinker."

Larry wrinkled his face in the dark. "A *what?*"

"A thinker. Some of them can think. They're the most dangerous ones."

James considered that. "That's probably the scariest thing I've ever heard."

Aaron nodded. "Where's the supply room on this floor?"

James carefully peered through the window. "It's to the right, away from that mob, thank God."

"Trust me. When that thinker gets a sniff of us, they won't stop. He'll have them all turning doorknobs to get to us."

"Which one is it?" Sam asked. "We'll put it down right now."

"I'm not sure. There's not really enough light to get a good look."

"Okay," James said. "There's another stairwell down the hall, across from the supply room. We just gotta get what we need, and get out of here."

Scott nodded. "I heard that."

They pushed the door open. Sam led everyone down the hall as fast as she could. Aaron stayed near the door just for a moment. The mob of corpses caught sight of the humans and grew agitated. Aaron could see which one was the thinker. A walker that was once a surgeon led the undead, a curious gleam in his one eye. He was missing half his face and part of his jaw.

As Aaron jogged down the hall to catch up, he saw James turning the doorknob to the supply room in frustration. He didn't know if it was locked or jammed. A corpse took a slow step behind the four of them. It was amazing how quiet they could be when they needed to. They didn't see it coming.

He stopped in his tracks and nocked an arrow. He drew back and aimed for only a split second, then released. The arrow sailed through the air and hit its mark. Sam let out a small shout as the walker fell to the floor. The walker missed taking a bite out of Larry only by a foot.

Aaron heard noise behind him. He turned to see the mob of about fifteen corpses, led by the surgeon thinker, slowly gaining ground.

"You'd better get that door open," he called as he joined the group.

James and Scott gave each other a look, then took a step back. They both kicked the door at the same time. It didn't fly open, but it did crack a few inches. They pushed as hard as they could. Something blocked the door from the other side, but it was finally moving.

They piled into the pitch-black supply room and closed the door behind them. James was the first one in, and tripped over something. Everyone else took a long step to get over whatever it was.

Scott pulled out a candle and lit it. The tiny flame threw shadows on the walls, open racks, and shelves. They saw what was blocking the door.

On the floor near the door were the bodies of two men. There was a gun nearby and an exit wound on the back of both their heads. They were nowhere near decomposed twenty years, maybe around one or two. James guessed they were there for the same reason, looking for drugs. They'd hidden in the supply room and taken their own lives.

They were now trapped, just like the two dead men.

Aaron heard the doorknob start to turn. He quickly dived at it and held it still.

"Scott! James! Move that rack over here!"

They slid the heaviest rack they could move in front of the door. Bottles and boxes fell all over the place. Sam grabbed the dead men by the feet and dragged them out of the way.

"That'll give us some time," Aaron said. "But once twenty of them start pounding on the door, we'll have problems."

James felt his heart sink. "They came out of nowhere."

Scott had never been so scared in his life. He'd killed plenty of corpses, but he'd never been in a tiny room with so many on the other side. He could hear their dreadful moans as they pounded on the door. The hair on his neck stood up.

Larry had accepted that they would die today, and he was okay with it. He knew that in the world of the dead, any day could be the last. He was going out like he always hoped, trying to help another person.

James was angry. Aaron's confident attitude made him believe they actually had a chance. Now he wondered whether Aaron's time in Baltimore had just made him crazy.

Sam had been in many bad situations in her life. Just a week ago she was trapped alone in the city, until Aaron showed up.

Still, even she had doubts about their survival.

"What do we do?" James asked.

Aaron looked around calmly. "Well, is what we need here?"

James was stunned. "You're thinking about Travis right now? How about thinking of how to get out of here?"

Aaron only smiled, which was the strangest thing the men had ever seen. Sam had seen Aaron's odd behavior around walkers before. She wasn't used to it herself. It frustrated her as well.

But she trusted him.

It's like they don't bother him, she thought.

"One thing at a time, guys. Let's get what we need."

James shook his head as he grabbed the candle from Scott and studied the shelves. It was hard to concentrate with a fate worse than death pounding on the door just a few feet away, but he forced himself to stay calm. He started filling his backpacks, getting several of everything. He grabbed a few splints, drips and bags, morphine, antibiotics, sutures, antiseptic. He had no idea if the liquids were still good, but a small chance was better than no chance at all.

"Okay. I think that's everything."

Aaron nodded. "Good. Time to go."

He walked past Sam and nimbly jumped onto the second shelf of the large rack against the wall. He stretched up and pushed a tile out of the way. No one had even noticed it was a drop-ceiling.

He held his hand out for the candle. Scott handed it over, then went back to forcing his weight against the rack blocking the door.

Aaron glanced around the area above the ceiling. The space wasn't that large, but it was sufficient for what he had in mind. There were sprinkler pipes that branched down the halls and offices, but he didn't think they would hold all their weight.

The walls of the rooms didn't run all the way up. They could stand on top of them in the dark space above the ceiling, if they were careful.

"Okay, up we go."

They were hesitant a moment, but the door opening a few inches got them moving.

Aaron helped everyone up one by one. They used the rack shelves as a ladder. Sam was the last one up, and took a quick glance at the space they were climbing into.

"The ceiling won't hold us," she said.

"Stand on top of the wall, right here," Aaron said. "Balance yourself however you can. Larry's got a hold of a support beam up there. Just lean on him."

She climbed into the ceiling, Aaron right behind her. Before leaving the supply room behind, he kicked the rack with all his strength, sending it tumbling to the floor. As soon as it landed, the door burst open. Walkers poured in.

The humans all crouched in a line on top of the wall. It was cramped and uncomfortable, but it was better than being eaten alive. Sam could feel her heart beating in her chest. She steadied herself by keeping a hand on Scott's back. She felt Aaron behind her with a hand on her shoulder. If any one of them lost balance there was a good chance they'd all tumble down.

"I can't see shit up here," Larry called back.

Aaron started kicking the tiles out around him for more light, on both sides of the wall. Sam fought panic as the tiles fell on the many corpses below. The supply room was full of them now. They reached up at the fresh food only a few feet away.

Aaron locked eyes with the surgeon thinker. He stood in the middle of the supply room. While the undead around him fought for position, he just looked around, like he was searching for something.

He's looking for something to climb on.

Aaron tapped Sam on the shoulder. "That's the thinker," he said, pointing. "That one right there."

Sam followed his finger, and for the first time, she actually saw it. She trusted Aaron with her life, but she wasn't with him completely on the idea of a walker that could think. Even the one he pointed out in the Pit back at Lexington, the one he called Sweatpants, didn't look special to her.

But this one, she could see it.

It wasn't so much what the surgeon was doing, but what it *wasn't*. He didn't roar or moan in frustration that he couldn't reach the humans, like the others. He had a gleam in his eye as he searched the supply room.

He stumbled into the corner and grabbed a chair.

Sam's eyes grew wide. She could see what it wanted to do. "We have to get moving."

"Where?" Larry said. "We have nowhere to go."

"James, where's the nearest stairs?"

"Back where we came from. Obviously we can't go that way. There's another stairwell down the hallway in front of us. But even if we stay up here, they'll just follow us all the way down."

Aaron knew he was right. "Alright, when I make my move, you all drop down and take off running. I'll be right behind you."

He maneuvered around Sam as best he could. She tried to grab his hand as he went by, but he shook her off.

"What are you doing?"

He didn't answer. He went around James, then Scott. He had to get to a spot near the hallway outside the supply room.

"I said what the hell are you doing?"

He kept one hand on the support beam Larry was using and kicked a few more tiles out. The hallway was right below him, near the supply room door. Undead were still piling into the room, but a few stopped in the hallway to look up.

He patted Larry on the back. "Okay, don't stop till you hit the stairs."

Before Larry could say anything in protest, Aaron dove from the ceiling onto the crowd of walkers near the door. Sam screamed in fear and surprise. Aaron and the undead crashed to the floor.

Larry didn't hesitate, and jumped down. There was a walker a few feet away that Aaron missed. Larry shot it in the head. He helped Scott climb down, then James. The two of them sprinted down the hallway. Sam jumped down on her own, then pulled against Larry's hand.

"We have to help Aaron."

Larry took a quick look at the pile. The walkers struggled to climb to their feet, fighting against their own lack of balance and rotting muscles. To Larry, it looked like they were swarming Aaron.

"We can't help him. Let's go!"

He grabbed her hand and pulled her along. He saw James and Scott just getting to the stairwell door at the end of the hall. A corpse tried to lunge at them from a side office, but a shot from Larry dropped it to the ground.

They were nearly to the door when Sam pulled free of Larry's grip. She gave him a hard look. She was numb, but she was certain of one thing.

"I'm not leaving Aaron."

Larry grabbed her shoulders. "He's gone. He sacrificed himself to-"

He stopped when he saw movement from where they had come from. Someone was running toward them, which he knew even the freshest of walkers had trouble doing.

"Holy shit," he said slowly.

Aaron stopped in front of Larry and Sam. He breathed hard, just a little winded from the ceiling dive. He'd had trouble pulling himself out of the pile of corpses. His foot pushed into one's stomach as he stood up, and he still had a bit of intestine on his shoe. He leaned over on his knees for a second while everyone just stared at him in disbelief. Sam dropped to one knee and held his face in her hands.

"Aaron?"

"Yes?"

"Are you bit?"

"No."

"How did-?"

He cut her off with a wave of his hand. The mass of undead led by the surgeon were slowly gaining ground, and there was another group coming from their right as well. "Come on, let's hit the stairs."

They moved into the darkened stairwell. James took a step going down, but Larry stopped him. He saw movement right before the door shut, and now they could all hear them, just ten steps down.

"Corpses," he said.

"Can we fight our way through them?"

Listening for only a second answered the question. They couldn't see them on the stairwell, but the walkers' moans told them there were more than they could handle.

"We have to go up."

They ran up the stairs to the third floor. Aaron peered through the glass window, knowing there were walkers right behind them.

They didn't see the single walker coming down the stairs from the fourth floor, just a few feet from them.

It jumped on James. The doctor panicked and started screaming. He couldn't see the walker attacking him. He tried to push back with his hands, and felt his fingers slide into the walker's eyes. He spun around, out of control.

Aaron moved in to help. James toppled over the railing, taking Aaron with him.

"We've gotta move!" Scott shouted.

Larry threw open the door. Enough light spilled in from the hallway to let them see what was happening.

James was all the way over the railing, hanging on by a single hand. His other hand clutched Aaron's wrist. Aaron had the two backpacks of medical supplies. James had dropped them when they went over the railing. The walker that attacked James had fallen to the bottom, three floors down.

A long way down.

Aaron looked to his left to see the walkers only about fifteen feet away, all gathered on the steps. The stairwell was full of them. They moved in from the first and second floors, their noses full of the delicious scent of fresh meat.

He saw the surgeon in the middle of the undead. Thinker or not, he was hungry.

Larry and Scott grabbed James' arm and started pulling. Sam held the door open. She fired at a few walkers limping toward them on the third floor. If they didn't hurry, they'd be surrounded on all sides.

Aaron looked up at James. The doctor's face was full of pain. He held on with all his might, but his grip was slipping, and Aaron knew it. Larry and Scott had a hold on him, but Aaron felt his wrist slip a bit in James' grasp.

He knew this was the end of the line. He was angry, and only had himself to blame. Everything could have gone differently, but he wasn't willing to give up his secret.

Aaron tossed the two backpacks straight up as hard as he could. Scott reached out and caught them.

James' strength finally gave out.

Aaron fell down the middle of the stairwell. They didn't hear him scream, or meet his fate at the bottom, because of the sound of the undead.

Sam still held her post at the door, shooting the walkers that stumbled closer. She risked a look back and saw them pulling James over the railing. The undead were almost on them. She waited for the men to pull Aaron up, but instead they moved past her into the hallway.

"Where's Aaron?"

James was trying not to fall apart. "I'm so sorry," he said, tears filling his eyes. "I just couldn't hold on-"

Sam took a deep breath. "Then we go and get him."

Larry grabbed her shoulders and pulled her inside the hall. He shut the stairwell door, knowing the undead had a tough time with doorknobs. If one of them could think, like Aaron said, then they had to keep moving.

"He's gone," he said. "I'm sorry, Samantha."

Larry knew Samantha was the strongest woman at Lexington. But her face twitched just a little as she fought emotions she wasn't used to.

"Come on," Scott said. "We have to get out of here."

Sam let them lead her through the hospital, but her mind was far away.

CHAPTER 13

Aaron woke up, but couldn't open his eyes. The pain immediately hit him, all throughout his head. He tried to sit up, but a wave of nausea washed over him, and he had to lay back down before he vomited. He groaned and tried to wipe the sweat from his forehead.

He felt a hand grab his own. It was warm, so not a walker. Sam? The hand felt too small.

"Charlie? I think he's awake."

He willed himself to open his eyes. He looked up at a blurry image of someone sitting next to him. Slowly, the world slid back into focus. A young girl, no more than ten years old, held onto Aaron's hand. She was a cute kid, even with her dirty face and tangled blond hair.

He tried to sit up again. A man knelt down and put a hand on his chest.

"Whoa there, friend. I wouldn't move just yet. You've been drifting in and out for a half-moon cycle. I doubt you're ready to be hopping up and down."

Aaron didn't bother fighting him. "Where am I?"

"Hell. But I'm sure you already knew that."

He sat up slowly and studied his surroundings. They were in a moving truck, similar to the ones they used at Lexington. There wasn't a sliding door to get to the front cab, and the rear door had been removed. In its place was a set of iron bars, welded together and secured to the back decades ago.

It was a mobile prison.

"Do you think you can stand up?" the man named Charlie asked.

Charlie and the little girl both helped Aaron to his feet. He lost his balance for a moment. He had to put a hand on the side wall to steady himself.

Aaron had so many questions. He looked at Charlie. Charlie looked about ten years older than Aaron. He had bright red hair and freckles. He wasn't wearing a shirt, but Aaron saw why. He had given it to the young girl at his side. He looked frail and malnourished.

"Who are you?"

"My name's Charlie. This little girl here is Amanda." Charlie pointed at a teenage boy standing near the bars with his back to them. "The grumpy guy over there is Derek."

Derek turned his head slightly and gave a short wave.

"Come on, Derek," Charlie said. "Aren't you even gonna say hello to the man?"

"Why? He's just more water we have to share."

Charlie and Amanda shared a look. Aaron got the impression Derek's attitude was something they were battling with.

"What's your name?" Amanda asked.

"Aaron. What exactly is going on here? How did I get here?"

"You're in a slave camp." He pointed outside. "These bastards make trips up and down the old east coast, taking people they find, and trading them for supplies. People as property. Kinda makes you sick, doesn't it? As for how you got here, well, I'm a little fuzzy on that. I can only go by what I hear when these pricks walk by. They found you while clearing out a hospital on the other side of town, near the front lobby where there weren't many corpses. You were real lucky."

Lucky, Aaron thought. *If they had left me alone, I would have woken up and walked back to Lexington. Now they think I'm a slave.*

Aaron had dreams of stumbling through the hospital from the stairwell after he'd fallen onto a pile of walkers. Apparently they were more than dreams.

He walked to the iron bars and leaned against them like Derek. He gave the young teen a nod. Derek sneered.

Aaron studied the place as best he could. They were in a fenced-in yard of some kind. There was a gate off in the distance, with the road leading away from the place. There were heavy trees surrounding them, but there were gaps where he could see houses just beyond.

Armed men walked around the yard. There were trucks, crates, drums of water. These men were surviving, just like Lexington, although their methods were much different.

A familiar scent touched Aaron's nose, right before he heard their song. He looked to what he thought was the center of the yard, and saw six walkers chained to an old light pole, like dogs on a leash.

"What is this place?" Aaron asked.

Charlie stood next to him and ruffled Derek's hair. The teen pulled away and joined Amanda near the front.

"I don't remember much about the old world, but when the snow was bad, they used to throw salt on the roads with these huge trucks. This place used to keep the trucks and salt."

Aaron nodded. A state highway facility. He'd read about them before.

He watched as a group of three men walked by the restrained walkers. They reached out in frustration. One of the men playfully held out his hand, teasing the creatures.

Charlie noticed Aaron staring at the corpses. "Four of those corpses used to be in the truck two down from us. They were planning an escape with two of the slavers helping them. They keep them as a little reminder in case we get out of line."

"There's other trucks here?"

As an answer, he heard a pounding on the wall from the truck parked next to them.

"Hey Charlie?" a female voice called. "Is the new guy awake?"

"Yeah, Sherry, he's awake." Charlie gestured with his head to the wall next to them. "They keep the women and men separate, for obvious reasons. Can't have any naked loving, right? I'm guessing there's probably fifteen slaves here."

An older man walked by. He carried a shotgun and chomped on a cigar. "Hey. Did anyone say you could talk back and forth in there?"

"Go away. No one's talking to you."

"Oh yeah? How about I talk to you with this here?" He pointed the shotgun at Charlie.

Charlie didn't flinch. "You're not gonna shoot anybody. We're worth too much, remember? You stupid piece of shit."

The slaver flashed Charlie an angry glare. His eyes shifted to Aaron. "Looks like the new meat is awake. Stay in line, maybe you'll stay alive," he said while walking away.

"I don't understand," Aaron said. "Why don't you all just fight back? They let you out to eat and piss, right?"

Charlie shook his head at Aaron's attitude. He pointed to a small hole near the back, three inches across, that emptied out to the ground. "*That's* our bathroom. So, please, try not to miss. And no, the only time they open this gate is to sell one of us off." Charlie's eyes fell to the floor. "My wife Jenny tried to fight when they sold her. They beat her right in front of me. Just in front of the bars, I could almost grab her hand. She was worth fifteen assault rifles, ten barrels of water, and a portable generator."

"You're married?"

"Yeah. *Really* married. We met an old preacher on the road. He married us."

Aaron grabbed Charlie's shoulder. "I'm sorry."

"Yeah. Me too. If I get out of here, I *will* find her."

They were quiet a moment. Aaron waited for two men with rifles slung to their backs to pass before speaking. He gestured to Derek and Amanda in the back. "What's their story?"

"These slaver bastards have a base in what used to be New York, where the border to Canada was. That's where they do most of their selling. Derek's been with me since then. They picked up Amanda somewhere in New Jersey I think. When they run into groups looking for a trade, the women usually go fast. I'm sure you can guess why." Charlie choked up a little, wondering what his wife was doing, if she was even still alive. "I don't know what's worse for the kids, staying here in this prison, or being *owned* by a group of men."

"Well, I don't plan on being here long, so they can come with me."

Charlie laughed. "I used to say the same thing. Now, I don't even know how long I've been here. I've looked at the bars, trying to figure out if I could take them off the hinges they made. Hell, you see those walkers over there? They had help, and couldn't make it out. I'm sorry, Aaron, you're trapped here."

He was quiet. Aaron remembered why he'd hidden in the city so many years. It was because people like the slavers existed. The people of Lexington, and how they took care of each other, were the exception, not the rule.

Aaron watched everything he could from the back of the truck over the next few hours. The slavers were in and out of the old office buildings and shoddy tents all day long. He thought he counted at least forty men. Every single one of them carried a weapon of some kind.

He didn't know where they were in relation to Lexington. They kept the front gate closed. There were two armed men stationed, and they only had to kill two walkers throughout the day. They'd picked a good location, close enough to a road, but the yard was tucked away down a hill, surrounded by heavy trees on three sides, and enough trees by the gate to keep them invisible.

The sun had gone down. Aaron kept a close eye out as the night went by. He looked for anything, manned patrols, a group dinner, anything at all that told him about the culture of the place.

Derek and Amanda slept near the front of the truck. It was a warm night. Amanda used Charlie's shirt as a pillow. He sat down across from Aaron.

"I know it's driving you nuts, being in this cage. But you're gonna have to get used to it. They'll drag you out of here and beat you if they feel like it. And if they think you're getting used to the beatings, then they'll beat someone close to you."

"Your wife?"

He nodded. "One time they gave a look to Amanda too. I begged them not to touch her, and they didn't. But it was then I knew they had control over me. They knew it too."

Aaron fought back anger. "A billion walking corpses around us, and it turns out people are the monsters."

They went quiet when they heard footsteps approaching. A man stopped at the bars. He didn't look too old, just a hint of gray in his hair and beard. Charlie relaxed when he saw who it was.

"Hey, Gibbons."

Gibbons nodded. "Charlie. I see your new mate is awake."

"Yeah, just today. Aaron, this is Gibbons. He's the only one here I probably wouldn't spit on."

"Gee, thanks." Gibbons looked around before pulling out two water bottles from under his shirt. "Here. Hurry up and drink a little. I have to visit the rest of the trucks."

Charlie grabbed a bottle through the bars and took a drink. He offered the bottle to Aaron, but he declined, not once taking his eyes off Gibbons. Charlie hated to wake the kids, but they needed to drink too. One of the slavers brought them their daily minimum a few hours ago, but Gibbons helped them whenever he could, with extra food and water.

Aaron lowered his voice as Charlie tended to the kids. "You found me at the hospital?"

"Not me, but some guys that went to clear it and look for supplies. Some of them are talking about you, trying to figure out how you didn't get eaten."

"Charlie says I was lucky."

"Yeah, right. You're so lucky you got brought back here."

Aaron could tell from his tone that Gibbons wasn't happy. "Well, why don't you help us get out of here, and we'll all leave together?"

He shook his head. "I hate it here, but I'm safe. You see those moaning bastards chained to the pole over there? They had the same idea. Look where it got them. It's risky enough slipping you guys extra water."

Aaron appreciated Gibbons taking the risk, but was still angry. "You're a coward."

"Hey, call me what you want. But I've gotta watch my ass. I think Allister already suspects I'm up to something."

Aaron felt the bottom drop out of his stomach.

Allister.

He'd heard the name spoken only once in his lifetime, but he would never forget it. The man who had murdered his family. He had fired a single bullet into both Uncle Frank's and his father's stomach, then left them to fend for themselves against the undead.

He still had nightmares about it, watching Denise, Margie, Frank, and his father die before his very eyes.

Allister was in charge of the slave camp.

Aaron reached through the bars and grabbed Gibbons by the collar. "*Who* did you say?"

"What? What's your problem, man?"

Charlie ran forward. He grabbed Aaron by the shoulders and tried to pull him back. He only succeeded in yanking Gibbons too, his face just a few inches from the bars. Derek and Amanda watched in fear.

"Aaron, calm down!" Charlie said. "Gibbons is on our side!"

"Who's in charge here?"

Two men stuck their heads out of their tents. They grabbed their guns and headed their way.

"Allister!" Gibbons said. "His name's Allister."

Charlie kept pulling on Aaron's shoulders. "Let him go! You're gonna get us in trouble!"

It was too late for that.

Aaron released Gibbons, who fell backwards.

"What the fuck is going on here?" the taller of the two men said. He eyed up Gibbons. "Why are you talking to them? Don't you got something better to do?"

"Bill, Taylor, just relax. I was checking on the new guy. He was confused for a minute, didn't know where he was. I popped him one, and now we have an understanding. Right, new meat?"

Aaron said nothing. Charlie took a step back to stand in between Aaron and the kids. He had a feeling this wasn't going to end well.

"He's talking to you," Taylor said. "You speak when you're spoken to, like a good little boy."

"Fuck you."

Charlie winced. He joined Amanda and Derek in the back. Amanda hid the bottle of water Gibbons gave them behind her. Charlie was worried about what Aaron's behavior would bring down on them.

Taylor smiled. "I hear you just woke up today. So you don't know how things work here. Well, let me explain."

He signaled to Bill, who went around the side of the truck. They kept the bars locked by a chain that stretched down the side and wrapped around a hook. Bill undid the chain and let it fall to the ground.

"Shit, Taylor," Gibbons said. "Just let it go."

"Shut up."

Taylor swung the bars open and aimed his gun at Aaron's head. "Get out of there, or I'll kill you, then your friends in there."

Aaron was mad at himself. He'd put Charlie and the kids in danger. He hopped down from the truck.

As soon as he landed, Taylor hit him in the head with the butt of his gun.

Aaron fell to the ground. His first instinct was to attack back. He wasn't that stunned, and Taylor's leg was in grabbing distance. He held back. Bill stood a few feet away with his rifle pointed at him.

Not the right time. Not yet.

Taylor and Bill said nothing else during the beating. It was the first one Aaron ever received. He covered up as best he could. Amanda tried to rush forward to help, but Charlie held onto her. Even Derek covered his eyes.

Gibbons just watched. There was nothing he could do. In the truck next to them, Sherry and the other women leaned on the bars and watched the beating. She wanted to say something, anything at all to make them stop. She didn't want to draw attention to the women. She knew they could do worse to them than beat them.

"Come on, guys, he's had enough," Gibbons said. "If Allister gets wind of this-"

Almost as if on cue, they heard his voice.

"What in God's name is going on over there?"

Aaron looked across the yard, not bothering to try to stand up. His right eye was swollen shut. Blood dripped from his mouth to the dirt. His entire body was sore from the kicks and punches. He saw men near their tents, not daring to move as Allister walked in between them.

Aaron recognized him immediately, even with only the moonlight.

Allister didn't recognize Aaron. He looked at the young man, bruised and bloody, clutching his ribs. He barely contained his anger as he looked at Taylor, Bill, and Gibbons. He knew Gibbons was too much of a pussy to have anything to do with a beating, one of the many reasons Allister was thinking about retiring him.

This was all Bill and Taylor's work.

"I know you have to let off steam sometimes. Hell, I do it myself. But do you really think we'll get any good trades out of a beaten, broken man?"

Bill and Taylor stared at the ground.

Allister looked at Gibbons. "Put him back in the truck. And you two." He pointed to Bill and Taylor. "Tomorrow, you're on shit duty. Clean up the shit under every single one of these trucks."

Gibbons carefully pulled Aaron to his feet. He lost his balance, and had to wrap an arm around Gibbons' neck. Bill and Taylor walked away, mumbling to themselves. The men vanished back inside their tents. Allister turned to leave, his hands clasped behind his back.

Aaron couldn't resist. "It was a pleasure meeting you."

Allister froze, but only for a second, then he resumed walking. He didn't speak to the property.

"You stupid bastard," Gibbons whispered.

He helped Aaron climb into the truck. Amanda put the water bottle to Aaron's mouth as he lay down. Gibbons gave Charlie an apologetic shrug.

"Thanks," Charlie said. "Thanks for the water."

Gibbons nodded, then went back to his tent.

"He's gonna get himself killed," Derek said while he paced. "Or worse, *us*."

Aaron barely heard them talking. It had been a long time since he felt raw anger.

"I'm afraid he's right," Charlie said. "You're gonna have to get that tongue under control. The last thing we need is Gibbons getting caught."

"You're right," Aaron said, coughing up blood. "Especially if I'm gonna kill Allister."

Sam woke up from her sleep for a brief moment, then pulled the sheet back over her head. She wasn't sure what time it was, but the sun peeking through the curtains and the sound of chores outside told her it was late morning. She still didn't move a muscle. She didn't plan on going anywhere.

It had been a month since she lost Aaron. The people of Lexington had barely seen her since then. She stayed in her room throughout the day, only going out to eat and drink at night. She didn't do anything but sleep, look through some books of Aaron's that she couldn't read, and cry. She hated herself for the crying part. She told herself when she was surviving that there wasn't a single person alive worth crying for. She was wrong, and her heart was paying for it.

There was a knock at the door. There had been a few knocks over the past month. She ignored them, and they eventually went away. That wasn't the case this time.

"Go away!"

The door opened. She turned over to see Richardson poking his head inside the door.

"Hi. Just wanted to make sure you were still alive in here."

"I am. Now leave."

She turned back toward the wall. The door closed behind her. She didn't know Richardson was in the room until she heard him speak.

"Travis is limping around now. James thinks he's gonna make a full recovery."

Sam shut her eyes to hold in tears. Hearing Travis' name only made her relive the trip to the hospital. "Good for Travis. I told you to leave."

Richardson sat on the mattress next to her. He half-expected her to get up and pace around, just to get away. To his surprise, she didn't move, but sat up next to him.

He didn't know what to say. He'd never seen Sam so upset since he'd known her. She didn't let anyone through her emotional walls. Aaron got through, and now he was gone. He'd consoled many people over the years, but Sam was different. He didn't think there was anything he could say to make her feel better, but he had to try.

"Samantha, Aaron wouldn't want to see you like this."

"Well, since he's dead, that doesn't really matter, does it?"

"We're *all* hurting. Everyone here liked Aaron. There was something about him. He was just so…happy. I could never figure it out."

"I really liked him."

She was angry at herself. She knew she liked Aaron, maybe even had that *crush* thing Mary talked about. But she didn't have the courage to say it aloud until he was gone.

I miss you so much.

Sam started crying. She tried to hold the tears in, but she didn't have the strength. She felt foolish and depressed. Richardson put an arm around her shoulder. She leaned into him and just cried.

"I don't know what to do," she said. "I'm angry one minute, then I'm crying all over myself. When will this go away?"

"It will *never* go away, not all the way. And it shouldn't. Aaron left a big mark on you."

"What do I do?"

He shrugged. "Just live," he said. He knew it sounded bad, but he didn't know what else to tell her. "You've got people to lean on here, and the kids are worried about you and look up to you."

Sam didn't think anyone gave her a thought at all, including the children. "What?"

He stood up and pulled the curtain open slightly. Sitting on the grass not too far away was Nikki with the rest of the children, all sitting in a circle playing duck-duck-goose. Every now and then one would look up to Sam's window.

"You're all they talk about," he said.

"That's weird."

"They like you, just like Aaron. He was one-of-a-kind. Everyone here was lucky to know him. And he wanted to be close to you."

Sam was quiet. Richardson was right. Aaron made her feel things she didn't know she was capable of.

She didn't want to honor his memory by becoming even more of a miserable person than she already was.

"I'm gonna take a shower."

He smiled. "Yeah, you do have some smell to you."

She pointed a finger at him before leaving her room. "You didn't see me crying."

"Of course I didn't."

The shower felt great. It had been weeks since Sam had taken a lukewarm shower. She didn't normally indulge in the water, but it had rained a few days ago, and they had more than their fair share of water.

She dried off outside the stall in her swimsuit. A few people passing by gave her a polite wave, some even a pat on the back. For the first time, she felt like she was part of the community.

She got dressed and headed for the garden. She was in the mood for a tomato. As she passed by the side of the school the children saw her. They erupted in cheers and ran straight for her. Sam was afraid for a moment, not knowing what was going on.

The twins Kyle and Kari tackled her first and grabbed her legs. She was able to stand up to them, but then the rest came. They knocked her to the grass and covered her. Sam laughed as she tried to climb out from under them. It had been a while since she heard the sound of her own laughter.

Nikki was smiling as she approached her. She held out her hands and helped Sam to her feet. The children still gathered around them.

"We missed you," Nikki said. "Are you okay?"

Sam took a deep breath. "No. But I will be, eventually."

The group broke up, but they didn't go very far. They started playing a game of tag while Sam and Nikki stood in the middle.

"I knocked on your door a few times," Nikki said. "Just to check on you."

"Sorry I didn't answer. I just needed some time."

"I miss him too."

They were quiet. They watched the children laughing and playing. Nikki noticed they were more lively now that Sam was out. Aaron was always the emotional leader. Now that he was gone, Nikki had a feeling Sam would have to fill that role, whether she wanted to or not.

"I thought you usually played in the library in the morning," Sam said.

"We did. That was before Garrett and his buddies took the place over."

Sam looked at her young friend. "What?"

Nikki shrugged. "You know Garrett. He's just an asshole. He's using the place as a rec room now."

Sam had heard enough. She walked away.

"Samantha? What are you--"

"You just watch the kids. I'll see you soon."

She went back into the school. She made a quick stop at her room before heading to the library.

She pushed the double doors open, and immediately felt her blood boil.

Ray was throwing a knife into the side of a bookshelf, for target practice. Don and Stanley, two men Sam didn't know very well, were boxing in the far corner with some gloves they'd found during the last supply run. Watching them, and knowing they'd kicked the children out, only irritated Sam.

It was Garrett that infuriated her.

He was stretched out on the couch, Aaron's couch. Garrett had tossed Aaron's books from the coffee table to the floor. He replaced them with a pile of pornographic magazines he'd found a long time ago in one of the teacher's offices. He grabbed the first one off the top and opened it up, letting the foldout fall to its full length.

"Hey!" Stanley said from the corner. "Look who's up and around. I was hoping Carrie would come over, but I don't mind looking at you."

Ray stopped throwing his knife. Garrett looked over at Sam. He tossed his magazine on the couch and stood up.

"What do you want?" he said. "No one invited you here."

Sam held her hands up in a show of peace. She really didn't want to fight. Aaron had worked hard to put the library back together, and he let the children play in it. As far as she was concerned, it was more their library than Garrett's.

"Look guys," she said. "Aaron would want this place to go to the kids."

"So? He's not here now, is he?"

"Garrett, the school is huge. Why don't you take that old shop class? You ever see how big that place is? Just gotta get the old equipment out of there-"

"We don't want the old shop class. We like it here. So what are you gonna do?"

Sam shook her head. She should have known better than to try reasoning with Garrett.

She pulled out her two Berettas she'd grabbed from her room. She aimed one at Ray, the other at Garrett.

Stanley and Don backed up a step with their hands in the air. Ray looked nervous, but Garrett didn't flinch. He thought she was bluffing.

"Really, Samantha? You're gonna kill four men over a fuckin' library?"

"No. But I will shoot you in the leg, and you can crawl out of here. Look, I myself will start clearing out the shop class for you. I'll get it all nice and neat. But this room is off-limits, okay?"

Stanley traded a look with Don. "We can respect that."

They left through the emergency room door without a word. Whether it was the guns in their faces, or Sam's offer of cleaning the shop class, she didn't know. Garrett and Ray didn't budge.

Sam couldn't believe what she was doing, holding up four men over Aaron's room. She wasn't doing it for herself. She was fighting for someone else for a change.

She hoped Aaron would have been proud of her.

"You're getting in over your head," Garrett said. "You do not want to get on my bad side. You're a hot little piece of ass, Samantha, but it's not smart to walk around alone and point guns at people."

"Good thing she's not alone then."

Sam didn't risk turning to look at the new voice, but she thought she recognized it. Garrett's face turned into a scowl when Scott stood next to her. He put a hand on her shoulder, showing her he was on her side.

"Did I miss something here?" Scott asked. "What's up with the guns?"

"Nothing's going on. We were just leaving," Garrett said, then looked at Sam. "Just give me a shout when you have that shop class all cleaned up."

She didn't lower her weapons until they left. She took a deep breath and looked at Scott. She hadn't seen him since the trip to the hospital.

She still had trouble showing gratitude. The only person she was ever comfortable with was Aaron. "Uh, I-"

Scott smiled. He knew what she was trying to say. "Don't mention it. I can't stand Garrett. Probably not the smartest idea, sticking a gun on him, though. What's going on?"

She gestured around her. "I just couldn't let him have this place. This is Aaron's. He wouldn't want Garrett messing it up."

"Speaking of Aaron, I've got something to tell you."

He motioned for Sam to follow. They walked over to Aaron's old living area. He was excited and nervous at the same time.

"Eric and I took the peddle bikes out today, to look for some supplies around town. We ran into a group of slavers."

Sam frowned. She'd encountered them before, back when she didn't have a home. They never stayed in one place very long. They were always moving, always looking to take weak people against their will and trade them for whatever they could get. She spent many days running and hiding from them when she was younger.

"Are you okay? Did you tell Richardson?"

"Yeah, we're fine. There wasn't any fighting. They had guns, and we had guns. They don't like messing with a dog that has teeth too. I told James, he's going to Richardson to spread the word."

Sam nodded. Whenever the slavers came back through town, the people of Lexington took extra care when going on supply runs. Richardson would also double the people on fence duty.

"Thanks for the heads up, Scott."

She stood up to leave. He motioned for her to sit back down.

"That's not all. They actually tried to trade with us. We talked for a while. They told me about some of the new slaves they have. They said the newest one they picked up is a young bald man they found at a hospital."

Sam said nothing. She opened her mouth, but no words came out.

"I think Aaron's alive," Scott finally said.

She forced the shock aside. There would be time to feel things later.

Now was the time for action.

"Do you know where they are?"

"Yeah. They said they're at the state highway facility on the other side of town, in case we ever wanted to see their *merchandise*. The sick bastards."

She stood up. She knew what she had to do. "Thank you, Scott. Thank you so much. I'll take it from here."

She left the library and headed for the storeroom. Mary was moving things around in preparation for the winter. She shoved sleeveless shirts into boxes, put sweaters out on tables. She gave a wave when she saw Sam.

"I'm glad to see you out of your room. Everything okay?"

"I need some weapons from the armory."

Mary was confused. "Well, okay. Didn't they already do a supply run yesterday? Just let me know what you take."

Sam stepped into the armory, which used to be the boys' locker room. They didn't have much, but it would be enough. Guns, rifles, knives, and ammunition were neatly spread out on the benches and shorter lockers. She still had her two Berettas. She grabbed a backpack and filled it with a set of binoculars and a Desert Eagle. The handgun was still in fine shape. She knew she had to leave room for water. She also grabbed the AR-15 leaning in the corner. She wasn't fond of the weapon for killing walkers, but for humans, it would do nicely.

"I thought I'd find you in here."

She turned to see Richardson. He stood in the doorway with his arms crossed.

"So you heard then? About Aaron?" she asked.

"Yeah. Scott found me." They were quiet a moment while Sam checked her weapons. "Listen, Samantha. You can do whatever you want. But I'm not sending anyone to go with you."

She nodded. "That's fine. I don't want help anyway. They'll just get in the way."

"What are you planning?" Richardson didn't think she was packing guns for trade.

"The plan. Well, the plan is to kill anything that gets in between me and Aaron."

Richardson felt a chill go up his spine. Her tone was cold, emotionless. She reminded him of the teenager that first found her way to the school. Alone, hungry, angry at the world. Now her anger was pointed at slavers who were keeping Aaron away from her.

He would not be the one to stand in her way.

"Take the truck," he said. "And be careful."

"Aren't you afraid I might die and you'll lose a truck?"

"I'm more afraid of what might happen if I say you can't take it."

She had the hint of a smile. She surprised Richardson by taking his hand.

"Thank you. I'm gonna go get my friend and bring him where he belongs."

With me.

CHAPTER 14

Aaron drifted in and out of sleep as he leaned his head against the bars. The night air had a chill to it. Amanda and Derek huddled together near the front of the truck, sound asleep. Charlie sat across from him with his eyes closed.

He looked up at the sky as two of Allister's guards walked by. He watched the beautiful stars on many nights. He wanted to see the sky again, but back at Lexington.

With Sam.

I need to get out of here.

He didn't know how much time had passed, but it was enough to give him a small head of hair. He watched the camp carefully every day. He knew when they ate, slept, where they kept their supplies, when they went out to town. He just needed a chance to get out.

"Still thinking of your escape plan?" Charlie asked, his eyes still closed.

"Sorry. Did I wake you up?"

"I can just hear you thinking over there."

He laughed. "I'll try to think quieter."

"Listen, Aaron." Charlie lowered his voice and leaned forward. "I know you still think you're getting out of here. And you're an idiot. But you have to keep that to yourself, okay? Derek thinks you're full of shit, but Amanda, well, she isn't as smart. You're getting her hopes up."

"When did you lose hope, Charlie?"

He leaned back. "When I lost my wife."

Aaron looked at his friend. "You can't lose hope."

"Can't lose hope? Are you kidding? We live in a world filled with walking corpses. I think hope got dead and buried a long time ago."

Aaron saw movement. He looked across the tents to see Allister touring his kingdom. He'd been studying the man who murdered his family, more than anything else.

Allister did very little work around the camp. While everyone else gathered supplies, cooked food, boiled water, Allister did nothing. He simply gave direction. He never looked at the slaves, his *property*. Aaron could see it pained him to even have to allot food and water for the slaves.

Allister never smiled or laughed once. He never showed any emotion. He was a hollow shell of a man, only concerned with surviving from one day to the next, at any cost.

Aaron was going to kill him. His only regret was that he couldn't kill him four times.

Allister disappeared as he moved closer to the perimeter fence. Aaron and Charlie finally nodded off to sleep, although it would be short-lived.

He woke up to the sound of a muffled cry. He heard it again, followed by what sounded like a slap. There was a loud bang against the wall in the truck next to them. His gaze fell on one of Allister's men, standing guard outside the women's truck. He looked around nervously while waving his gun. Aaron heard a male grunt, followed by flesh smacking flesh. His tired mind immediately put the pieces together.

"What's all that noise?" Charlie mumbled, just barely awake.

"Hey!" Aaron shouted. He grabbed the bars and shook them. "What the hell are you doing?"

He recognized the guard, a man named Keller. He peered into the back of the truck.

"Hurry up you guys!" he said. "The property is waking up out here!"

Aaron had gotten to know the two women in the truck next to them, Sherry and Dana. He talked to them every day. Sherry was a child when the corpses first rose, and she spent some time each day telling them about the old world. Dana was sick, but refused to take more than her share of food and water from Sherry.

"Help! We need some help over here!"

Keller looked nervous, but no one in their tents made a move. Aaron was shocked. There was no way every slaver was sleeping. Charlie checked on Derek and Amanda.

"What's going on?" the young girl asked.

"Just stay back here. Derek, you both stay here, okay? And please, cover her ears."

Derek's eyes were fearful. He nodded.

Aaron paced back and forth, his eyes never leaving Keller. Hearing Sherry's and Dana's cries for help, just ten feet away, threatened to send him over the edge. If he could get out, he would kill everyone in the camp.

"Why aren't they coming?" Aaron asked. "Why aren't they helping?"

Charlie put a hand on his shoulder to stop his pacing. "Look, they don't care, Aaron. As long as the *property* isn't harmed, Allister doesn't care. This shit happens every now and then. Keller doesn't even really need to stand guard out there."

Aaron grabbed at his hair in frustration. "What can we do?"

"Nothing."

Aaron shook the bars some more, just wanting to be as loud as possible. The only response he got was someone in a tent telling him to shut up.

Sherry went quiet. Only Dana cried out in pain. Aaron could hear more of the rape. Charlie put a hand on his shoulder as a tear ran down his face.

"They're strong," he said. "They'll get through this."

A loud throaty moan, followed by a terrified scream, erupted from the truck. Aaron and Charlie went to the bars to see as

much as they could. Keller was shaking as he pointed his rifle
into the darkness.

The planned rape had gone horribly wrong.

Harold, the man who had picked out Sherry earlier in the day,
lost control. He was too rough on her, beat her too much. He
never realized that Sherry didn't just pass out, he had killed her.
He didn't know until, in mid-thrust, Sherry came back to life and
sank her teeth into his throat.

She shook her face violently, ripping flesh away. Blood shot
from his neck and sprayed over Sherry's face. Harold tried to
shout, but nothing came out. Andy, the man who picked out
Dana, couldn't see what was happening next to him, but he
heard the feast. He pushed himself away from Dana and crawled
toward the open bars. His pants were still around his ankles.

Keller slammed the bars in his face and chained them shut.

"What the fuck?" Andy screamed. He reached through the
bars. "Open the gate!"

Keller panicked. He disappeared in between the trucks into
the shadows. Andy shouted in pain as Sherry bit into his bare
leg. Dana cowered at the front of the truck, screaming as loud
as she could.

"You've got walkers killing your damn *property*!" Aaron
shouted.

Only then did he finally see a head poke out of a tent.

Harold twitched as Sherry gnawed on Andy's arm. He slowly
crawled toward Dana, who tried to keep quiet in the corner.
Harold couldn't see Dana, but he could certainly smell her.

Aaron and Charlie said nothing as men finally ran to the truck.
Amanda and Derek were both crying. Aaron reached out to hold
Amanda, and she nearly jumped in his arms. Charlie put an arm
around Derek as he wiped his eyes.

Aaron wondered who was worse, humans or undead.

It was mid-morning, and Allister was pacing back and forth near the trucks. His men were gathered around, both anxious and afraid of what he had to say. The undead corpses of Sherry, Dana, Harold, and Andy reached through the bars as he passed by. The women weren't wearing any pants, a sick reminder of the prior night's events. Andy still had his pants down, and would fall and pick himself back up, over and over again. Some of the men had trouble keeping in their laughter.

Allister said nothing. He was so angry he couldn't speak. What he wanted to do was cut every man loose, and wave goodbye to the slave trade. He knew he couldn't do that, not yet. They needed to get back to the old border that used to separate the United States from Canada and trade every last slave they had. Whichever ones didn't sell, it was easy just to kill them. Then he would retire to a nice little corner and watch the corpses kill everyone.

As he paced by the last truck, the newest slave kept giving him that hard look. Allister never looked at the slaves. He didn't really consider them people. For some reason, the newest slave got under his skin, and he wasn't sure why.

He stopped by the truck full of corpses and fired off four shots from his pistol. The rest of the men flinched as the corpses collapsed on top of each other.

"I want to know who helped with this last night," he said. "The gate didn't just close itself."

No one said anything.

"If you want to fuck the slaves, fine. I don't care. But you *kill* them, you take food out of my mouth. So, again, who was part of this?"

Silence.

He stopped in front of the last truck, Aaron's truck. As always, they kept the children near the front. Aaron and Charlie said nothing as they leaned against the bars. Aaron knew he could spot Keller if he saw him, but he didn't know his name. Only Charlie knew, and he wasn't talking.

"I know you saw," Allister said, looking right at Aaron. "I know it was you making all the noise. Who was it?"

He said nothing. He just kept his eyes locked on Allister.

Allister finally figured out what it was about the young man that unsettled him. He wasn't afraid. The camp was full of people that were afraid of him, even his own men. Whenever he passed by someone, they would dip their head or lower their eyes.

But not Aaron.

Allister needed to get everyone back to the border in one piece. He needed them to behave, plain and simple. He thought the six walking corpses he left chained up in the center of their camp would have deterred unruly behavior. Obviously, he was wrong. He needed another example, and Aaron would serve that purpose.

He gestured to two of his men whose names he didn't know. Allister pointed his gun at Aaron after they opened the gate.

"Get down."

Amanda wrapped her arms around his waist. "No," she whispered.

Aaron patted her on the head and pulled himself free. "It'll be okay."

He stood in front of Allister. He was so close, just an arm's length away from avenging his family. He could do nothing, not with forty men standing around with guns.

Allister pistol-whipped Aaron across the face.

He dropped to one knee. Allister circled around him.

"Who was it?"

Aaron truly didn't know, but he wouldn't utter the words. He wouldn't say another word to Allister until he had his hands wrapped around his throat.

The beating continued for a few minutes. Charlie wanted to say something, but he was too afraid. He had Amanda and Derek to think of, and he could only imagine what the other slavers would do to them if he gave one of them up. Allister tried to control the men, but Charlie knew they were all out of control, except for Gibbons.

Aaron was on his knees, still looking defiantly at Allister. Allister stepped forward and kicked him square in the face.

"Get some rope," Allister announced. "We're gonna play a little game."

Two men hauled Aaron to his feet. He spit blood to the ground. He'd just recovered from the beating he took on his first day at camp, now he had to deal with another. A few men tied two pieces of rope around his waist.

Charlie started shaking the bars. He knew what Allister had in mind. He'd seen it before. He couldn't let Aaron die such a horrible death. Even Derek was scared.

"It was Keller!" Charlie shouted. "It was dark, but I'm pretty sure it was Keller!"

Allister laughed. "It's a little late for that now. Shit, we've already got the rope tied. But grab Keller, he's next."

He signaled, and the two men holding onto Aaron began to pull him by the rope. The rest of the slavers started cheering and whistling. They cleared a path to the chained corpses.

They're gonna feed me to the walkers.

He tried not to smile.

His chance had finally arrived.

He looked around quickly while digging his heels in the ground. He was still weak from the beating. He needed time.

"Please, wait!" he shouted. He tried to sound desperate, even though the corpses didn't look at him.

"Let's place bets on how many times we'll hear that!" Allister said.

Aaron searched around as they dragged him back another few feet. He could finally see the entire camp. Three men had grabbed Keller and were kicking him on the ground. They were in the middle of the yard. No matter which direction he chose, it would still be a long run to the fence. Climbing the fence wouldn't be fast either.

His eyes fell on some crates against the rear fence. That was his best chance.

He met Charlie's gaze. He was trying to shield Amanda from what she was about to see. He saw the rest of the slaves he'd never met watching from behind bars. Only the slaves and Gibbons looked horrified. Everyone else was having a fun time.

Aaron dug his heels once again in the ground, to plot out his escape. His only immediate danger was the slavers realizing the corpses were more interested in them than him. He leaned forward and tried to crawl on the ground.

"Allister! Listen to me!"

Allister smiled. The men took his advice and were placing bets now. Some bet on how long it would take for the walkers to kill him. Others bet on how much he would beg. Allister was pleased. This would teach a lesson about staying in line, and let the men blow off some steam.

Aaron was blinded by a light.

He glanced to his left. In the trees, just a short distance behind the rear fence, was a flash. It disappeared, then hit him again in the eyes.

Someone was signaling him. He had a good idea of who it was.

"Please, stop!" he shouted, more for his accomplice's benefit than his own.

He gave one final look around camp. Most of the men had holstered their weapons.

Allister knelt down in front of Aaron. He made sure to keep his distance. The walkers stretched and reached for the camp leader, but to everyone, it seemed they were reaching for Aaron.

Aaron struggled against the rope, which made it hard to breathe.

"Nothing personal, young man," Allister said.

Aaron looked up at him. Something scratched at the back of Allister's mind. His instincts, which had kept him alive from the very beginning, were telling him something was wrong.

Through the bloody nose, swollen eyes, and bruised jaw, Aaron gave Allister a bright smile.

"You don't know me at all, do you?"

Allister did not. He looked at the young man through narrowed eyes.

"You have no idea how personal this is."

Allister had had enough. "Kill him!"

The men pulled the rope with all their strength. Aaron surprised everyone by turning around and running directly at the walkers. They made no move for him as he passed by. He grabbed the first person in the crowd he saw and tossed him back into the hungry undead. The slavers let go of the rope.

Aaron heard screams of pain as he ran through the crowd toward the fence. He dragged the rope tied to his waist behind him, slowing him down. He was almost to the fence, but he could hear the confusion behind him disappearing as Allister shouted at everyone to grab their weapons.

They never had the chance to fire.

Aaron heard the explosion and felt the heat at his back as he raced for the crates near the fence. Men behind him shouted and jumped behind any cover they could find as the first drum of gas exploded. He was halfway over the fence when the second larger drum near the front gate went up in flames.

Men dove for cover while others caught on fire. They rolled on the ground to try to put out the flames.

He shed the rope from his waist and stayed low in the trees. He tried to head in the direction he thought the light came from. He could see the slavers gathering more weapons when he heard a voice above him.

"Aaron! Up here!"

He looked up to the treetops and saw the light signaling him. He slowly pulled himself up using the sturdy limbs. Every movement brought pain. He could feel the blood still oozing out of his nose.

As he neared the top a hand reached out and clutched his wrist, helping him the rest of the way. He straddled the limb and leaned back against the tree. Squatting on the limb just a foot away was Sam.

He didn't know what was happening until he felt her hugging him. She kept one hand on a higher limb for balance, and the other around his neck. He could feel her breath in his ear.

The world stopped for a moment as he wrapped a free arm around her. He was conscious of keeping balance, and how high up in the tree they were, but it felt great to hold onto Sam.

She pulled back to look him in the eye. She saw the blood and bruises, and her face went cold with anger. She nimbly jumped to a nearby limb, where her bag of weapons hung. She grabbed her rifle and took careful aim at another barrel of gas.

Aaron stopped her with a frantic wave of his hand. "Not yet."

Sam shouldered the rifle while he took another look at camp. They'd recovered from his escape and were searching the woods. Every walker in the yard was dead. He had trouble seeing, but he could see the rest of the slaves talking in the four trucks.

He looked beneath them. He wouldn't have seen Sam in the trees at all if she hadn't signaled him with an old mirror she'd found. They were as high as they could go and were surrounded by plenty of green. They were safe.

Aaron and Sam stayed silent for over an hour. Allister's men searched all around them. They cursed and yelled at each other. He noticed that despite all the noise, no walkers showed up. Allister definitely picked a good spot for his camp.

In the early afternoon the slavers finally gave up their search. He watched as Allister paced around camp. Aaron knew he'd gotten under the skin of the slave camp leader when he murdered Keller in cold blood in front of everyone.

He looked at Sam. He wasn't surprised at all with her preparation. Multiple weapons, thick, tight clothes, and bottles of water she constantly handed to him.

"At nightfall, we'll head out of here," she whispered. "This place is buried in trees, but there's actually houses not too far away. I parked there and snuck over here."

"No walkers?"

"Very light. About four streets over is the main road. Plenty of them there."

"How did you find me?"

She smiled. "Scott did. He ran into some slavers trying to make a deal."

"How's Travis?"

She gave him a confused look. Despite everything, Aaron was worried about someone else. "He's fine."

He nodded. "Good."

"Are you okay? You have enough strength to leave?"

"Yes, but we can't leave yet."

"Why not?"

"There's people in there that need our help. You see them in the trucks?"

"Aaron, listen, I'll be honest. I don't care about them. I came here to get you. And now I have you. That's all I care about."

His face took on an expression Sam hadn't seen before. He was angry.

"There's another reason. The man running the camp, he's the one who killed my family."

Sam was quiet. She could see Aaron's determination. She wanted to go home. She wanted to eat dinner with Aaron, listen to him read, watch a talking picture, hold his hand, sleep next to him. Maybe even kiss him.

But he wasn't ready to leave yet. So she would stay with him. She knew she would always stay with him.

"What do you have in mind?"

Aaron smiled. Sam felt her heart beat harder. She had missed his smile.

But this smile had something else in it. Something sinister.

He thought back to Allister leaving his family as bait for the undead. The sounds of the horrific rape, not even a night ago, flashed through his mind.

A very simple plan formed in his mind.

"They don't know who they've pissed off."

"Well, whatever you got in mind, you'll need this. Sorry, couldn't find a bow and arrow."

She tried to hand him a gun, one of her Berettas. He waved her off.

"I've got better weapons. I'm gonna be gone a couple of hours."

"What? Are you serious?"

"Yes. Listen, when the shit starts, I need you to cover the trucks. Don't let anything happen to anybody in there. Okay? And there's one slaver that's alright." He used her binoculars to point out Gibbons. "Try to cover him."

He made a move to scale down the tree. She grabbed his arm before he could leave. "What are you gonna do? There's a lot of people with guns down there."

"They don't have a chance."

"*Don't* get yourself killed. We have a lot to talk about."

He nodded, then slowly worked his way down the tree.

Sam sat in the tree the rest of the afternoon, into the early evening hours. She watched the camp as they prepared for night. They sat around tables, ate dinner, played cards by candlelight. While they feasted and enjoyed the night, someone gave the slaves in the trucks a single bottle of water to share. Her anger started to rise again, thinking of what Aaron had to endure.

Where the hell are you?

She started to worry as she stretched her legs. It was completely dark. The only light came from the candles and torches in the camp below. The wind blew through the trees, giving Sam goosebumps. What was Aaron doing? He should have been back by now. Why was she foolish enough to let him run off by himself?

She knew the answer to the last question. She believed in him.

She wondered how he was alive in the first place. He seemed to have a talent for avoiding death by undead.

She had a lot of questions for him when they made it back to Lexington.

"Allister!"

The voice cut through the quiet night. It was Aaron. Sam stopped breathing for a moment, trying to listen for where he was.

The men in the camp started mobilizing. They grabbed weapons and ammunition. Sam looked at the man giving the orders. She guessed he was Allister.

"Allister!" Aaron called again. "I wake you up in there?"

His voice came from Sam's left, deep in the trees. He sounded like he was out of breath. He didn't sound elevated, like she was. She grabbed her binoculars to get a better look at the trucks, and the slaver named Gibbons. He didn't grab a gun like everyone else. He stayed back near the slaves.

Allister checked his gun and slipped on a bulletproof vest. He kept his distance from the fence and yelled into the woods. "We didn't think we'd see you again. Coming back to be a hero, free your friends? Not a good idea."

"I told myself I would kill you, but I'll give you a chance to surrender. Run away, now, as fast as you can. Leave all your supplies behind, and the slaves. You don't have much time."

Allister looked at his men around him. Sam could see him laughing.

"Fuck you."

She was quiet as she waited to hear Aaron again.

"That's what I was hoping you'd say."

Silence. There was only the wind, some crickets, and movement in the camp below. Sam thought she heard a moan, just over the rustling of the trees. Then there was another, just below her.

In a matter of seconds, the sounds of nature were pushed aside by the song of the undead.

She watched the slavers start to panic.

"Walkers! They're everywhere!"

Sam's jaw dropped as the undead assaulted the fence. It stood its ground for a few seconds, then the old metal started to give and the walkers poured in. The slavers fired wildly, getting a few lucky head shots, but more took their place. She didn't know how many there were, but judging by the sound, the slavers were far outnumbered.

She grabbed her rifle and did exactly what Aaron told her to. She kept an eye on the slaves, occasionally taking a second to kill a slaver that wandered in her sight. Ironically, the trucks that were modified to be a prison were the only things separating the slaves from a gruesome death from the undead.

Damn, Aaron, what have you done?

Aaron kept low to the ground and stayed in between the corpses as they pushed their way into camp. A few maggots and a worm fell on his head that he quickly brushed off. With the darkness and mass of undead around him, he had no idea where he was going, but he didn't need to. Once the undead he gathered had the scent of fresh meat in their noses, there was no stopping them. All he had to do was go with the crowd.

It had taken him longer than he thought to find a thinker, a corpse the others would follow. The thinker was an auto mechanic in the old world. There was blood instead of grease on his uniform. Aaron recognized the glimmer of intelligence in his eye, and dragged him by the bony hand through the streets, gathering corpses as they went.

Aaron guessed there were at least two hundred undead.

He heard slavers dying all around him. They fought with guns, knives, their bare hands, but in the end, it was useless. The undead started to scatter as they attacked and feasted, leaving Aaron more exposed than he would have liked.

He just dropped to the ground and laid still. The corpses would ignore him, and the slavers would think he was already dead.

He looked around the camp. The attack was quick and brutal. He saw five undead slowly rip apart a slaver. Another managed to kill four or five corpses before he was overwhelmed. Someone headed for the trucks, either to hide with the slaves, or kill them. Before he could undo the chain, Aaron heard a gunshot, and saw his corpse fall to the ground.

Sam was still covering the slaves from the treetop. He smiled in her direction, knowing she couldn't see him. There was no one else he wanted watching his back.

His eyes fell on Charlie, Amanda, and Derek. They were huddled together near the front of the truck, away from the gate. He needed to get everyone away and safe.

Then he would deal with Allister, if he was even still alive.

A familiar figure ran across camp, not too far away. Aaron jumped to his feet and ran toward Gibbons, tackling the man. They fell a short distance away from some corpses ripping at the chest of a dying slaver. Gibbons fought for a moment until Aaron slapped him across the face.

"Shut up, Gibbons! It's me."

"Aaron? What the hell?"

"Be quiet! It's dark. The undead can smell, but not see great. Just keep still for a few minutes."

"You *led* them here?"

He smiled. "Every last one of them."

They were quiet as the chaos unfolded around them. Gibbons tried to fight back tears as he heard the men being eaten alive. He didn't like any of them, but it was still horrible to hear them die.

Any moment, he knew the corpses would stumble over them, and they would be next.

Gibbons heard a moan. He looked up to see an old corpse hovering over them. There were just as many bones exposed as rotting flesh. Gibbons raised his hands to shield himself, but Aaron was already moving. He jumped to his feet and held the corpse by its ribcage.

Aaron held the corpse back as easily as holding a small child.

Gibbons watched, stunned, as he climbed to his feet. The walker made no attempt to bite Aaron. It tried to reach for Gibbons.

Aaron looked at the fighting and corpses shuffling around them. They could wait out the battle, but the longer the trucks were around, the longer the slaves were in danger. He knew Sam was a good shot, but he didn't know if the truck prisons could hold out against a mass of undead.

"It's time to go," he told Gibbons, still holding onto the corpse. "Those trucks can move, right?"

Gibbons nodded. "Yeah. The keys are inside. Makes it easier to move camp fast."

"Perfect. Talk to the slaves. Find anyone that can drive, and help them get behind the wheel. And damn, man, get a gun."

"*You* don't have a gun."

"Well I'm different. I'll help out Charlie. You get moving."

Gibbons ran to the last truck. Aaron tossed the corpse to the ground and headed for Charlie. He peered into the darkness, barely seeing movement near the front.

"Charlie? You in there?"

He recognized a familiar female voice. "Aaron!"

"No, Amanda! Don't move." Charlie held Amanda back and took a few steps toward the bars.

"Charlie, stay there. Are you okay? Is anyone hurt?"

Charlie froze. "Aaron, is that you? We're all okay."

"Yes, it's me. Listen, can you drive this truck?"

"You're damn right I can."

Aaron glanced around to make sure no corpses were nearby. They were still chasing and feasting on the slavers, but that particular food was quickly running out. Many undead wandered about, looking for a meal.

He quickly undid the long chain that held the gate closed.

"Okay, hop out of there. Amanda, Derek, I'm gonna lock you back inside. You'll be safe in here."

"I'll watch over Amanda," Derek said.

Aaron escorted Charlie around the side of the truck. There was one corpse in the way. Aaron tossed it to the ground with barely any effort.

"How did you-"

"No time. It's safe a few streets over. Just head there, I won't be too far behind."

As Charlie jumped in the truck, Aaron heard a gunshot and a shout of pain. He ran to the back and saw Gibbons lying on the ground near the truck that used to keep the female slaves.

He ran to Gibbons. Gibbons held up his hand, motioning for Aaron to stop. Aaron glanced at the bars on the truck, and immediately knew what happened.

The chain the slavers used to lock the bars in place was being pulled *inside* the truck. Someone was inside, holding the bars closed. Whoever it was shot Gibbons as he ran by.

Aaron didn't slow down. He grabbed Gibbons' feet before the gunman inside could react. Aaron dragged him away, out of range. Charlie drove by, riding over anything in his way. Aaron gave him a quick wave.

"He shot me in the shoulder," Gibbons said. "I'll be okay."

"Did you see who it was?"

A voice shouted from the truck. "You double crossing son of a bitch!"

It was Allister. He hid in the same truck where his men had raped Sherry and Dana. He was in there with their bodies, they'd never cleaned them out.

"This day just keeps getting better," Aaron said. He saw one truck left. Slaves he'd never met stuck their hands through the bars. "Can you drive that?"

Gibbons could barely move his right arm, but that wouldn't stop him. "Yeah."

"Okay. Stop by the gate on the way out. You're gonna pick up a passenger." Gibbons opened his mouth to question, but Aaron shoved him by his good shoulder. "Get going."

Gibbons ran around the front to avoid getting shot again. Aaron sprinted across the yard. Allister shot at him. Aaron dove to the ground, taking a quick look behind him. He could only see darkness inside Allister's truck. He moved with the walkers until he made it to gate. He had to jump over two corpses sharing a severed arm.

He circled around the fence, quietly calling Sam's name. He heard branches rustling from above, then Sam dropped to the ground just in front of him. Her bag of guns was still slung over her shoulder. They gave each other a quick hug.

"Aaron, I couldn't see too good, but were you running with the walkers?"

"No time to talk now."

He grabbed her hand and they circled back toward the gate. Gibbons had parked the truck near the fence. Two corpses were beating on the driver's door, but he was safe. Sam took careful aim and shot both of them in the head.

Gibbons opened the door and slid over so Sam could sit behind the wheel. She held her hand out for Aaron, but he shook his head.

"Go without me. I'll be right behind you."

Sam glanced behind them. Nearly everyone in the slave camp was dead, and the corpses were heading their way.

She flashed him an angry glare. "Aaron, I came here for *you*. Now come on, we have to get out of here."

He smiled. Sam had had her suspicions for a while, but she knew then for certain he was keeping a secret.

"Trust me," he said. "This won't take long."

She didn't move the truck forward until Aaron turned and walked calmly back to camp, toward the walkers. Most of the corpses were up and wandering now, with only a few feasting on flesh. Some of the slavers who weren't completely devoured stood up and joined the other corpses. Sam watched Aaron in the side mirror as he stood near the camp gate, like he didn't have a care in the world.

"He's a freak," Gibbons said.

Sam glanced at the ex-slaver. "He's definitely something."

Aaron surveyed the camp as he heard Sam drive away behind him. The trucks were gone, and the fighting had stopped. No more gunshots or screams, just the song of the undead.

He watched as the corpses turned and stumbled in the direction of the last human in the camp.

Allister's truck.

Aaron took a step past the gate to join the corpses, and his foot caught on something. He looked down to see the rope the slavers used in his attempted murder earlier in the day.

He laughed out loud.

Allister had watched the massacre from the safety of the prison truck. He gripped the chain attached to the bars as hard as he could. His plan was to let the corpses get distracted chasing everyone else, then sneak out and drive away.

He checked the ammo in his clip, only four rounds left. He had to fire more than he wanted to at the wandering corpses that got too close to the bars. He also had to put a slug in Gibbons, the back-stabbing bastard that helped the slaves escape. Hopefully he was bleeding out somewhere.

Finally, the screams in the camp died down. The walkers were slowly finishing their feasts. It was time to make his move. He stepped over the dead body of one of the old female slaves he shot earlier in the day and carefully peeked through the bars. Some of the corpses were heading his way.

Before he could push the bars open, a voice rang out over the walkers.

"Was that really your plan, Allister? Hide like a coward until it was safe?"

He backed up into the shadows and gripped the chain tighter. A walker made it to the bars. Allister shot it in the head.

He looked out over the camp. The voice sounded like it was coming from the crowd of walkers. That was impossible.

"You don't even know my name, do you? It's Aaron. Aaron Thompson."

Allister thought it was odd, a young man with a last name. People didn't care about last names anymore.

"You've destroyed everything," Allister said, looking at his ruined camp. Tents were on fire, throwing shadows over the corpses as they slowly marched to him.

"Well, this is how it goes now. This is how you survive in this world. Does that sound familiar?"

It didn't. Allister had done what he had to do to survive over the years, and that involved a lot of killing. Obviously he'd killed someone close to the young man, but he didn't care.

He saw a silhouette standing upright near a tent not too far away. Its posture didn't seem like a walker to Allister.

He kept one hand on the chain while aiming with the other. He fired a single time and watched the skull explode. The body fell to the ground.

"Not quite," Aaron called out. "Not even close."

"You little shit," Allister whispered. "Look, kid, let's make a deal. No one has to die here."

"That's not true. *You* have to die."

Aaron's voice was eerily close.

A head leaned in near the side of the bars. "Boo!"

Allister fired twice. The first shot only caught part of the cheekbone. The second took off the top of the head. He would have fired a third time, but the gun only clicked.

He smiled when he saw the body fall to the ground, but his joy didn't last long.

"Oh no. Gun's empty?"

Aaron dropped the corpse torso he'd held up as a decoy.

Three of the walkers started pounding on the bars. They weren't smart enough to pull, but Allister kept his grip anyway. It only took a second for a few walkers to turn into many, and they blocked his escape from the truck. The walkers pushed around each other to get to the bars. He recognized a few men that used to work for him and look up to him. Now they wanted to eat him.

He saw someone making his way through the bodies, slowly pushing them out of the way. The walkers made no move to attack him or slow him down. Allister watched in disbelief as Aaron made his way to the back of the truck and pulled himself up on the back step.

"They smell terrible," he said. "But it's still nice having them on your side."

"Who the fuck are you?" Allister asked.

Aaron smiled. "Do you want to see the scariest thing?"

Allister watched as Aaron jumped into the mass of corpses. He still had trouble accepting what he saw, a human walking among the undead.

Aaron grabbed a corpse in the middle of the group, one that used to be an auto mechanic. He handed the corpse a rope, the most absurd thing Allister ever saw. Aaron tied the other end securely around the bars.

"What are you doing?" Allister shouted.

He watched as Aaron gave the rope a few tugs. He grabbed the auto mechanic walker by the hands and showed him how to pull. Allister was horrified when he saw the mechanic imitate Aaron's motion. But the bars barely moved, and Allister laughed.

"Oh yeah, kid, I'm terrified."

"You should be."

The former auto mechanic pulled again. Allister held the bars in place easily. Another walker grabbed the rope, followed by another. He felt a lump in his throat as more walkers joined in. Weak or not, the numbers were catching up to Allister. The chain started to slip from his hands as the bars cracked open a few inches. At least ten walkers were lined up on the rope.

Aaron stood there watching with a smile on his face. "They like to play tug-of-war too."

Allister lost a few more inches of chain. A corpse managed to climb halfway in the back, keeping the gate from closing. "Listen, kid. Aaron, you said? We can work something out."

"It's a little late for that now. Isn't that what you said earlier?"

Allister lost his grip. The bars flew open, and walkers pulled themselves inside. He put up a fight, but only for a few seconds. A walker bit into his arm, then his leg. He screamed in agony as walkers tore into his flesh. He felt a hand reach into his stomach and feel around for juicy tissue.

Before he died, he remembered murdering Aaron's family.

"He's not coming," Charlie said.

Sam shot another walker as it shuffled toward them from the end of the street. The slave trucks were scattered around. Some were parked on the curb, others on old front lawns. Gibbons checked everyone for injuries. Amanda held Derek's hand. The slaves, even though they were free, still stayed close to the people they were grouped with at the camp. They hugged each other and enjoyed viewing the world without bars in the way.

"Is Aaron dead?" Amanda asked.

"No," Sam said. "He'll be here any minute."

Charlie gestured for Derek to watch Amanda as he grabbed Sam and pulled her aside. "Listen, I want Aaron to be alive. He saved us all. But we have to get out of here."

"You can go wherever you want. Drive all over the world for all I care."

Charlie looked at the heavy firepower Sam had. "Maybe I'll stay a few more minutes."

It didn't surprise Sam when a truck slowly drove toward them. The slaves started cheering and shouting. Sam had to motion to keep the noise down.

"Holy shit," Gibbons said. He helped a slave sit down on the road. "The man is unbelievable."

Sam smiled as Aaron jerked the truck back and forth trying to park it. They locked eyes as he climbed out. He had a small beard and a head of hair. His face was beat up and swollen. But he was alive.

She stepped forward and hugged him harder than she meant to. He lost his breath for a moment before returning the hug. She didn't want to let go.

"I told you I'd be right behind."

She gave him another gentle squeeze. "Looks like walkers have a tough time killing you."

He picked up the hint. She knew he was hiding something.

Aaron spent the next few minutes getting swarmed by the slaves he helped set free. Charlie was the first to greet him with gratitude and a strong handshake. Amanda held onto his leg. Gibbons, and even Derek, gave him a smile and thanks. It was nice to finally be able to put faces with the voices he'd heard the past month.

There was an awkward silence as everyone calmed down and stared at Aaron.

He leaned close to Sam. "Why is everyone looking at me?"

Sam smiled and cupped a hand to his ear. "Everyone *always* looks at you, Aaron. You better get used to it."

"Right." He raised his voice. "Okay, guys. I don't know how you want to work this, but we got plenty of transportation here. Sam and I live at an old high school. That's where we're heading. You're welcome to come back with us, or go your own way."

He was surprised at the reaction.

"We'd like to go with you."

"Would you take us with you?"

"Just lead the way."

The only person who had different plans was Charlie. He stepped forward and put a hand on Aaron's shoulder.

"I won't be coming along."

Aaron nodded. He understood completely. "Your wife?"

"Yeah. She's out there, and I will find her. Just like your girlfriend found you."

"Charlie, she's not my-" He turned to face Sam, embarrassed. "I never said that."

She smiled, then pulled the AR-15 off her shoulder. She handed it to Charlie. "Take this. It's not much, but hopefully it'll get you to your next stop."

He took the rifle. "Thank you."

Amanda tugged at Charlie's shirt. "Is it okay if I stay with Aaron?"

"Me too," Derek said. "I'd like to stay too."

Aaron saw a glimmer in Charlie's eye as he fought off tears. Aaron knew Charlie had taken care of the two children for a long time, and now it was time to say goodbye.

"Of course it's okay, guys," he said. He knelt down to look Amanda in the eye. "You take care of Derek here, okay?"

Derek laughed. Aaron had never heard the teen laugh before.

"I will, Charlie. I'll take care of Derek and Aaron, and his girlfriend too."

"What's this girlfriend shit?" Aaron mumbled. He looked at Sam. "I don't know where they're getting this girlfriend stuff from."

She shook her head. "Shut up, Aaron."

"Okay."

Charlie gave Amanda and Derek a tight hug. He said goodbye to everyone he'd spent so much time with. Gibbons gave him a handshake and a hug.

"I'm sorry. For everything," Gibbons said. "None of you should have ever been in a cage."

"Hey, when walkers were everywhere, you helped get us out of there."

Sam gave Charlie quick directions to I-95, using as many landmarks as she could remember. He thanked her.

"Good luck," Aaron said.

Charlie climbed behind the wheel of one of the old prison trucks. "When I find my wife, maybe I'll swing back through this way."

Aaron nodded. "We'll be here. Just find Lexington High School."

He gave everyone a final wave before driving away. Amanda and Derek cried as the truck disappeared down the road.

Aaron was a little choked up himself. "Okay, guys," he said. "Anyone that can drive, pick a truck. Everyone else just climb in back. But don't ride in the one I came in. There's, uh, just a little bit of blood back there."

Sam and Aaron climbed in the truck she took from Lexington. Aaron was surprised to see Derek take the wheel of a truck. He saved a spot for Amanda next to him. Aaron didn't know Derek could drive.

Aaron leaned back and closed his eyes. It felt good to just rest. He looked forward to getting back to his library. He turned to look at the woman who had saved his life. She wasn't the same person he first met, the woman who took pride in only looking out for herself.

He felt ashamed. She was willing to risk everything to save him. But Aaron still kept his secret to himself. It didn't feel like a fair trade.

He knew the time was coming soon to change that.

"Are you okay?" she asked.

"Yes. Thank you for coming for me."

She put a hand on his shoulder. "We're friends."

He didn't believe that. He cared about her more than any friend, and he had a feeling she felt the same way. He squeezed her hand.

"You ready to go home?" she asked.

"Yes. Home sounds good."

CHAPTER 15

It was a whirlwind of activity when Sam returned to Lexington with not only Aaron, but fourteen other people. It took a few days for the new arrivals to acclimate. Amanda wanted a room close to Aaron, but she also wanted to share a room with Derek. They settled for an old classroom around the corner from the library.

Some of the ex-slaves were full of surprises. An older man named Tom turned out to be just as good a gardener as Susan. Everyone worked hard to help out.

Sam wasn't ready for the attention she received.

Everyone was happy to have Aaron back. She'd known that would happen. What she hadn't expected were the people of Lexington walking up to her throughout the day and giving *her* a hug, complimenting her for saving Aaron's life. It was attention she was neither used to, nor comfortable with.

Sam hadn't seen Aaron in nearly a week. Everyone was wrapped up in their own world, their own chores. The week kept her busy, but there was so much she needed to talk to him about. She also missed him. She was no longer afraid to admit it to herself.

The sun was slipping away on a warm day. She passed through the cafeteria, then the storeroom. Mary was on duty, relaxing in a chair with her feet propped up on another.

"Hey, Samantha," Mary said. "I'm so bored in here. Would you please take something so I can at least write?"

"Don't need anything right now. Listen, have you seen Aaron lately?"

She nodded. "I saw him heading out to the Pit. I have no idea why. Who the hell wants to spend time with a bunch of walkers?"

"Yeah. Just plain weird, isn't it?" Sam almost left the storeroom when she had an idea. "Uh, Mary, do you still have any of those makeup kits I found for you a while ago?"

"Yes, a few. I keep them over with some of the bathroom stuff. Do you want one?" As soon as she asked the question, Mary knew what was going on. "Oh, Samantha? Really?"

Sam tried to hide her embarrassment. "I just want to try some."

Mary smiled. "You want to impress Aaron."

She knew there was no sense in hiding it. Whether she wanted to or not, she had feelings for Aaron. She wouldn't be surprised if everyone at Lexington knew by now. "Yeah. What's the word you used? Crush?"

Mary knew it went far beyond a simple crush. "You went through town and busted him out of a cage in a slaver's camp. Sounds like more than a crush, and I'm sure you have no problem impressing him. But sit down, let me work some magic."

"Uh, thank you."

Sam felt silly and strangely vulnerable as Mary applied a small amount of eye shadow and lip gloss. She almost told Mary to stop a few times, but Mary seemed to be enjoying herself.

"Good choice, wearing some jeans with holes in them. Interesting way to show some leg."

Sam's clothing choice wasn't on purpose. "Everything else is dirty right now."

Mary tried not to laugh. "I'll put some clothes aside. Just stop by later to pick them up."

Sam tried not to fidget.

"Okay, just relax," Mary said. "You're nervous, and it really shows."

"I don't even know how he feels."

It was strange to share her feelings with Mary. The two seldom talked, except when they worked together in the storeroom.

"You don't see how he looks at you, do you?" Mary asked.

Sam shook her head. She had a good guess that Aaron had feelings for her, but she was too afraid to believe it.

"He cares about you, Samantha. It's easy to see, trust me." She held up a mirror. "What do you think?"

Sam was amazed. She knew men found her attractive. Looking at Mary's work, she could see it for herself. Just a light shade of purple lip gloss, with some purple eye shadow. She liked it.

"Wow, Mary."

"Thank you. Now, go and get him, before the light goes away."

Sam stopped and turned around before leaving the storeroom. "Mary? I, uh, I know I haven't always been the friendliest person..."

Mary laughed. "What? You? No way."

"Yeah, yeah, I know. Thank you for helping me."

"Hey, we ladies have to look out for each other."

Sam gave her newest friend a smile.

Sam pushed the dread aside as she left the storeroom and crossed the field. She was thankful that most everyone was already inside. She didn't want anyone except Aaron seeing her with makeup on.

She stopped as she drew closer to the Pit.

Aaron was there, but so was every child in Lexington. She recognized the two newest arrivals, Amanda and Derek, keeping a safe distance from the fence covering. Nikki stood next to Aaron, and Sam thought for sure she saw her youngest friend staring at Derek.

She was one second from turning around and walking away when she heard her name.

"Sam? Is that you? Get on over here."

She gave a sheepish wave, then half the children ran to her and swarmed her. They grabbed her by the hands and slowly dragged her to the Pit. She already felt embarrassed and mortified. They spoke all over each other.

"Samantha, come with us."

"Aaron's teaching us all about corpses."

"What's that stuff on your face?"

Aaron wrapped an arm around Sam's shoulders. Goosebumps danced across her skin. She had been a survivor all her life, but standing next to Aaron with so many eyes on her, she thought she would fall over dead.

"Everyone knows Sam here. When you all get older, we'll see if we can talk her into having a little gun class."

Everyone cheered. Sam laughed at their enthusiasm.

"Okay, guys, we're losing light, but there's one last thing I want to show you. I want everyone to look at that one corpse there near the back, with the dirty torn sweatpants. That one's very dangerous, and you need to watch how she acts."

Amanda gripped Derek's hand tighter. "Those noises they make are scary."

"I know. Just don't let it get to you. Now keep your distance, but watch old Sweatpants there."

The children talked amongst themselves and studied the walkers while Aaron grabbed Sam and pulled her aside. They gave each other a quick hug. Sam pulled away when he winced in pain, still a little sore from being beaten at the slave camp. He had the clean look she had grown used to, having shaved his head and face a few days ago, and his bruises were almost healed.

"Hey, where have you been?" he said. "I've been looking for you."

"We keep missing each other. So, you're teaching the kids now?"

He nodded. "They're a little scared, but they need to know." He noticed her face in the setting sun. "Is that makeup?"

"Just something I'm trying. Mary helped me."

"It looks nice. Very pretty. But you're *always* very pretty."

More like beautiful, he thought. He had never seen her looking so good. He remembered telling her before that she was beautiful without even trying. She even made jeans with holes in them look good. He wondered why the sudden desire for makeup.

"Thank you." She looked at the ground for a moment. "Listen, when you're done with the kids here, do you want to get something to eat?"

"Sure. I want to talk to you about some things."

"Me too."

Aaron tried to control his nerves. He didn't know where to begin. Did he tell Sam about his secret? Did he tell her he missed her when she wasn't with him? Did he tell her that in a world full of the walking dead, that he was falling in love for the first time?

Nikki kept a close eye on Aaron and Sam. She smiled as she watched them look into each other's eyes.

"Okay, guys," Nikki announced. "The sun is almost gone. Let's get to the cafeteria and play some games."

The children cheered as she led them away. Sam smiled at Nikki. Aaron and Sam were alone at the Pit. He led her away a few steps so the walkers would quiet down.

"Okay, listen," he said, "I have to get this out of the way before I lose my nerve."

"No, me first. Aaron, when I thought you were dead, I, uh…" Sam didn't have words. She'd been waiting to see Aaron, wanting to talk to him, and now she didn't know what to say. "Aaron, do you know what a *crush* is?"

Aaron shook his head. He'd read plenty of books, but didn't know what she was talking about. "You mean like to squeeze something?"

She laughed. Aaron felt his heart melting. He had missed her laugh so much.

"No. It's something Mary told me-"

She didn't get to finish. Neither Aaron nor Sam saw them coming.

Garrett swung the broken table leg as hard as he could. He connected with the back of Aaron's head, dropping him to the ground. Sam was surprised for a second, then charged toward Garrett. She meant to tackle him, but Ray got to her first from the side. He forced her hard to the ground, just a few feet away from the Pit.

Ray knocked Sam unconscious with a few punches to the face. He tied her hands behind her back while Garrett continued to beat Aaron.

"You just couldn't stay dead, could you?" Garrett said. He gave Aaron a kick in the ribs. "You take Samantha all for yourself, then bring *more* people back here? More people we have to feed? Are you fuckin' crazy?"

"Careful, Garrett. Don't kill him. We don't need to deal with a walker."

Garrett smiled at the idea Ray gave him. He pointed at the fence covering the Pit. "Open that up."

Ray did so, peeling one corner of the fence back. The corpses reached upward.

Garrett kicked Aaron one more time, then slapped his head as a final insult. He shoved him into the Pit.

Aaron smacked the ground hard. He was still hurt and disoriented, but he had enough sense to know Garrett expected a scream. He let out the best fake scream he could. He grabbed two walkers and pulled them on top of him to help with the illusion. Their struggle to stand up and get away only helped make it look like an attack. It was dark now, but he could see Garrett leaning over to stare into the Pit.

"I should have killed you when you first got here."

Aaron kept still and was as quiet as his aching body would allow. The stench and filth of the two walkers on top of him almost made him vomit, but he somehow held it in. Ray stood next to Garrett with Sam slung over his shoulder. He thought for a moment Ray would dump her in the Pit, but he saw her bound hands, and knew they wanted her alive.

"Is he dead?" Ray asked.

"Yeah, they're having a nice little meal down there. Let's go pack our shit and get out of here. Cover this thing up, they'll never even find the bastard."

"I'm carrying Samantha."

"Well, pass her hot little ass over here and I'll carry her."

Aaron almost lost it when he saw Garrett rub Sam's leg as he tossed her over his shoulder. Anger was starting to replace the aches and pains.

Ray secured the fence back in place. They kept to the shadows as they headed to the back of the school.

Aaron pushed the two walkers away from him and stood up. The only thing he felt was rage. He was getting used to beatings, but to see Sam hurt was too much.

He heard voices approaching.

"Amanda! Stay back!"

"Aaron! Are you alive in there?"

It was Nikki, Derek, and Amanda, who had not gone to the cafeteria with everyone else. They'd instead hidden under the bleachers, hoping to see Aaron and Sam kiss. Derek and Nikki peered into the Pit, Amanda a few steps behind.

"Yeah guys, I'm here."

"We'll get you out of there."

"No! The walkers will get you. Don't reach in here."

"But they're not hurting you."

"I know. Just listen. Go find Richardson." He had to think of where Garrett and Ray stayed. They shared a room together in the school's basement, away from everyone else. "Tell him to go to Garrett's room, that Sam's in trouble."

"Okay, Aaron, we'll get him."

Derek grabbed Nikki's hand and ran away, Amanda right behind them.

Aaron jumped as high as he could, but he couldn't reach the top of the Pit. He took a deep breath as he looked at the walkers mindlessly moving around.

"Sorry, guys."

He grabbed a walker and shoved it to the ground against the dirt wall. Before it could stand up, he tossed another on top. He stopped when the pile of walkers was five corpses high.

He climbed onto their backs and grabbed a spike holding a corner of the fence down. The walkers moaned and moved beneath him. He managed to fight the pain enough to lift the fence off the spike and climb out, making sure to secure the fence back in place. The pile of walkers collapsed as he ran across the field. His nerves were raw from pain and anger.

The walker Aaron called Sweatpants watched every move the human made.

🖐 🖐 🖐

The first thing Sam felt was the pain in her head. She struggled to open her eyes, and found the left one almost swollen shut. She was lying on an unfamiliar floor, her wrists and feet bound, a smelly shirt tied around her mouth. She looked around for Aaron, but didn't see him.

I'll kill them if they hurt him.

Garrett and Ray walked back and forth, packing old suitcases and bags. The room was well lit with candles.

"Where we heading?" Ray asked.

"Anywhere but here. This place can rot in Hell."

Sam had a change of heart. *I'm going to kill them anyway.*

"Why we taking Samantha?"

"The slave guys will give us good shit for her. Young, pretty little thing like her. We can name our own price."

"I heard they killed all the slavers."

"There's others out there. Toss me my magazines."

"I thought you wanted to fuck her?"

"That bald dickhead probably already had her. I'm not going in after him."

Ray laughed. "He's worm food now, anyway."

Sam struggled against her bonds. Garrett heard her.

"Well, look who's awake."

Garrett stood over her. He grabbed her by the shoulders and forced her into a sitting position.

"Your boyfriend's dead," he said. "In a few days, you're gonna belong to someone else. None of this had to happen. This is all your fault."

Sam would have spit on him if she could. Looking back and forth, she could see they were in the school's basement, in an old storage room they'd converted to a living space long ago. No one ever visited Garrett and Ray. They could pull a truck up to the back and no one would ever see them leave.

Garrett and Ray went back to packing. Sam looked around for a weapon of any kind. There were plenty of things to grab, tables, chairs, she just couldn't move her hands at all.

"Hey, Garrett," Ray said. "Since you don't want her, could I have her?"

"Have you ever even had sex?"

"Yeah."

"Whatever. Just don't mess her up too much. If we're gonna trade her, she needs to be in good shape."

Sam saw the sick look on Ray's face. She kept calm. She had killed men who tried to rape her before. He would have to cut the rope around her ankles if he wanted to entertain his dark thoughts. Then she would kick with everything she had.

He dragged her by the feet to the middle of the room. "I always thought you were really pretty."

He pulled out a knife.

The door to the storage room flew open. Everyone looked up to see Aaron, his hands and face covered with dirt.

Aaron stood motionless for only a second. He saw Sam tied up and gagged on the floor. She was bruised and hurt, with Ray standing over her with a knife. That was all he needed to see.

He charged forward, screaming in rage. Ray held the knife up to defend himself, but he was too clumsy and slow. Aaron tackled him around the waist, and they tumbled to the floor. The knife flew across the room. Aaron pounded on Ray's face again and again with the bottom of his fist.

Garrett pulled out a knife of his own and ran toward Aaron. Sam scooted across the floor as fast as she could and stuck her legs out just in time. Garrett tripped over her and landed hard on the floor. The wind rushed out of him, but only for a second. He spun around and swiped at Sam with the knife, cutting her shoulder. She cried out in pain against the shirt in her mouth.

Aaron heard her. He stopped beating Ray and turned to see Garrett stalking Sam on the floor as she scooted away. Blood flowed from her shoulder and soaked her shirt. Aaron jumped to his feet. Garrett spun around to face him.

"I'm gonna kill you," he said. "I was gonna sell your woman, but I'm just gonna kill her now, too."

Garrett held the knife out defensively. Aaron didn't hesitate. He grabbed a small end-table next to him and swung it as hard as he could. The knife flew out of Garrett's hand and stuck in the wall. Aaron swung again, this time aiming for Garrett's head. He connected, and the end-table broke into pieces.

Aaron didn't utter a word, not a single taunt or threat. He just beat Garrett with the broken table leg. They had hurt Sam. Anyone that hurt Sam was going to die. It was that simple.

After seven or eight hard swings Aaron tossed the table leg aside. He went to Sam and checked her shoulder. It was only a slice, but it would need stitches. He grabbed Garrett's knife from the wall and cut the rope around her wrists and ankles. She pulled the shirt out of her mouth and tried to hug Aaron. It was an awkward hug, as Aaron was busy putting pressure on her shoulder.

"They said they killed you," she said.

"They were wrong."

"My shoulder hurts like hell."

There was a new voice behind them.

"Ray, you drop that gun. Right now."

Aaron turned to see Ray standing upright. His face was almost unrecognizable. His nose was twisted, both eyes nearly swollen shut, his face covered with blood. He aimed a gun at Aaron.

In the doorway stood Richardson and Larry. Richardson aimed a gun at the back of Ray's head, while Larry had a rifle.

Aaron shifted in position to cover Sam completely, in case he decided to shoot. He would die for her, but it turned out that wasn't necessary. Ray dropped the gun to the floor.

"Well, well," Garrett said, climbing to his feet. He was a broken and bloody mess, just like Ray. "Look who came to see us off."

Richardson looked over the room. He saw the ropes, the blood. He could picture the scene in his head.

"Larry, take Samantha to James. Get him to stitch her up."

Larry handed Richardson the rifle. He and Aaron both helped her to her feet.

Aaron went to leave with Sam, but Richardson motioned for him to stay. Aaron put a hand on her good shoulder. "You'll be okay without me?"

She nodded. "Yeah. Just come find me later."

Larry and Sam left. Aaron picked up the gun Ray dropped on the floor. He planned on firing a gun for only the second time in his life.

"Aaron, we don't kill people in cold blood," Richardson said.

"Look around. Does this look like cold blood to you?"

Garrett smiled, showing off some missing teeth. "You ain't gonna kill us, Richardson. You're too much of a softie. Always have been."

Richardson looked hard at both of them. He settled on Garrett and gave him an angry glare.

"You've lost your privilege to live here. You've both just been evicted."

Garrett threw his hands in the air. "Hey, we were leaving anyway. Already got our shit packed."

"No. You don't get anything. You're leaving now with what you're wearing. That's all."

"Are you shittin' me, Richardson? You should just kill us now, then."

Richardson passed the rifle to Aaron. "We can do it that way, if you want. Aaron's already beaten the piss out of you. I can get Samantha here, lock you both in a room with them. How long do you think you'd last?"

Aaron stared at Garrett and clenched his fists. For all his talk, all his attitude, Aaron could see Garrett was afraid of him.

"This place is bullshit, anyway," Garrett said. "We don't need any of you. Fuck you."

"Believe me, the feeling is mutual."

The exile went without incident. Aaron stayed close to Richardson, in case they tried anything. Richardson led them by gunpoint through the school's back door. They marched across the fields to the locked front gates. Paul Sorenson was on watch duty. He didn't say a word, just opened the gates when they drew near.

"Listen, Garrett," Richardson said as Paul fumbled with the chain, "don't ever come back here. I'm telling everyone if they see you, they have permission to kill you. You didn't make any friends here. You're not welcome."

"Go to Hell, old man."

Garrett and Ray left and started the long walk down Honeyton Road, both dripping blood to the ground. Paul shook his head.

"What the hell happened to those two? Looks like somebody gave them what-for."

Richardson let out a small smile and gestured to Aaron.
"There's your what-for, right there."

Aaron didn't smile. "They hurt Sam. So I hurt them back."

Richardson patted Aaron on the shoulder. "You want a
drink?"

"I want to see Sam."

"James is taking care of her, I'm sure. Just give me a few
minutes of your time."

Aaron thought it over. "Okay."

Richardson nodded. "Goodnight, Paul."

"Night, fellas. And hey, get someone to come relieve me. I
gotta hit the outhouse."

Aaron followed Richardson back into the school. Richardson
grabbed a candle near the front door and took the lead through
the darkened hallways. A few people touring the halls gave them
polite greetings. Nearly everyone was gathered in the cafeteria.
As they passed by the open doors Aaron heard a voice.

"Aaron!"

He stopped to see Nikki, Derek, and Amanda jogging toward
him. Amanda reached him first and gave him a tight hug around
the waist.

"Are you okay?" Nikki asked.

"We found Mister Richardson!" Amanda yelled.

Aaron laughed. "Yes you did. You saved both me and Sam's
life."

Derek almost smiled. "I guess we're even now, huh."

"Yes we are. Thank you."

He gave Nikki a hug, and pretended to reach out for Derek,
just to watch him cringe away. The three disappeared back into
the cafeteria.

Richardson led Aaron to his room. Appropriately enough,
Richardson used the old principal's office. Aaron had to stop
and admire the place as Richardson lit a few candles spread
throughout the room. He noticed the simple things, bed in the

corner, couch against the wall. It was the walls that caught Aaron by surprise.

The walls were littered with information. There were handmade calendars, lists of people's names and jobs, maps, sketches of improvements.

Aaron had to smile when he saw different sketches of windmills, built on top of the school.

"You definitely like to plan, don't you?"

Richardson laughed as he poured himself a shot of whiskey in an old glass. He offered a glass to Aaron. Aaron only took a small sip. It felt like pouring fire down his throat. He tried not to cough and gag.

Richardson looked over his own sketches and ideas. "You always have to plan, always have to think ahead. Thanks to you and Samantha, we have eighty people here now."

"Uh, sorry about that."

"No, don't be. That's what we need. We need good people. If we don't want to become extinct, we need to grow."

"It almost sounds like you have hope for the future. I haven't seen much of that lately."

Richardson gave him a look. "You want to know what gives me hope? You and Samantha."

"Really? Why?"

"When the dead first started jumping around, I thought our days were numbered. But seeing that two people can still find each other, and fall in love, well, that makes me think maybe we're not done yet."

"Love? What? Sam and me?"

"Yes. Everyone already knows it, Aaron. It's our little entertainment. She blew up a slave camp to get to you. I couldn't even get her to cut the grass without giving her something before."

Aaron didn't know what to say. He was surprised, a little embarrassed. But he didn't argue with Richardson.

"Have you two talked about it yet?"

He shook his head. "Not yet. I, uh, have some stuff I've kept to myself."

Richardson laughed. "Of course you do. No man survives the way you do without a few secrets."

"Well, I don't know how Sam will react."

"She'll be fine. She's a tough woman."

"Don't I know it. And speaking of Sam…"

"Yeah, you'd better go find her before she hunts you down. Tomorrow, I'll try to convince you to take over the supply runs."

"Uh, okay. Until tomorrow then."

Aaron handed his half-empty glass to Richardson and left.

Richardson wondered how long it would be before Aaron took over his job.

Aaron quietly knocked on Sam's door. He almost opened it, like he always did, but remembered the last few times he made that mistake. He didn't think she was in, and was a few steps down the hall when he heard her voice.

"Yeah? What do you want?"

He pushed the door open. There were two candles lit on opposite sides of the room. Sam was lying on her mattress. She perked up when she saw Aaron.

"Oh, hey. Come on in. Just come in next time."

He shut the door behind him. In the dancing light he saw she wore the same jeans from earlier and a sports bra. He had to check his anger again when he saw her swollen eye and stitched up shoulder.

"Hi. How you feeling?"

She barely rolled on her side. "I don't feel, right now. James gave me morphine. A walker could rip my throat out and I wouldn't feel a thing."

"Nice thought."

"I know. Help me up."

He grabbed her by her good arm and pulled her up. He held her shoulders gently while he moved her toward a candle to inspect her wound. She didn't pull away. The slice was about three inches across, going across the shoulder and a little into her chest. James had done a good stitch job.

"That's gonna leave a scar."

"I'll live. Not my first scar, won't be my last. It's funny. I've killed walkers all my life, and I almost get taken out by two assholes."

"You won't have to worry about them anymore. Richardson kicked them out."

"I won't have to worry about them because you're here."

They stared at each other. She was so beautiful. Aaron couldn't imagine anyone, even in the overpopulated old world, that was more beautiful or stronger than Sam.

"I didn't forget what we were talking about," she said. "But my head feels like it's floating. So we'll do it tomorrow."

He nodded. "Okay. I'll see you tomorrow then."

He turned to leave.

"Wait a minute. I didn't say you should leave."

He laughed. "You got something in mind?"

She pulled the checkers board from under her end-table. He smiled as they laid on the mattress on opposite sides of the game.

They played for at least an hour. After Sam hesitated on taking a jump Aaron looked up at her. She was sound asleep.

He carefully moved the board off the mattress and scooted just a little closer. She sighed contentedly as she rolled onto her stomach and threw an arm over him. He gave her a gentle kiss on the forehead before falling asleep himself.

CHAPTER 16

Aaron woke up nearly the same time as Sam. During their sleep they'd somehow gotten into the position of him spooning her. He pushed himself away from her as a familiar scent moved through the air.

"Corpses," Sam said.

Aaron got up and pulled the curtains open.

"Oh no."

"What is it?"

She stumbled to her feet and saw what Aaron saw. It was too dark to make out details, but they could see just enough to let their imagination fill in the rest.

In the field, near the bleachers, they saw a lone shape on the ground. Kneeling over the shape was a silhouette. Its hands worked feverishly as it pulled flesh from the shape's torso.

"They're inside," Sam said.

"Walkers!" Aaron shouted as loud as he could. "We've got walkers!"

Aaron and Sam ran to the door. She swung it open and nearly bumped into Scott. She couldn't see his face, but knew it was him. He was the tallest, largest man at Lexington.

"Scott?"

The walker that used to be Scott lunged forward, but Aaron was just a little faster. He stepped in between Scott and Sam and pushed her out of the way. Scott sank his teeth into Aaron's arm. Aaron shouted in pain while dragging Scott into the room.

Scott didn't like the taste of Aaron's flesh. He let go, but the damage had already been done. Aaron cradled his arm and backed up near the mattress.

The gunshot almost hurt his ears.

Scott fell dead to the floor. Sam lowered her Beretta she grabbed from the table. Aaron ran forward and slammed the door shut. He could hear screams now, out in the halls.

"Are you okay?" Sam asked.

Aaron took a deep breath. He carefully hid his arm from view.

"Yes. We need to get outside. We can fight there."

He helped Sam out the window, then climbed out himself. Other residents of Lexington had the same idea, as more people climbed out of the windows and gathered on the field. Aaron could sense the panic and chaos.

"They're everywhere!"

"Is anyone bitten?"

Aaron gestured to Sam as more people started lighting candles. Two walkers stumbled out of a side door. Aaron's heart sank when he saw it was Susan Lively and Paul Sorenson.

Sam killed them both.

Richardson's voice rose over the confused crowd.

"Okay, everyone! Group up, stay together. Point out any corpses you see coming."

Aaron grabbed Sam's hand and pulled her through the crowd to Richardson. He was passing out the few weapons he had to anyone who wanted one.

He looked up at the young couple. "Are you two okay?"

Aaron nodded. "We're good. Are there people still inside?"

"I'm sure. I woke up to their moans. There were three or four right outside my room. We all just rushed out here."

Aaron looked at the group. He knew there were people missing. He saw the children gathered in the middle, but three in particular were missing.

Sam noticed the same thing.

"Nikki," she said. "And your new friends."

"We have to find them."

Richardson grabbed him by the arm. "Not a good idea. You can't fight the walkers and the dark inside those halls at the same time."

"I won't let them die."

Sam touched his shoulder. "Would they be together?"

He thought a moment. "I don't think so, not at night. Amanda and Derek have a room near mine. Nikki sleeps in a classroom right outside the auditorium."

"Okay. I'll get Nikki. You get Amanda and Derek."

Aaron held her hand for a moment. He didn't want to let go. He didn't want her going back into the school, but he couldn't be in two places at once.

"You be careful."

She nodded. "I will. You too."

Sam took an extra gun from Richardson, and they ran together to the front door. Aaron took a right toward the library. Sam had to go in the opposite direction. She watched as he ran down the hall, not even bothering to light a candle. She wanted to kiss him, but the moment was lost.

She hoped she'd see him again.

She headed down the hall with a candle. It was quiet to the point of making Sam nervous. She kept a steady grip on her Beretta, with the spare gun she'd taken from Richardson tucked in her jeans waistband. She felt completely exposed. She didn't have two layers of clothes, her cap, her favorite knife. She still wore her torn jeans and a sports bra.

She carefully scanned the rooms as she passed each one. There was a body up ahead, lying in the middle of the hall.

It twitched.

The walker moaned as it rolled over and tried to sit up. Sam didn't recognize who it was, and she couldn't waste time bothering to try. It actually hurt to pull the trigger, something she didn't think she'd ever feel. She knew these people now. She was one of them.

The gunshot was loud in the quiet hallway. No other walkers came. She picked up her pace as she headed for the auditorium. Sam had never seen Nikki's room, despite the younger girl's constant invitations. She felt guilty for that now.

She shot two more walkers as she made her way through the school. She could see through one of the classrooms that the sun was coming up. That would help in some halls, but not all of them.

She made it to the auditorium. There were classrooms on both sides of the hall. She leaned her head into the first one she came to.

"Nikki? Are you in here?"

Silence.

Sam kept moving. She jumped over a corpse she thought was dead.

She was wrong.

The corpse grabbed her ankle. It was a weak grip, but enough to trip her. She landed on her bad shoulder and felt a stitch or two pop.

The walker pulled itself along Sam's body. She pressed the barrel of her Beretta to its skull and pulled the trigger before it had a chance to bite. It fell lifeless against her legs.

She shoved it aside and stood up, gore all over her. She heard a voice.

"Help me!"

"Nikki? Is that you?"

"Samantha? I'm in the bathroom!"

Sam had lost the candle when she fell. Only a little light spilled in from the side classrooms. She could barely see in front of her.

"Nikki, I can't see. Keep talking so I can find you."

"I'm in the boys' bathroom. Hurry up!"

She kept a hand on the wall and followed Nikki's voice. "I *am* hurrying."

"Are Derek and Amanda okay?"

"Aaron's getting them now. Just worry about yourself."

"Believe me, I am."

Sam found the bathroom door. She opened it and was surprised to see light. The bathroom had a small window. It was too small to escape through, but large enough to let Sam see what was happening.

Nikki was lying on a large sheet of plywood placed on top of two bathroom stalls. Four walkers stood underneath her, trying to shake her off. Nikki swatted at them to make them let go. One walker tried to climb up using the toilet in the stall next to her. She kicked it in the face.

"Samantha!" she said. Tears streamed from the teenager's eyes.

The walkers were so preoccupied with Nikki they didn't pay any attention to Sam. She shot all four without a problem. Only the last one turned just in time to see its death.

Nikki clung to Sam as she jumped down from the plywood. Nikki cried and shivered as Sam wrapped her arms around the girl. Sam looked up to see the plywood was nearly cracked in half. In another few minutes Nikki would have been dead.

She quickly pulled herself together. She looked at Sam and wiped the tears from her eyes.

"Thank you."

"You're welcome. Let's get the hell out of here."

They stepped out into the hallway, and almost ran right into two walkers. The corpses stumbled forward with their arms outstretched. Sam shot them both. She recognized one walker as Helen, who sometimes watched the storeroom.

Sam could have sworn she'd seen the second walker before in the Pit.

She felt the gun being pulled from the back of her jeans. Nikki let out a small scream, then fired. The walker that had been sneaking up behind them fell to the floor.

Nikki trembled as she held the gun out. Sam gently pulled it from her grip.

"Nice shot."

She could barely speak. "Thanks."

They went to the nearest classroom and climbed out through the window. As they rounded the corner they saw the rest of Lexington still gathered in a group in the middle of the field.

James and Eric were checking everyone for bites and wounds. Richardson and Larry kept an eye on the school, weapons ready. Mary was with the children. Sam was relieved to see Derek and Amanda with them.

She didn't see Aaron.

Derek and Amanda ran to Nikki when they saw her. It was obvious that Derek and Nikki had been spending more time together than she realized. Sam only gave them a second to hug each other before she knelt down and looked at Amanda.

"Where's Aaron?"

"He's inside."

"What?"

Derek was frustrated. "He saved us from three of those things. Then he went back inside. He keeps saving people. He won't stay out here. Richardson keeps screaming at him."

Sam stood up and grabbed her hair in frustration.

He's gonna get himself killed.

She led everyone back to the group. Mary gave her a quick hug, then she marched up to Richardson.

"I'm going inside. Give me one more gun."

Richardson hesitated. "Samantha, he's reckless. I don't know what he's thinking, but you should stay away from him right now."

"I will *not* stay away from him."

She took the gun from Richardson and walked toward the front door. She was halfway there when it opened and Aaron stepped out into the early morning sun.

He looked terrible. He had his bow slung over his shoulder and the quiver on his back. His clothes were covered in thick walker blood. He had Carrie in his arms, her arms wrapped around his neck. Blood poured from a wound on her leg.

Sam ran forward to help. Larry and a few others were right behind her. They took Carrie and helped her to the ground. Aaron was exhausted. Sam had to hold him to keep him from falling over.

"She wasn't bit," he said. "In all the confusion, she got shot."

He dropped to one knee to catch his breath. Sam held onto him the entire time.

"James!" Richardson called. "Get over here."

The doctor emerged from the group and checked on Carrie. He shouted orders while digging for the bullet in her leg. She screamed while holding onto Larry's hand.

"The school is clear," Aaron said between breaths. "You can get your tools, whatever you need."

Richardson looked at him. "You killed *every* walker?"

"Well, you guys killed a few. And I'm sure Sam did. But yeah, I finished the rest of them off."

"How?" Larry asked.

Amanda stood near the front of the group in between Derek and Nikki.

"Well, the walkers like Aaron, right?" she said.

Everyone ignored Amanda. The only one who gave her a look was Sam. Aaron locked eyes with Derek and Nikki, and they could read his face. Nikki leaned down to tell Amanda to keep his secret.

Richardson gestured to the half-open gate off in the distance. "Who was watching the gate?" he demanded. "How did this happen?"

Aaron felt a heavy weight on his shoulders. He knew what happened.

While he was escorting survivors outside, and killing walkers, he recognized where some of them came from.

He motioned for Richardson to follow him. Most everyone stayed back to help Carrie. They ran inside to fetch drugs and James' tools. Carrie would be fine.

Richardson, Sam, most of the children, and a few others followed Aaron across the field to the Pit.

Richardson let out a breath when he saw a corner of the fence covering the Pit peeled back. They heard moans as they approached, but not as many as they should have. Aaron was horrified, but not surprised.

Only five walkers were left in the Pit, just enough to make a body ladder.

"Did someone set them free?" Richardson asked.

Aaron had secured the fence after climbing out the night before, but it didn't matter. The walker that could think watched him, copied his actions.

It's all my fault.

"No," he said. "They climbed out on their own."

Richardson wiped a tear from his eye. He paced a moment, then pulled his gun and killed the five remaining walkers. The children jumped at each shot.

Larry jogged across the field.

"We just did a count," he said. "There's walkers all over the school, but it looks like only ten are people we know."

Richardson lowered his head for a moment. "This is a terrible day, and this is awful news. But it could have been worse. We all worked together, and we survived. Losing ten of us, we'll find a way to get past it."

Larry frowned. "*Eleven* of us."

He pointed at Aaron's arm. Aaron had tried to wipe the blood off as much as possible, but now the wound was noticeable. There was a tiny amount of blood on his arm, leading to the bite wound, which was red and swollen.

"Ah, shit," Richardson muttered, and turned his back to the group.

Everyone was silent. Sam couldn't say anything. She saw the wound on Aaron's arm, and instinctively backed away. She immediately felt guilty for doing so.

Nikki wiped tears from her eyes. Derek put an arm around her shoulders. Amanda was confused. She looked up at her new family.

"Does this mean Aaron will turn into a monster?"

Richardson turned back around and stared at the gun in his hands.

"Get the kids out of here," he whispered.

The group slowly walked away. Amanda cried loudly, sobbing and calling Aaron's name. Derek had to pick her up and carry her away. The only two who stayed behind were Sam and Richardson.

Richardson had never felt so defeated. To lose any of their number was heartbreaking, but to lose the person he hoped would take his place was overwhelming.

Sam could see the pain in Aaron's eyes. He kept staring at his arm, then looked around at the place he now called home.

She said nothing, just kept a close eye on him.

"How do you want to do this?" Richardson asked. "I can shoot you, or give you the gun. Or do you feel more comfortable with Samantha?"

"I've only killed something with a gun once in my life. That was enough for me."

"Aaron, look-"

"I'll just leave."

"You *want* to become one of those things?"

"Of course I don't. But I don't want a bullet in the head either. I'll be dead in an hour, maybe two. I'll leave right now."

"I'm so sorry, Aaron. You are one of the best bright spots to hit this place in a long time."

Richardson looked at Sam. He expected her to say something, but she was quiet. Aaron stepped forward to give her a hug that she barely returned.

"I'll miss you," he whispered in her ear. He looked back at Richardson. "When you sweep the school, make sure you find that walker wearing sweatpants. I didn't see it in there. Maybe someone else killed it. But make sure you find it."

DEAD LIVING259

He turned and walked away. He waved farewell at the people
he passed, and some of them broke down and cried. Even Carrie
forced James to help carry her so she could get a hug goodbye.

"Sam, I know you're hurting," Richardson said. "But don't
you even want to say goodbye?"

She said nothing. She looked at Richardson, then back
at Aaron as he left through the front gate and walked down
Honeyton Road.

"Something's not right," she finally said.

He laughed, but it had an angry edge to it. "Tell me anything
about this damn world that *is* right."

Sam ran down Honeyton Road. She headed in the direction
she saw Aaron walking. It was quiet on the road, away from the
school. She heard birds flying overhead, but no walkers.

She ran nearly the length of the entire road. She knew if she
went just four or five more houses, she would start running into
walkers. She had no way of knowing where Aaron went. He
could be long gone, in the woods behind the houses, for all she
knew. She wanted to call his name, but knew any sound could
possibly bring corpses down on top of her. There was always
the possibility there were stray walkers even in the houses on
Honeyton Road.

She heard a door slam, just to her left.

She turned to see Aaron leaving an abandoned house. He set
his bow and quiver down and sat on the front step. He had an
old bottle of whiskey he'd taken from the house.

Sam slowly walked up to him. He noticed her as he unscrewed
the top, and gave her a small smile.

"My father said they used to do this back in the old west," he
said. He poured the liquor on his wound, and winced in pain.
"He didn't tell me it would hurt like hell."

She put her hands on her hips and stood in front of him. "You're not acting like someone with a death sentence."

He thought the setting would be different, but it was time to be honest.

Finally, the truth.

"I've been bit so many times, I've lost count. All by accident, though. You can't get in between a dog and food."

"And you won't turn?"

"Nope." He held up his arm. "This doesn't really feel good, but it'll heal, and I'll be fine."

She nodded, not exactly the reaction he expected.

"You control the corpses, don't you? Or something like that?"

Aaron sighed. He should have known it was only a matter of time before Sam suspected his secret.

"Or something," he said. He patted the step next to him. "Sit down."

She did so, and gave him her undivided attention. She looked into his eyes, the same eyes she stared at while he was deciding which move to make in checkers.

"I don't control them," he explained. "They just ignore me. They see me, they know I'm there, but they don't attack me. They never have."

She put a hand on his knee. "How?"

He shrugged. "I don't really know. I have guesses, but there's not exactly a lab or something I can get checked out at."

"What are your guesses?"

He lowered his head. He was about to share details of his life he'd never shared with anyone.

She saw how hard this was for him. She put a hand on his shoulder and squeezed gently. He put a hand on top of hers.

"My father told me I was born right when this all started happening. They hadn't even cut the umbilical cord yet when my mother died. Maybe that changed me somehow."

"What's your other guesses?"

"I might be a sign of how everyone will be. I've read it in history books. Life can change, depending on the environment. Maybe one day, walkers will ignore everyone."

Aaron was quiet while Sam took everything in.

He was terrified as he waited for her. The truth was he wasn't a courageous corpse killer. He had an easier life than most. He didn't have to fight for survival. He wasn't strong and brave, like Sam.

"Okay," she said. "This means you don't have to leave. We can go back, right now."

He shook his head. "No."

"Why not?"

"How do you think people will react? They'll be afraid of me. They'll hate me."

"What do you mean?"

"I'm different, Sam." He looked her up and down. "In the old world, because of your skin color, people would have thought you were a terrorist. Imagine what they'll think when they find out about me."

"What's a terrorist?"

"A bad person. They used to kill people."

"What's that got to do with skin color?"

"Exactly. People hate for the strangest reasons."

"No one will hate you. Don't you see? You're the best thing that ever happened to that place."

Her words were flattering, but he was just too scared. Sharing his secret with Sam was one thing. Sharing it with all of Lexington was something else. He would miss everyone, especially Nikki, Derek, and Amanda. But he wasn't ready to expose himself.

"I might go back to Baltimore," he said. "Start over again there."

"You were just gonna leave me behind?"

He was surprised. "No. I was gonna stay in one of these houses until nightfall, then sneak back into the library and get some things, my pictures. I would have stopped by your room."

Sam stood up and paced in front of him. Her thoughts were going in different directions. She'd known for a while that Aaron was hiding something, but she didn't imagine at all that he was immune to walkers in every way. She didn't agree with Aaron's idea of people hating him, but that was something she'd work on over time.

There was one thing she was absolutely sure of.

"Okay. We'll stay here today. When the sun falls, we'll sneak back, get some stuff, say goodbye to the kids. Maybe we'll steal a truck. They've got six now, anyway."

Aaron stood with her. "We?"

"Yeah, we. I'm going with you."

"You are?"

She wouldn't stop pacing. "So much shit going on, almost too much. Okay, let's see-"

She stopped for a second to collect her thoughts, then paced again.

"Me and you," she said. "I can't believe we're doing this here. How do I say this?"

He smiled. "Richardson thinks me and you are in love."

She stopped. "Whoa, hold on there. Let's not go throwing big words around. Love, no. It's just that I can't live without you. I need you."

Aaron laughed. "My father would probably call that love."

He took another step toward her and grabbed her by the arm to hold her still. She loved his closeness, and was afraid at the same time. Aaron could see it. She didn't pull away from him.

Sam stuttered. Aaron tried to hold in laughter. Sam, always in control of every situation, couldn't get her words out.

"I, when I thought you were dead, I fell apart," she said. She put a hand gently on his cheek. "I can't go through that again."

He smiled and looked in her eyes. He put a hand on the back of her neck. Her hair was a mess, her clothes torn. Her sports bra and slim stomach were caked in dried blood. She had the beginning of a black eye forming.

She was still the most beautiful woman Aaron had ever seen.

"How do you feel about me?" she asked carefully.

He leaned in and kissed her gently. It had been years since either one of them had kissed another person. Aaron pulled her to him and wrapped his arms around her waist. She let out a satisfied sigh and pressed her body to him. The walkers, the dead world, everything else faded away.

They didn't know how much time passed. Aaron finally pulled away, but only by an inch. He rested his forehead against hers as they both caught their breath. Sam let her hands float up inside his shirt and gripped his back.

"Since you won't say it, I will," he said. "I'm in love with you."

She squeezed him hard and kissed him again. She cared for him so much, and now struggled with her passion. She didn't want to come on too strong. Her entire body also ached.

"I love you too," she said with a smile. "Happy now?"

"Yes, I am."

Aaron noticed the blood dripping from her shoulder. He took a step back and looked at his arm. They were both beat up and bruised.

"We're quite a pair, aren't we?"

She smiled and held his hand. "Yeah, we are."

Aaron wanted nothing more than to kiss Sam for the rest of the day, but there were things they had to do. He led her to the river just behind the houses, the same river they followed returning to Lexington from Baltimore. He left her behind to wash up while he searched the nearby houses.

The houses had been picked clean long ago, but he did manage to find some useful items. He found a relatively clean sheet they could use as a towel, some shorts and shirts, and an old brush. He went back to the river and was worried when he didn't see Sam. Then he noticed her, waist deep in the river. Her clothes were hung on a nearby tree branch, *all* of them.

She took a complete dip in the water for a brief moment, and came up shivering. Her back was to him, but he still couldn't keep his eyes off her.

"Aaron? Is that you back there?"

"Uh, yes, it's me."

"You've seen me naked before."

"Yes, but it was dark. And now there's water, and sunlight, and, wow."

"This water is freezing. Turn around so I can get out."

He did so, holding out the sheet for her to grab. He kept his eyes clenched shut.

"Hurry up before I lose my willpower."

She smiled as she wrapped the sheet around her. It felt silly to brush her hair, but she took the brush from his hand. Things felt different between them now, more playful.

"You can open your eyes now."

He didn't make eye contact with her. He kept his gaze focused on the clothes he held. "I've got some tee shirts, shorts, some mismatched socks."

"My jeans are fine. It's my sports bra that got ruined. Aaron, you can look at me."

He lifted his head up. Even in a white sheet, she was a gorgeous woman.

She stepped forward and gave him a hard kiss on the lips. She smiled and took the clothes from him.

He pulled his shirt off and splashed water on his face from the river. She watched him with a grin. She didn't know what the future had in store for them, but she knew they would be together.

Aaron turned to look at her. She was already dressed in her jeans and a tee shirt.

"Should we take the kids with us?" she asked. "Derek and Amanda are at the school because of you. And we're both pretty close with Nikki."

Aaron smiled. It was amazing how far Sam had come. When he first met her, she wanted nothing to do with anyone.

He thought it over. "I think the safest place for them is Lexington. But we can ask. If they want to come, I won't stop them."

They went inside one of the old houses to kill time and lay low. They threw another sheet on top of a couch and laid across from each other with their legs intertwined. Both their bodies hurt, but neither of them had ever felt better.

They took naps and watched each other. Aaron didn't think Baltimore was a good idea, especially if the children came along. He wouldn't have a problem, but corpses would be a constant danger to everyone else.

He smiled as he wondered if Uncle Frank's cabin was still in good shape.

"You've never been in any danger, have you?" she asked. "Baltimore, all the way back to here."

"Well, I wasn't exactly having a fun time in that slave truck."

She was happy, knowing she did save his life.

"Why did you stay in Baltimore?"

He didn't expect that question. "After my family was murdered, I just had enough of people. So I found the place I was sure I wouldn't find any."

She wanted to share something with him, but there wasn't much about her life he didn't already know.

"I'm, uh, glad I found you," she said.

It was getting easier to say, but she still felt foolish. She'd always kept her feelings bottled away.

He laughed at the memory and rubbed her leg under her jeans. She liked that.

"I found you, actually."

She rolled her eyes. "Whatever. You get what I mean."

"I know. Listen," he lowered his eyes, "are you sure you want to come with me? I don't have much to offer."

She couldn't believe what she was hearing.

She was quiet, just watching him. He looked up slowly, almost afraid to meet her eyes.

She caught him by surprise when she dove across the couch. She was on top of him in a second. She pinned her body against him and kissed him. It didn't take long for Aaron to respond. He kissed her back as their hands roamed all over each other. His ribs throbbed from the beating Garrett gave him the night before. Sam's shoulder and eye hurt. Neither one of them slowed down.

Sam sighed quietly as Aaron kissed her neck. They'd been dancing around each other's feelings for a long time. Something always got in the way, but not anymore.

"You've got plenty to offer," she whispered in his ear.

She pulled her shirt over her head. She helped him out of his shirt, and he caressed her sides gently. It felt wonderful to touch her, but he was nervous.

"It's been a while for me," he admitted.

She held his face and smiled. "Me too," she said. "But we'll be fine."

CHAPTER 17

Aaron and Sam did better than fine, several times.

She lay asleep in his arms on the couch. They were both still completely naked, only covered by a sheet. Her rhythmic breathing threatened to put him to sleep as well. He smiled as he looked down at Sam's beautiful face. Now he could finally understand what his father felt, all those years ago, when he looked at Denise.

Sam was simply an incredible woman. Strong, tough, gorgeous, and whether she wanted to admit it or not, sweet and caring.

She stirred and gave him a squeeze. She flashed that amazing smile and ran a hand down his chest.

"Hi."

He kissed her.

"Is it late?" she asked.

"The sun's still up. We've got some more daylight before it gets dark."

She strategically rested her hand on his hip. "So we've got some time?"

He smiled as he held her tight and shifted under her, not bothering to fight the arousal he felt.

Aaron stopped when he heard something outside. Sam saw his expression and stiffened.

It was a walker moan, followed by dragging feet.

They both quickly got dressed, staying low to the floor the entire time. He grabbed her hand and they crawled to the shattered living room window.

Aaron stood up, and Sam felt a flash of panic. She had forgotten that Aaron was entirely safe from the undead. She stayed low, leaning against the wall next to the window. She watched Aaron's face, and saw his jaw drop.

She didn't utter a sound. She grabbed Aaron's hand and gave it a light pull. He looked down at her, and she questioned with her eyes.

What the hell is going on?

"Peek very slowly," he said in a normal speaking voice. "Don't make any noise."

She carefully moved just enough so she could see out the window with one eye. She didn't like what she saw.

Corpses slowly moved down the street toward Lexington High. There were so many Sam couldn't get a good count. She had never seen that many bunched together all at once, except in Baltimore. They moved with a purpose, slow and steady. It was the most terrifying thing she'd ever seen.

"The school," Aaron said. "They have to be heading there."

Sam pulled him down close to her and leaned forward to whisper. "We have to go help."

Aaron was proud of her. "Yes, we do."

He grabbed his bow and quiver from the floor and led Sam through the house to the back door. Aaron kept Sam behind the house with his arm as he stood in clear view for the walkers to see. It was strange to watch Aaron move. She had to keep reminding herself he was different.

Aaron watched as the horde of corpses kept marching down the street. He knew it had to be a thinker leading them. His eyes went wide as he realized which thinker it was.

"Oh shit," he said.

"What's going on?"

He grabbed her gently by the shoulders. "You make your way back to the school. Keep to the backyards. They're all slow, so you should be able to beat them there. Warn everyone, get them ready. I'll slow them down as much as I can."

"Be careful."

He kissed her on the lips. "I'll be fine. *You* be careful."

Aaron watched Sam as she sprinted away. Richardson told Aaron he feared this day, the day the walkers came in force. He knew the easiest thing to do was go in the opposite direction. But that wasn't in Aaron's nature, and not in Sam's anymore either.

A horde of corpses destroyed Allister's camp in minutes. He couldn't let the same thing happen to Lexington.

He ran to the street and joined the corpses. He shoved as many to the ground as he could while making his way to the front of the horde. There were so many he didn't feel he was slowing them.

He finally pushed his way to the front and saw Sweatpants. Aaron felt a twinge of anger as he realized he was outsmarted by a corpse. Sweatpants had climbed out of the Pit, and simply left the school to gather more undead.

Aaron stood on the sidewalk and let loose an arrow. The arrow pierced the thinker's head through the ear. It fell to the ground, tripping up other corpses.

The corpse horde didn't slow down.

His spirits fell. The corpses already had the scent of flesh in their noses. They didn't need a thinker to guide them the rest of the way.

"Oh no."

Aaron could see the high school up ahead.

He tripped some more walkers in the front before sprinting away. He killed a few more as he gained ground, but there were at least two hundred walkers. He didn't have two hundred arrows.

As he ran toward the gate he could see two trucks moving in position to block it from the inside. Travis and Larry parked the trucks nose to nose, tight against the gate. He scaled the fence as Richardson ran across the field carrying guns. Sam was right behind him.

"Aaron!" she shouted as he jumped down.

She gave him a hug. He saw the stunned look on Richardson's face as the older man stared at Aaron's wrapped up arm.

"I killed the thinker," he explained. "But they're still coming."

Richardson sighed as more of Lexington's men and women ran across the field. Not everyone had a weapon. Aaron wished he had found more guns during his supply run.

"Carrie's with the kids," James said. "We got the bullet out of her leg, but she won't be walking for a while."

Richardson gestured to the horde approaching. "If we don't solve this problem, she won't ever walk again."

James' eyes grew wide. "Shit. Samantha said a few corpses were coming."

"She exaggerated."

James looked at Aaron. "I heard you were dead."

"They exaggerated."

Richardson held his hands up to get everyone's attention. He could see the fear in their eyes. They had about fifty people present, and only twenty guns.

"Okay, everyone," he announced. "Everyone with a weapon, get up front. Everyone else get behind and hold ammo. Aim for the head."

A voice came from the crowd. "We're all gonna die."

Richardson wanted to calm the people he had known for years, but unfortunately, he thought the same thing.

"No, we're not," Aaron said. "We've all worked too hard to get where we are to give up now."

Sam held Aaron's hand for a moment, then stood near the fence.

The walkers were twenty feet away. Aaron heard some cries and whimpers among the crowd. Some of them hadn't seen a corpse in the wild in years.

Richardson fired the first shot, and everyone else followed. Nerves and shaky hands were a problem. Only a few corpses fell.

"The head!" Sam shouted. "You've gotta get the head! Come on, guys."

The firing continued, and more corpses fell. Aaron fired arrow after arrow.

It wasn't enough.

The corpses made it to the fence. They spread out and pushed against the metal. Sam and the rest continued to fire. For every corpse they killed, another took its place.

"Reload!" Sam called.

Aaron handed her a clip.

He dropped as many corpses as he could. His stare passed over two he recognized. Garrett and Ray.

Even in the afterlife, Ray followed Garrett wherever he went. Aaron shook his head. They couldn't even last a full day.

He shot Ray clean through the head. Before he could kill Garrett, a bullet penetrated his forehead. Aaron looked over at Sam, who had a tiny smile on her face.

"You don't know how long I've wanted to do that," she said.

Aaron grew agitated as he saw Nikki, Derek, and Amanda running across the field. Their arms were full of knives and blades. Amanda carried a backpack.

"There aren't any bullets left," Derek said. "So we brought these."

Sam pointed to the school. "Get back to the storeroom."

"We want to help," Nikki said.

A corner of the fence near the gate started to pull away from the metal framing. Aaron watched in horror as the walkers slowly forced the fence to the ground more and more. Sam killed a few, but there was nothing stopping them from getting inside.

"Everybody back to the school!" Richardson shouted. "Go to the storeroom."

Everything broke down as panic began to set in. Some people ran for the storeroom's outdoor exit while others ran for the school's front door. Some tried to get off that last shot, kill that last walker, and paid for it with their lives.

It took Sam a moment to find the children. She grabbed Nikki's hand and pulled her along. They had a chain going, as Nikki held Derek's hand while he held Amanda's. There were screams of death all around them, but Sam kept her eyes forward, staring at the open doors to the storeroom.

She saw the storeroom was already compromised. A few walkers trickled inside the open doors. She knew she couldn't stop. The storeroom was still their safest bet.

"Wait!" Derek shouted.

Sam didn't hear him over the sounds of death and the undead feasting.

They made it to the storeroom to see three corpses moving toward Carrie and the children against the wall. Larry arrived just behind Sam, and the two of them killed them.

"Go over with Carrie," Sam said.

Derek grabbed Sam by the shoulders. "We lost Amanda!"

"What!"

Derek was crying. "I don't know what happened. She tripped or something."

Nikki made a break for the door. "We have to get her."

Sam and Larry both grabbed her. Sam scanned the fields. Walkers were still pouring in through the fence. They tackled people within reach and took chunks out of their flesh.

She almost took a step out of the storeroom. A corpse came out of nowhere, behind the open door. It grabbed Sam's hair and had its teeth almost to her neck before Larry put his gun to its head and pulled the trigger.

The closeness of the shot hurt Sam's ears. She pulled back into the storeroom and dropped to a knee.

"What the hell is he *doing* out there?" Larry asked.

She looked up to see Aaron still among the undead, fighting walkers with his bare hands. He would shoot one at range with an arrow, then knock another to the ground.

"Aaron!" Larry called. "Get your ass in here!"

Aaron looked in the direction of the voice calling his name, and so did every walker on the field that wasn't already eating.

"Shut the door," Sam said. "Trust me, he'll be fine."

"What about Amanda?" Derek said.

Sam said nothing. Her lower lip shook at the thought of the walkers tearing into the young girl.

Larry grabbed the door to close it, and a hand grabbed his wrist. A walker pulled itself around the door, followed by three more.

"Help!"

Sam was on her feet and moving. She wrapped her arms around his waist and pulled with everything she had, but he didn't budge. Four more walkers grabbed Larry, one by the shirt collar. More walkers slowly made their way to the open storeroom door.

Someone tackled the walkers holding Larry from the side. Larry and Sam fell backward onto the floor as the grip on him loosened. She looked up to see Richardson climbing to his feet. He grabbed two walkers that were close to the door and threw them to the ground.

"Richardson!"

He took a step toward the storeroom. Larry was climbing to his feet to help him inside.

No one saw the walker approach Richardson from the side. It bit into his hand and ripped his pinky finger off.

Richardson screamed in pain as he cradled his hand. Larry shot the walker in the head, Richardson's finger still in its mouth. More walkers slowly funneled toward the storeroom door.

He looked at Sam and Larry with sad eyes. His face went stern as he accepted his fate.

"No!" Sam shouted.

The last thing Larry saw was Aaron being swallowed up by walkers in the distance.

Richardson slammed the storeroom doors in Larry's face.

Aaron saw everything from across the field. He couldn't get to
Richardson in time. The undead didn't harm him, but they were
so thick he had trouble moving.

He finally managed to push through the corpses and saw
Richardson lying on the ground not far from the storeroom. A
walker chewed on his arm while he beat on it with his free hand.
Another walker dropped to its knees and started ripping at his
clothes.

"Get away from him!"

Aaron threw both walkers off Richardson. The stump where
his finger was shot blood across the grass. Aaron hooked him
under the arms and started dragging. He only made it a few feet
before another walker fell on top of them. Aaron had to let go
of Richardson to push the walker away.

Some corpses still headed for the storeroom door, while
others moved toward Richardson.

"Get out of here, Aaron," he said.

Richardson watched as another walker came from Aaron's
left. The corpse didn't go for the young man at all. It tried to
walk around Aaron to get to him. Richardson saw it with his
own eyes.

"I knew there was something special about you."

Aaron said nothing. He tried to drag Richardson again, but
the walkers were just too many. He shoved one away, but another
fell on Richardson's chest. It took a bite out of his shoulder.

Aaron kicked the walker and dropped to his knees to put
pressure on Richardson's wound.

Richardson felt a tugging at his feet. A walker was trying to
bite his leg.

He reached into his coat and pulled out his gun. He slipped it
into Aaron's hand.

"Saved one bullet for myself," he said.

Aaron felt tears welling up in his eyes. He looked down at the man he respected, the man who had spent the past twenty-three years saving people's lives.

"You take care of them," Richardson said. "You and Samantha both."

Aaron couldn't speak. He could only manage a nod.

Richardson took a deep breath, then gave Aaron a nod of his own, telling him he was ready.

Aaron put the gun to Richardson's head and killed for only the second time in his life.

He stood up and shouted. He threw the empty gun against the school's brick wall as hard as he could. He was numb as walkers moved around him to get to the storeroom doors. They pulled on the handles, but the doors didn't move. Other walkers feasted on fresh kills littered about the field.

Aaron thought for a moment he might have lost his mind, as he could have sworn he heard crying.

He scanned the field, and thought he saw something through the horde of undead, not too far from the fence. It was a small figure laying on the ground in a fetal position.

Aaron ran through the walkers, pushing them out of the way. He was stunned when he saw who it was.

Amanda hugged her knees to her chest and cried. The backpack she'd taken from the storeroom with Derek and Nikki lay just next to her. She kept her eyes shut tight, not wanting to look at the horror around her. A corpse picked at a fresh dead body not too far away.

"Amanda?"

He bent down to touch her shoulder. The little girl flinched and hugged herself tighter. She reminded him of himself just after his family died.

He looked up at a corpse as it walked by, ignoring both of them.

He pulled the girl into a sitting position and checked for any injuries. She still kept her head buried in between her knees.

"It's me, Aaron," he said. He gave the girl a hug. "You're gonna be okay."

She pulled her head up enough just to reveal her eyes. "The monsters-"

"Listen to me. You're like me, sweetie. The monsters won't hurt you. Remember last night at the Pit? It's the same with you."

Amanda sniffled. "Where is everybody?"

"Don't worry about that. Let's get you out of here."

He picked her up in his arms. She opened her eyes just enough to point at the backpack on the ground.

"I got that for you."

He picked it up off the ground and heard metal clanging against metal. He carried her to one of the trucks parked near the gate. He opened the door and slid her into the passenger's seat.

"Okay, Amanda. I want you to stay here, okay? I'll shut the door and crack the window for you a little. You'll be safe here." He heard the metal in the backpack one more time. "What's in here?"

Aaron opened the backpack to see it was full of knives. One of them had a striking resemblance to the blade Sam was so fond of.

"Did you take this from Sam's room?"

She nodded.

Aaron patted her on the head. He surveyed the schoolyard again. Walkers beat on every door they saw, while others wandered in through the open front door. Some of the former residents of Lexington stood up and searched for fresh meat.

He clutched the backpack in his hand.

"Amanda, you might have saved everyone."

She smiled proudly.

"You're gonna hear a lot of noises. Just stay in here, and don't come out till I get you."

She hugged him around the neck. "Please don't die."

"No chance of that."

He closed the truck door.

Aaron had a lot of work ahead of him.

Sam looked at Larry as he nearly pushed the storeroom doors open. She ran to his side and grabbed his wrist.

"We can't go out there," she said.

"Richardson is out there."

"Richardson is dead."

Derek looked at the both of them from behind. "What about Amanda?"

There was more light as candles were passed around and lit. Sam turned to look at the teenagers and slowly shook her head. Derek held Nikki in his arms as she cried against his chest. Behind them, Sam could see the rest of Lexington's survivors. Six months ago, she barely knew any of them. Now, the only ones she didn't know were the former slaves they just brought home. People huddled together and cried. Others were too shocked to do anything, just leaning up against the walls. James walked around and checked everyone.

Sam knew lives had been lost, but the storeroom was still packed full of people. Larry stood next to her. Carrie sat on the floor with the kids. She tried to climb to her feet, wounded leg and all. Mary was locking the other entrance to the storeroom that led inside the school's halls. Travis checked and reloaded his gun.

Somewhere, she knew Aaron was still alive.

The fight hadn't been lost yet.

They all looked to her.

"Okay," she said. "First things first. Secure both exits. Make sure they can't open. Wrap chains around the handles, whatever you gotta do. Do we have anything to nail some tables to the doors?"

Travis lowered his eyes. "Uh, no. I took all the nails to work on the smokehouse. They're out there."

Sam sighed. She grabbed her gun from her waistband. "Fine. Now, who here has been bitten?"

No one said a word. They went to work following Sam's orders. Larry's hands shook as he wrapped a chain around the outside exit's handles. He could hear the corpses on the other side, pounding on the door.

"I'll take that as no one is hurt. But if someone is, and they're hiding it, all you'll end up doing is killing us all. So please, last time, is anyone injured?"

Silence. Derek and Nikki stepped up to Sam.

"What do you want us to do?" he asked.

"Take the kids and Carrie. Go to the girls' locker room. Take some of these tables, barricade yourselves in."

"It's gonna get dark soon," Nikki said.

"I know. If they get that far back, it means we're dead. If it's dark, they won't be able to see. You'll have a chance to maybe get out."

Nikki wanted to cry more, but she held it in. "Okay." She turned toward the children and tried to put on her best smile. "Let's go guys. We're gonna go in another room."

Carrie leaned against the wall with her weight on one leg. "I'm not going," she said. "I'm staying here and fighting."

Sam never had liked Carrie, but now she had a new respect for the woman.

Mary walked up to Sam and gave her a hug. "I'm glad you're alive."

Sam returned the hug quickly. "You too. Did you get that other door locked up?"

She nodded.

Sam looked over everyone again. "What weapons do we have?"

Travis laughed sarcastically. "Just what we have on us. Most of the rifles are gone."

Sam saw the knives Nikki and Derek had on them when they ran outside. She picked them up and started handing out what she could.

"Samantha, this is ridiculous," James said as he took a knife. "Did you see how many of them there were? We're just waiting to die in here."

She put a hand on his shoulder. "If we're gonna die, I want to kill as many of those things as I can."

He took a breath, then slowly nodded.

The doors that led into the school started shaking. The chain held, but the doors cracked open enough for a hand to slip through.

"Make every shot count," Sam said. "Use blades first, if you can."

Sam pointed to the other door leading outside, and several people ran over to watch it. Their numbers were divided fairly evenly. They had a good number of people watching both doors.

The inside door cracked a little further, and more hands slipped through. Travis beat at them with the butt of his empty rifle. Sam and Larry pushed on the doors as hard as they could. A walker managed to get its head halfway through. Larry stabbed it through the forehead, and remembered to pull the knife out. Sam shut the doors completely, but she knew that wouldn't last long. Even with her and several others pushing against it, the doors shook.

"Wrap that chain tighter! Do we have anything to lock it with?"

Larry shrugged. "No, we don't. We never kept any locks."

Sam looked to the other side. "How are you guys doing over there?"

"Not too bad," Mary called. "This door, they have to pull to open it. They're not too good at pulling."

"Some of you come over here then."

They kept them out longer than Sam thought they would. The problem was Sam and everyone grew tired, a problem the walkers didn't have. Weak or not, they could push forever. Sam ended up dividing everyone into shifts to hold the door. Thirty minutes passed.

Hope began to dwindle.

"Samantha, this isn't working," Larry said. "We have to run."

"There isn't any other way out."

"We should fight then."

Before she could respond, the door flew open on the other side. The walkers finally managed to pull it open. There were screams followed by gunfire as walkers flowed into the storeroom.

A few walkers died, but not enough. Sam felt the door shaking at her back as two corpses barely missed grabbing Mary and Carrie.

Sam noticed some walkers moving toward the locker rooms.

Toward the children.

"No!" she shouted. "Everyone get over here! Don't lead them to the kids."

The rest of Lexington grouped near Sam, trying to stay as close to the wall as possible while still blocking the door. Her shout drew the corpses' attention, as the walkers shuffled in their direction. Some still had fresh gore on their faces and hands from earlier kills. Travis and several others opened fire, dropping a few of them.

Sam couldn't count their numbers. She thought they had a chance to make it out of at least this battle, but they'd lose many people.

She didn't notice the pounding on the door behind them had stopped.

She jumped when a loud, steady knock came right behind her, followed by a muffled voice she recognized.

"Hello? Got room for one more in there?"

Sam shook as she ripped the chain away. Larry and Travis continued to shoot corpse after corpse, but they kept coming. The low light made it difficult to get a clear head shot.

She threw the doors open. Aaron stood with his bow slung over his chest. He held two long blood-covered knives, one in each hand. Sam recognized one as her own. He had a few more sticking out of his quiver.

She threw herself in his arms. Larry turned from shooting walkers long enough to give him a surprised look.

"Sorry it took so long," Aaron said.

Sam pulled away and pointed to the storeroom. "They're inside."

Aaron squinted to see. It was difficult to see anything with the few people holding candles moving to the door. All he could make out were shadows and moans.

"It's clear out here. Everybody move out." He looked at Sam and gave her a quick kiss. "The halls are clear. Just give me five, maybe ten minutes."

He jogged forward and kicked at the feet of the horde while the rest of Lexington filed out into the school's halls. The undead tripped and fell over each other, giving everyone precious seconds to get out. Travis and Mary brought up the rear as they helped Carrie walk. The last two standing at the door were Sam and Larry.

Aaron turned around and gave them a nod. "Ten minutes, I think."

"The kids are in the girls' locker room."

"I won't let anything happen to them. Don't worry."

Larry shook his head. "Is he insane?"

Sam smiled. "I used to think so too."

She closed the door behind her.

Sam didn't know how much time had passed, but it felt longer than ten minutes. She stayed by the storeroom doors while everyone else spread out in Lexington's halls to see Aaron's work.

He had killed every walker he saw. Some had arrows in their heads, but most were killed by blades.

She couldn't wait anymore. She opened the storeroom doors to see dead corpses everywhere. Aaron emerged from the hall leading to the locker rooms, the children right behind him. He flashed her a bright smile.

She ran to him and they embraced as hard as they could. Sam gave the children a glare as they whistled and made noises over the display of affection.

"Is it over?" she asked.

"I mean, still be careful, but I think I got all of them. Just takes a long time to stab two hundred brains."

Sam locked eyes with Derek and Nikki, who stood right behind Aaron. She saw the sadness in their eyes.

"We lost some of us. Richardson and Amanda are gone," Sam explained.

Aaron nodded and put a hand on Derek's shoulder. "I'll miss Richardson. But you're only half right."

He led everyone through the storeroom to the outside. They had to step over corpses as they walked. He waved to the truck near the gate, and Amanda climbed out.

Derek almost knocked Aaron over as he ran to the girl he thought of as his little sister. Nikki stopped just long enough to give Aaron a kiss on the cheek, then ran to Amanda as well.

Aaron put his arm around Sam's shoulders as she watched the three embrace. He wasn't surprised when Derek gave Nikki a long kiss.

"That's not a bad idea," Aaron said, pulling Sam close to him.

Sam wrapped her arms around his neck. "We thought Amanda was out here with the walkers."

"She was."

It took a moment to understand his meaning. She looked over at Amanda as she hugged Nikki's leg. "You mean-"

Aaron nodded.

Slowly, the people of Lexington started to gather around Aaron. They looked at the dead corpses with stunned surprise. Larry was the first one to talk.

"Aaron, how the hell did you *do* this?"

"Richardson's gone. What are we gonna do?"

"Aaron and Samantha should be in charge now."

"Are more walkers coming?"

Aaron held up his hand to get everyone's attention. He still held Sam's hand. People started to light candles as it grew darker. He was surprised at how fast everyone quieted down and looked at him.

"Okay, we have a lot to talk about," Aaron said. "Between last night and today, it's been pretty shitty lately."

"You can say that again," Travis said.

"But I've got a plan. It'll take work from all of us, but things will get better around here."

The questions came at a fast pace.

"How did you kill all the walkers?"

"What do you have in mind?"

"I heard you got bit by a walker."

"What do we do now?"

Aaron laughed. "First thing out of the way, about me and the walkers..."

EPILOGUE

Six months later . . .

Aaron hoisted the last generator onto the back of the truck while Amanda dragged two pillowcases of supplies behind her. He took them from her and placed them neatly near the back.

He took a quick drink of water from his canteen and handed it to her.

"You doing okay?"

The young girl nodded, although Aaron could see she was tired. Amanda was definitely a tough little girl. She pushed a lock of blond hair out of her eyes. She would need a haircut soon, something Aaron wasn't looking forward to. When Mary cut her hair three months ago she cried for almost an entire day. It took two showings of an old movie called *The Lion King* to calm her down.

"What do you think?"

He gestured to the back of the truck. It had been a long four days from home, but it was a productive four days. The truck was full of wood, water, blankets, light clothes, tools.

Amanda smiled. "We got a lot of stuff."

"Damn right we did. Put her there."

They gave each other a high-five.

"What are we doing next?"

He pulled the sliding gate down.

"Now it's time to go home. Mission accomplished."

Her eyes lit up. "Really? We're going home?"

"Yup." He felt guilty at her enthusiasm. "You know you don't have to come out here with me, right?"

"I have to help you."

He laughed. Amanda watched him kill corpse after corpse, what she called monsters. He didn't really want her to watch, but it didn't seem to bother her. She was growing up too fast.

He hopped over a dead corpse as he climbed behind the wheel. Amanda sat next to him and buckled her seat belt. They started the drive away from Home Depot back to Lexington High School.

"Next time we come out, can we bring a sleeping bag? Sleeping on these seats is hard."

Aaron smiled. He'd tell her later that this was the last excursion away from home.

They drove with the windows down. The winter was finally over. It was a beautiful spring day. Aaron was going to enjoy the next few months.

He enjoyed keeping Sam warm during the winter. He'd enjoy cooling her off in the summer too.

They heard activity as they drove down Honeyton Road and made the turn into the high school. Aaron glanced at Amanda to see the girl was almost bouncing on the seat with excitement.

The windmill on top of the school was steadily turning in the breeze. Mary shouted Aaron's name and waved before disappearing into the greenhouse near the second garden. He heard the sounds of chickens clucking. It was good to be home.

Travis, James, and Carrie were chatting near the front gate. They gave Aaron and his young partner a wave as they drove by. They were already peering into the back of the truck as they got out.

"Aaron, you guys got a haul here," James said.

Aaron walked to greet them, Amanda at his side.

"I couldn't have done it without my sidekick here."

Amanda smiled proudly, then looked up at Aaron. "Can I go find Derek and Nikki?"

"Sure."

Carrie smiled. "I saw them over by the bleachers. But be careful. They were tongue-touching the last time I saw them."

"Tongue-touching?"

"Kissing."

"Yuck!"

Amanda ran away. The adults laughed. Others joined in near the back, ready to help unload. Aaron saw Larry jogging their way.

"Did it go okay?" Larry asked.

They walked together inside the school. Kids played in the halls. Some of them stopped long enough to give Aaron a hug. Everyone missed him.

"It went well. Got plenty of supplies."

Larry unfolded a list he'd been working on. "I hate to tackle you right when you get back, but I'm afraid another list is already growing. Gibbons isn't gonna be able to handle the cows at the end of the street by himself. We're gonna need some more fluorescent lights. One of the panes in the greenhouse is busted. We're down to only two electric chainsaws and-"

"Larry, you can go get all that stuff yourself."

"Huh? What?"

Aaron slapped him on the back and pulled a map of Lexington out of his back pocket. He handed it over.

"The circle I drew is walker free."

Larry stopped in the hallway to study the map. They faced each other as Larry looked up at Aaron.

"Are you kidding me? This is almost all of Lexington."

"No joke. There's still bodies in the streets we'll have to clean up, and I might have missed a bathroom or two. But yes, it's clear. Just be careful, as always, but my days of being away from my girlfriend are over. Speaking of my girlfriend, where is she?"

Larry laughed and motioned for him to turn around. Aaron looked behind him to see Sam leaning against an old locker, a small smile on her face.

His jaw dropped, and he remembered why he was looking forward to the summer so much.

Sam wore tight sweatpants and a white tee shirt that was too small for her, showing off her stomach and fine curves. She was gorgeous, and gave him a look that told him she had thoughts involving the two of them.

"Larry, you're dismissed," she said.

"Yes, ma'am."

He took one step toward her, but she was already moving. She tackled him and pinned him against the row of lockers. She kissed him so hard he almost lost his breath. He pulled himself together and kissed her back. She ran her hands up his sides as he grabbed her hips and pulled her closer to him.

She leaned in to nibble his ear and whisper. "We need to get back to our room. Right now."

He laughed. He thought back to the night before he left. He was surprised he could move the next day.

"I've only been gone four days."

"Four days too long."

Sam knew no undead in the world could harm her boyfriend, but that didn't stop her from missing him when he was gone. She shoved a touch of jealousy she had for Amanda aside, who could go with Aaron among the walkers.

"Is it true what you said?" she asked. "You're done running around out there?"

"I'll still help out, but you can come with me."

She kissed him again and playfully ran her lips over his neck. She was pleased with his response.

"Me and you. Bedroom. Now."

They walked hand in hand for only two steps when they heard a voice behind them.

"There you are. Hey guys, you got a second?"

They turned to see James. James could see from their faces he was interrupting something.

"I'm sorry," he said. "But we've actually got visitors."

"Oh really?" Aaron said. He looked at Sam. "I guess we'd better go say hello?"

She sighed, but knew he was right. It had taken a while, but she'd accepted the fact that everyone looked up to her. "Okay, let's go."

They left the school through the front door. Next to the trucks was an old minivan. A man and woman that didn't look much older than Aaron and Sam were cautiously looking around. They had two children with them, a boy and girl. Everyone kept unloading the truck while keeping their distance.

"Good afternoon," Aaron said.

Sam smiled and squeezed his hand. Those were his first words to her when they met.

"Hi," the man said. "I'm Kevin. This is my wife, Lori. These are our children, Ronnie and Linda."

Aaron took the time to shake everyone's hand, including the children.

"I'm Aaron. This is my girlfriend, Samantha."

He smiled. "We saw the sign on the beltway. Is it true? Is this place really walker free?"

Sam looked at Aaron. He and Amanda had just put up the sign the day before.

"It's very close. We're proud of what we've done here."

"How is that possible?"

"Stick around, maybe you'll find out. Are you good people?"

Kevin nodded. "We'd like to think so."

"Then you're welcome to stay. Hey, Larry? Would you mind giving Kevin and his family here a tour?"

Larry helped lower a generator from the truck, then walked over to introduce himself. He led Kevin and his family away.

Sam leaned her head on Aaron's shoulder. "We're gonna get bigger, aren't we?"

He nodded. "This is a good place, and it'll attract good people. And the bad people, well, that's why I've got you with me."

She laughed and grabbed his hand. She was done waiting. "You and I have things to do. Let's go."

She led him to the bedroom they shared in the library.

Aaron had a feeling it was going to be a good day.

ABOUT THE AUTHOR

I live in Maryland with my wonderful wife and four cats. I love gaming, computer technology, movies, and of course, reading and writing. I love science fiction and especially horror. Ghosts, vampires, werewolves, zombies, anything supernatural, all beautiful subjects.

I've been writing since I was twelve years old. There's just something about creating a story that I like. It's always fun to try to come up with something that hasn't been done, or is unique in some way. It's fun to build a character, give him a personality and background.

Visit my website at www.glennbullion.com

PERMUTED PRESS
needs **you** to help

SPREAD (THE) INFECTION

FOLLOW US!

f Facebook.com/PermutedPress
🐦 Twitter.com/PermutedPress

REVIEW US!

Wherever you buy our book, they can be
reviewed! We want to know what you like!

GET INFECTED!

Sign up for our mailing list at
PermutedPress.com

PERMUTED
PRESS

14

Peter Clines

"A riveting apocalyptic mystery in the style of LOST."
- Craig DiLouie, author of The Infection

PETER CLINES

Padlocked doors.
Strange light fixtures. Mutant
cockroaches.

There are some odd things about
Nate's new apartment. Every
room in this old brownstone has
a mystery. Mysteries that stretch
back over a hundred years.
Some of them are in plain sight.
Some are behind locked doors.
And all together these mysteries
could mean the end of Nate and
his friends.

Or the end of everything…

PERMUTED
PRESS

THE JOURNAL SERIES
by Deborah D. Moore

After a major crisis rocks the nation, all supply lines are shut down. In the remote Upper Peninsula of Michigan, the small town of Moose Creek and its residents are devastated when they lose power in the middle of a brutal winter, and must struggle alone with one calamity after another.

The Journal series takes the reader head first into the fury that only Mother Nature can dish out.

PERMUTED
PRESS

Michael Clary
THE GUARDIAN | THE REGULATORS | BROKEN

When the dead rise up and take over the city, the Government is forced to close off the borders and abandon the remaining survivors. Fortunately for them, a hero is about to be chosen...a Guardian that will rise up from the ashes to fight against the dead. The series continues with Book Four: *Scratch*.

Emily Goodwin
CONTAGIOUS | DEATHLY CONTAGIOUS

During the Second Great Depression, twenty-four-year-old Orissa Penwell is forced to drop out of college when she is no longer able to pay for classes. Down on her luck, Orissa doesn't think she can sink any lower. She couldn't be more wrong. A virus breaks out across the country, leaving those that are infected crazed, aggressive and very hungry.

The saga continues in Book Three: *Contagious Chaos* and Book Four: *The Truth is Contagious*.

PERMUTED
PRESS